Caught!

"Zephyr!" Mercedes points straight at me, her eyes wild.

I am freaking out. I'll have to make a run for it. Get away. Hide in the subway like a rat. But what if I get caught? Where will they take me? What will they do to me?

"What about her?" Ari demands.

"The ELPH camera!" Mercedes yells.

At the mention of the word "elf" I spring to my fingers and toes in a runner's stance. When I hear the word "camera" I scan the room for recording devices, then locate the doors, planning my escape, praying I can outrun whatever surveillance they'll use to track me so I can get home in time to warn my family. We'll have to flee. This is terrible. My mom and dad were right. This was too much for me to handle. I should've never thought I could be normal. Now I've ruined everything. Just as I push into my feet to take off, I slip on a paper napkin and wind up sprawled on the floor like a squashed bug.

Ari grabs my arm and pulls me up. "Perfect!" he yells. He looks deeply into my eyes. "Zephyr," he says urgently. I squint, turn my head away, afraid of what he'll say. "Do you have an agent?"

I open one eye and peek at both Ari and Mercedes, who are inches from my nose. "Huh?" I ask, trying desperately to figure a way out of this mess. This is the time when knowing how to lie would come in handy. Or being able to cast a backward timespell. But since I can't do either, I'm stuck.

other books you may enjoy

me, my elf & i

heather swain

speak

an imprint of penguin group (usa) inc.

SPEAK

Published by the Penguin Group

Penguin Group (USA) Inc., 345 Hudson Street, New York, New York 10014, U.S.A.

Penguin Group (Canada), 90 Eglinton Avenue East, Suite 700, Toronto, Ontario, Canada M4P 2Y3
(a division of Pearson Penguin Canada Inc.)

Penguin Books Ltd, 80 Strand, London WC2R 0RL, England

Penguin Ireland, 25 St Stephen's Green, Dublin 2, Ireland (a division of Penguin Books Ltd)

Penguin Group (Australia), 250 Camberwell Road, Camberwell, Victoria 3124, Australia
(a division of Pearson Australia Group Pty Ltd)

Penguin Books India Pvt Ltd, 11 Community Centre, Panchsheel Park,
New Delhi - 110 017, India

Penguin Group (NZ), 67 Apollo Drive, Rosedale, North Shore 0632, New Zealand
(a division of Pearson New Zealand Ltd.)

Penguin Books (South Africa) (Pty) Ltd, 24 Sturdee Avenue,
Rosebank, Johannesburg 2196, South Africa

Registered Offices: Penguin Books Ltd, 80 Strand, London WC2R 0RL, England

Published by Speak, an imprint of Penguin Group (USA) Inc., 2009

1 3 5 7 9 10 8 6 4 2

LIBRARY OF CONGRESS CATALOGING-IN-PUBLICATION DATA

Swain, Heather.
Me, my elf, and I / by Heather Swain.
p. cm.
Summary: Zephyr, a fifteen-year-old elf, moves with her family from
their home in the Michigan forests, determined to adjust to living in
Brooklyn among humans so that she can attend the Brooklyn Academy of
Performing Arts High School.

ISBN 978-0-14-241255-8
[1. Elves—Fiction. 2. Identity—Fiction. 3. Self-actualization (Psychology)—Fiction.
4. Interpersonal relations—Fiction. 5. Conduct of life—Fiction. 6. High schools—Fiction.
7. Schools—Fiction. 8. Brooklyn (New York, N.Y.)—Fiction.] I. Title.
PZ7.S9698934Me 2009
[Fic]—dc22   2008054209

SPEAK ISBN 978-0-14-241255-8

Printed in the United States of America

Many thanks to Jennifer Bonnell, Kristin Gilson,
and their fabulous team at Puffin/Speak,
plus Stephanie Kip Rostan and
Monika Verma for all their help.

4 LJ + Em. BFF. Thnx.

me, my elf & i

chapter 1

"ARE YOU LOST?" The man is big. Bigger than any other man I've ever seen in my life and for a moment I can't say anything. My grandmother, back in Alverland, would call this man an ogre, even though he's the only person out of all the people rushing past me in this subway station nice enough to notice that I'm completely confused.

Everyone else just jostles on by, jabbing me with elbows and banging me with overstuffed shoulder bags. I feel as if I'm caught in the middle of a moose stampede during a forest fire. (Only instead of being surrounded by burning trees, I'm in a smelly underground passage with dirty walls covered by advertisement posters for a million things I've never heard of.) I hug my bag to my chest and nod without making a sound. The man leans down closer to me. It's not just that he's tall. I'm used to tall people. Everyone in my family is tall. He's also wide, soft, pillowy. I think of sinking into my grandparents' large goose-feather bed with my brothers and sisters and cousins surrounding me, anticipating my grandmother telling us a tale about giants and ogres.

The man's skin is dark, too, and I'm captivated. Everyone in Alverland is fair. Our hair is light and straight and our eyes are almost

1

always green. Drake, my father, who's been out of Alverland more than anyone else, told us that there are many kinds of erdlers (that's what we call people who aren't from Alverland) and you can judge them based only on their actions, not on how they look. So I know I shouldn't stare at this guy. Or any of the people rushing past me. Especially because I know how it feels to be different.

"Where are you trying to go?" he asks.

It's bad enough that I took the wrong subway three times. I mean, how was I supposed to know? I'd never even ridden a bus before today. But now that I'm finally at the right station, I can't find my way outside. I unclutch the piece of paper wadded in my fist and show it to him. I clear my throat and try out my voice. "The Brooklyn Academy of Performing Arts High School," I tell him, but the words come out tiny, as if I'm six years old. Great, my first time alone in Brooklyn and I can't even talk like a regular fifteen-year-old girl. How will I ever make it through a day of high school?

He takes the paper from me and studies it with a frown. "Never heard of it," he mumbles, and I think he'll walk away, leaving me stranded forever. I wonder if I give up now, could I find my way back to our house near the park? Tell my mom and dad that they were right. I'm not ready for a regular school. I should let them teach me at home like they wanted to in the first place.

Then the man looks up and nods. "But I do know this street, Fulton Avenue. Come on. I'm walking that way. I'll show you." He takes off and I hesitate. Everyone back in Alverland warned us not to talk to strangers, never to go with people we don't know, and to keep to ourselves. But this guy has my paper with the school's address on it. So I force my legs to move and I skitter after him, weaving through the rushing people in this dingy underground passage.

He leads me to a stairway and I can see sunlight again, although the air doesn't smell any cleaner up there than it does down here. I press my sleeve over my nose and mouth to keep from gagging on the car fumes. He takes the steps two at a time and I run to keep up with him. He glances over his shoulder and smiles kindly at me.

"New to the city?" he yells over the roaring traffic. I see him chuckle.

"Yeah," I yell back, defeated. "First day of high school."

"Sheez." He shakes his head. "Rough start. But it'll get better." He points to a street packed with cars, trucks, motorcycles, blue-and-white buses, and bicycles. A flood of people spill out of the underground stairways. Like ants on a mission, scurrying over rocks, past sticks, through gullies just to get their crumbs, the people keep moving along the crammed sidewalks, across the streets, and into the hulking buildings surrounding us. He and I join this throng and I realize that his size is a plus because at least I won't lose sight of him. On the opposite corner he stops and points. "This is Fulton Avenue. The address says four thirty-six, which has to be down this way on the left side. If you get lost, ask somebody. New Yorkers aren't rude. They're just in a hurry, but somebody'll always help you if you ask." He hands me my piece of paper and walks off into the crowd.

"Thank you!" I yell after him. "Thank you for helping me!" I wave my paper over my head as he disappears beneath the shadows of skyscrapers. Then I'm alone again in the middle of hundreds of people. For a moment I consider zapping everyone around me with a hex, maybe some kind of skin pox or limping disease of the knees so that they'll all fall down moaning and I can step over them, one by one, as if walking on rocks across a stream to find my way to school. But of course I don't. First of all, I'm not really old enough to hex an entire crowd of moving people, and secondly, my mother warned me, No magic in Brooklyn!

* * *

I finally find the school, but I'm late, of course, even though I left my house hours earlier. In Alverland, nothing is more than a ten-minute walk away, so spending this much time getting anyplace seems absurd. Standing in the middle of the empty hallway I wonder why I insisted, fought, begged, bartered, made promises, and endlessly cajoled my parents into letting me attend public high school in a new place. Am I out of my mind? Did somebody put the donkey hex of stupidity on me? I thought this was going to be easy. All I'd have to do is dress like an erdler and I'd fit right in. As if I could waltz into this school, playing my lute, and everything would be fine. Obviously I'm an idiot.

I'm about to turn around and head out the big green doors of the school. Back into the chaotic, smelly street, where I'll probably wander around lost for years before I find my way to the subway, let alone all the way home. I'm about to chuck it all, tell my parents they were right, and hole up for the rest of my existence in my new cramped bedroom at the top of the stairs in our house, when someone says, "Why are you out of class?"

I turn around to face a tiny, angry woman scowling at me. She has small sharp features like a mouse. Her hands are balled into fists, which she holds on her hips like weapons. Plus she's wearing all green. She looks just like the mean little pixies my grandmother used to tease us about. "I said, what are you doing out of class? Do you have a hall pass? What's your name?" the pixie lady demands.

That's when I lose it. Lose it like a snot-nosed, diaper-wearing, thumb-sucking, toothless, babbling baby. I drop my bag to the floor, let my knees go weak, slump over into a heap of quivering jelly, and cry miserably. The pixie lady stares me down while I wail. I swear she checks her watch and taps her foot impatiently until I pull it together enough to lift my head and squeak, "I don't know where to go."

She rolls her eyes. "Do you always get this worked up when you're lost?"

I suck back the snot streaming down my face, wipe my hands across my moist eyes, and say, "I've never been this lost before."

"For God's sake, girl," she hisses. "You're inside a school. How hard can it be?"

This only makes me cry harder, because I know she's right. "But I, but I, but, but . . ." I sputter. "First the trains . . . and I went the wrong way . . . was it the F or the A or the 2 or 3 . . . and who can figure out those maps with all the colors? Red! Blue! Orange! How was I supposed to know which platform, which staircase, which end of the train I'm supposed to get on? Not to mention the subway stations! There are rats down there. And it smells. Terrible. And all those people? Where are they all going? Where could so many people be going?" I come out of my rant clutching my hair and stamping my feet as if I'm having a temper tantrum, which, actually, I am.

The pixie grabs me by the upper arm and pulls. I scoop up my bag and go tripping behind her. "How many drama queens can one school hold?" she mutters to herself as she drags me down the empty hall.

We pass closed doors through which I hear teachers' voices over groups of kids laughing. I also hear music (drums, pianos, a trumpet from far away) and feet stomping in unison as if dancing. Posters cover the walls inviting me to "Join Student Government" or "Come to the First Chess Club Meeting Tonight" or "Help Plan the Halloween Dance!" I drag my feet to slow the pixie down so I can read every flyer on a large bulletin board. This weekend there's going to be a film festival and an "open mic night," whatever that is. And today after school I could go to a free talk about poverty in Africa or even learn how to crochet. I could never do those things in Alverland, but here, I can do anything, and that's why I came today.

The pixie stops and I bump into her, nearly sending her to the floor. "Good God!" she says to the ceiling. "Not even nine o'clock yet and this is my day already." She points to a half-open door and gives me a little shove. "In you go," she says. "Tell it all to the shrinky dink, drama queen."

I'm inside a bright, sunny office with a wilting jade plant in the window and sad yellow daisies in a vase. Without thinking I whisper one of the first incantations my grandmother taught us, "Flowers, flowers please don't die, lift your heads up to the sky!" Slowly the jade plant unfurls its drooping leaves and the daisies stand tall in the vase. Then I remember that I shouldn't be casting spells, no matter how harmless. What if someone saw me? How would I explain? I consider undoing the incantation, but that would be more magic. I have to be careful now. I must remember to act like an erdler.

I hear quick footsteps in the hallway. I peek out the door and see a couple hurrying by, holding hands. The girl's hair flies over her shoulder as she looks up at the guy. "We're so late," she says, and they both laugh, then they're gone around a corner.

I'm left with a tingly feeling in the pit of my stomach. Before my family left Alverland, my cousin Briar and I spent hours in the branches of a sycamore tree, talking about how erdlers fall in love, date, fight, and break up with broken hearts. Or so we've heard.

"Do you think you'll have a boyfriend there?" Briar had asked me a hundred times.

"That's not why I want to go," I told her as I picked layers of shaggy bark off the peeling tree trunk. "I just want the chance to see another part of the world, try new things, eat food I've only heard of." But secretly I wondered if I would find an erdler boy in Brooklyn. Then again, I can barely find my way to school, so how will I ever find a boyfriend? I need to focus on the real reason I'm here: music, art, experience! All of the things missing in Alverland.

I drop onto a little couch and try to regroup. I need to break the problem into manageable steps, as my mother likes to say. I take a deep breath and try to remember My Plan for Life in Brooklyn. First, make friends. (But how?) Second, get a boyfriend. (Yeah, right!) Third, and most important, find as many ways to perform as possible. I have one year here, and I'm not going to waste it.

I look around the office again. Beside me on a little table is a big black binder titled "Upcoming Auditions." It's filled with dozens of pages with information about trying out for plays, musicals, bands, ensembles, improv troupes, and commercials. I get prickly chills up and down my back. *This is it!* I think. The real reason I'm here. In Alverland we do the same pageants and plays every season—to welcome in the harvest, to give thanks for bountiful hunting, to celebrate the equinox. It's always the same songs, in the same order, on the same day. Nobody writes plays about a different topic or makes up new songs except my dad. It's not that I don't like singing in the sugar shack when we make syrup for the Festival of Maple Trees, but there's more to life than pancakes!

As I browse through the binder of possibilities, a door across the room opens and a woman walks in. She's too preoccupied with reading the paper in her hands to notice me, so I take a second to get a good look at her. She wears a full, rippling purple skirt with tiny bells sewn on the hem that jingle as she moves. On top she wears a long flowing white shirt, not unlike what we wear in Alverland. She has three necklaces of brightly colored beads, lots of bracelets on both wrists and even around one ankle above her soft leather sandals. She tucks a loose strand of her brown hair behind one ear and I see that she has silver rings on nearly every finger. I like her already.

"Are you the shrinky dink?" I ask.

"Yow!" she shrieks, and gives a little jump so that all her bracelets, necklaces, rings, and bells clink and clatter. "The shrinky dink?" she asks, as if she can't believe I said that.

"Sorry." I cringe. "That's what that woman told me." I point to the door where the lady in green left me, but of course she's long gone, vanished just like a mean little pixie would. "Am I in the wrong place?"

She narrows her eyes to study me. "Who are you?"

"My name is Zephyr," I tell her, then remember how the erdlers always use last names, too. "Zephyr Addler."

"Ah ha!" She grins. "So you are Zephyr. I've been looking forward to meeting you."

"You have?" I ask, and for the first time since I kissed my mom goodbye this morning, I smile.

She nods. "I'm Ms. Sanchez, your *guidance counselor,*" she tells me carefully. I get the hint that "shrinky dink" is not what I should call her. I imagine how the pixie will look after I zing her with a nasty little hairloss spell for embarrassing me like this. Then I remember my no-magic promise to my mom.

"So you made it," Ms. Sanchez says as she perches on the edge of her desk.

"Barely," I admit.

Ms. Sanchez pulls a red file folder off her desk. I see my name printed on the tab. "So you've never been to a regular school?"

I shake my head, more embarrassed now. "I didn't realize everyone in the universe would know that about me."

Ms. Sanchez laughs. "Only your teachers and I know that about you. And you're not the only homeschooled student we've ever had. It's nothing to be ashamed of. Especially with test scores like yours."

"Thanks," I mumble. "But being smart hasn't stopped me from being an idiot today."

"Don't be so hard on yourself," she tells me. "It's tough coming to a new school as a sophomore, especially a week after everyone else started."

"Oh no," I groan and clutch my knapsack to my chest. She makes it sound so terrible!

"You're going to do just fine," she assures me as she flips the pages in the red folder. "Let's see where you're supposed be now and get you started."

Ms. Sanchez knocks on a classroom door and goes inside. I wait in the hallway but I hear people murmur, papers shuffle, and someone laughing inside the room. "Settle down," an adult says, then a girl comes out in the hall with Ms. Sanchez.

"What's up, Aunt Nina?" the girl asks. Ms. Sanchez frowns for a moment until the girl rolls her eyes and says, "Ms. Sanchez," in a silly voice that makes Ms. Sanchez snicker.

"Mercedes, this is Zephyr. Zephyr?" She turns to me. "This is my niece, Mercedes. She's also a sophomore here and she'll be your official tour guide today."

When Ms. Sanchez steps aside, Mercedes and I face each other as if we're looking in an opposites mirror. I am tall. She is short. I'm as pale as milk. Her skin is the rich, beautiful brown of acorns. My stick-straight, so-blond-it's-nearly-translucent hair hangs down below my shoulders. Her thick, dark ringlets are cropped just above her chin. I am all points and angles: cheekbones, collarbones, elbow, knees; she is soft curves from her round cheeks down to her feet.

And it's not just how we're built, it's how we're dressed. I've taken great care today not to look like some hippie wood sprite straight off the commune (which is what most erdlers think of us when we leave Alverland). I purposely left my soft deerskin boots and handwoven tunic dress at home. I didn't even wear my hat or the amulets my grandparents made for me. I gaze at Mercedes in her red-striped tank top over a white T-shirt and skinny jeans riding below her hips and pegged above her silver ballet flats. I realize I look nothing like a regular erdler kid. My navy blue pants are too fitted, too new, too stiff, too high up on my waist. I have on a bona fide blouse, aquamarine with pearly buttons all the way up to my chin. And I'm wearing white sneakers. I'm so embarrassed that I wish someone would turn me into a bird so I could fly away and never ever see these people again.

"My aunt told me about you," Mercedes says. "You're the girl from Michigan, right?"

"The U.P.," I say hopefully, but Ms. Sanchez and Mercedes look at me blankly. "See, Michigan has two parts." I hold up my right hand like a mitten with the thumb sticking out to the side. "This is the main part where Detroit and stuff like that is." I hold my left hand sideways over the top of my right fingertips. "And this is the Upper Peninsula, the U.P." They blink at me. "All this space between my hands is the Great Lakes. And up here?" I point to the pinky knuckle on my left hand. "That's where I grew up."

"Close to Canada then?" Mercedes asks.

"That's right!" I say, impressed with her grasp of geography. Most people in Michigan have no idea how close we are to Canada.

"Yeah," she says, smirking. "I can hear your accent. 'Out and about.'" She laughs because she pronounces it like "oot and aboot."

I press my lips together as my cheeks grow warm, embarrassed by how obviously weird I seem, even in this school where the brochure says diversity is a good thing.

"But that's okay, yo, because I'll have you talking Brooklyn in no time flat." Mercedes snaps her fingers in front of her face and grins at me, this time nicely.

Ms. Sanchez hands Mercedes a green slip. "Here's a hall pass. Show

Zephyr her locker, the cafeteria, her homeroom, then escort her to her classes for the rest of the day."

Ms. Sanchez turns to me. "You can stop by my office anytime if you have a question." She slips her arm around Mercedes's waist. "Mercy will be a great tour guide, won't you?"

Mercedes wiggles out of her aunt's embrace, but I see her smile. "Yeah, yeah, Aunt Nina."

"*Ms. Sanchez,*" Ms. Sanchez says playfully over her shoulder as she walks away.

First I ask to stop in the bathroom so I can do something about how I look. I stand in front of the mirror and sigh. "I look like . . ." I say to Mercedes.

She sits on the countertop, kicking her feet into the big rubber trash can stuffed full of used paper towels. "A dork," she says. "Which is weird because, you're like, so freakin' gorgeous and everything. Does your mom make you dress like that so boys won't be looking at you?"

"No. I mean, I just didn't know what to wear." I untuck my shirt and undo the top button. I take off my belt and shove it in my bag. (A *belt*! She's right. I am a total dork.) I try to squiggle my pants down around my hips, but it's hopeless. "Is that better?"

Mercedes raises her eyebrows. "Yeah, better, but . . ." She hops down from the counter. "I don't know what kind of malls they have up there in the U.P., but girl, we're gonna have to take you shopping or something."

I follow her out of the bathroom. "Please," I beg. "I would really, really appreciate that."

Mercedes snorts a little laugh. "'I would really, really appreciate that!'" she mocks, and I have to give her credit, she truly does sound like me. "For real you talk like that?"

I stop and tower over her. "How am I supposed to talk?"

She shrugs. "I don't know. However you talk, you talk, I guess. It's sweet, kind of. Real nicey nicey. Polite sounding."

"Is that a bad thing?"

"Naw, just different," she assures me. "But maybe you want to tone it down a little bit with people you don't know. Otherwise, you know, they might get the wrong idea."

"That I'm nice?" I ask. "What's wrong with being nice?"

"Too nice. Like people can take advantage of you. Push you around. You know. Like that. You gotta be able to hold your own here."

"Right, hold my own." Then I realize that again I'm lost. "Hold my own what?"

This time Mercedes cracks up. She leans into me and shakes my arm as she laughs. "Girl, you crazy! 'Hold my own what?'" She imitates me perfectly again. "You really are from someplace else, aren't you?"

"You have no idea," I tell her. "No idea at all."

chapter 2

I'M OVERJOYED TO see Mercedes waiting for me after my algebra class. "Mercedes! Mercedes!" I jump up and down and wave. Everyone around me moves away and stares. I stop hopping.

"Dang, *chica*," Mercedes says. "Simmer down."

"Sorry, I just got so excited," I say. "What are we doing now?"

"Lunch, I guess. How exciting is that?"

I think about this. "Can I eat with you?"

"If you promise not to jump around," she says, starting down the hall.

I promise, but I'm still excited. I follow her. I'm so grateful that she's letting me come with her that I want to give her something. A garland of wild roses to wear in her hair. A bouquet of sweet sage and honeysuckle to tuck into her belt loop. But those are the kinds of things we do in Alverland and I have no idea how erdlers show their appreciation. So I just say thank you, over and over again until finally Mercedes stops short.

"Jeez, Zephyr!" she says loudly. The crowd of kids parts around us. "Stop with all the thank-yous, would you? I get it! I get it!"

"Sorry." I hang my head.

"Man, you apologize more than anyone I've ever met. 'Sorry, sorry, so sorry,'" she says, mincing around, bobbing her head, exactly like I do. Then she jabs me in the ribs with her elbow and howls with laughter. "You got me bugging, girl! But it's all good."

"Mercy, Mercy, Mercy me!" someone bellows from behind us. I turn around to see a chubby boy, not much taller than Mercedes, with wild dark strands of hair over his eyes. He's wearing black baggy clothes from head to toe, and has even painted the fingernails of his right hand a dark smudgy color. He zigzags through the other kids, singing Mercedes's name.

"Ari!" Mercedes screeches, and holds open her arms. They envelop each other in a long embrace, then begin to dance, hips close together, cheek to cheek, sliding elegantly across the floor. He dips her dramatically and looks up at me through his messy bangs.

"Is this her?" he asks.

Mercedes pops upright. "That's right. This is Zephyr."

"Are you Mercedes's boyfriend?" I ask, full of romance and envy, but also a little bit relieved to think that I finally understand something. But from their reactions, clearly I'm wrong. Mercedes and the boy snort and howl, slap their knees, and nearly fall down they're laughing so hard. People passing by us stare and snicker.

"She's funny," Ari says to Mercedes.

"Yeah," says Mercedes. "She's all right." They each loop one arm through my elbows and pull me down the hall.

"So you're not?" I ask, confused again.

They both crack up, then Ari asks, "Is she for real?"

"I don't know," says Mercedes. "But she's a trip."

"And gorgeous!" Ari runs his fingers through my hair. *"Oy vey es mir.*

What I would give for such hair. And that *punim*?" He tweaks my cheek. "Look at that bone structure!"

"Stop with the Jewish granny routine," Mercedes says.

"I love your hair, too." Ari reaches around to tousle Mercedes's pretty curls.

"Get your grubby hands off my head." Mercedes shakes viciously, but I can see the grin lurking on her lips. Ari takes that as an invitation to slip behind her and maul her with his fingers deep into her hair, massaging her scalp. Mercedes leans into him, purring like a cat.

"She loves it," Ari says to me. And as suddenly as their shenanigans started, Ari stops. They both stare at me. "I think we should make her our mascot," Ari says. I can feel a stupid grin frozen on my face because I'm so excited that they want to be my friends. Sort of. I try to rearrange my mouth and eyes into something less "nice," but I can't really. Nice is who I am. So I shrug, helplessly grinning at them.

"Good golly, Miss Molly!" Ari says with overexaggerated zeal. "Just how tall are you anyway?"

"She's gotta be like six feet tall," Mercedes says, peering up at me as if I'm a tree.

"And those legs. Up to her armpits with those legs." I slouch a little, trying to seem less tall as Ari rubs his chin and eyes me. "No boobs." I cross my arms over my chest. "No butt either. You're a model, aren't you?" he asks.

"You're teasing me, right?" I venture from my tight self-hug.

"For real, you a model?" Mercedes eyes me suspiciously.

I have no idea if they're trying to compliment me or if they're being mean, so I stay quiet.

"If you're not, you should be," Ari says.

"You could make mad money," Mercedes tells me as we join the last few stragglers on their way to lunch.

"We should get her on *America's Next Top Model*," Ari says.

"Can you see her talking to Miss Tyra?" Mercedes asks. "'Yes, Tyra! Oh thank you, Tyra! I'm so sorry, Tyra!' Then Tyra'd be like, 'Cut the crap, girl, and pose!'" Mercedes shoves one hip out to the side with her hands in the air and sucks her cheeks in.

Ari pretends to take pictures of her while shouting, "Work it! Work it!" as Mercedes hits silly pose after silly pose, making her way down the hall. I scurry behind them, desperate not to be left behind.

When they're tired of the strange Tyra game they're playing, Ari turns to me and asks, "So, not a model. Why'd you come to this school then?"

"I want to perform," I say.

"Duh," says Ari. "What kind of performing?"

I stare at them blankly.

"Music? Dance? Drama?" Mercedes asks.

"Everything!" I say. "All three!"

"A triple threat," says Ari. "I get it."

"Broadway bound," says Mercedes.

"But which do you like the most?" Ari asks.

I think for a moment. "Music," I say.

Ari brightens. "I'm a musician, too."

"So is my dad," I tell him.

Mercedes rolls her eyes and blows a puff of air into her bangs. "Musicians," she snorts.

"Mercy here wants to be a *theater diva*," Ari says with a British accent, and Mercedes bows deeply. Ari shoves her and she flings herself across the hallway, arms flailing, bumping into passing kids, who bump her back, so that she ends up banging noisily into lockers.

"Oh, I'd love to try acting!" I tell Mercedes, thinking back to that big black binder of auditions in Ms. Sanchez's office. "I'll try anything new."

"Whatever," says Ari. "Let's talk about real art. What instrument do you play? Wait. Let me guess." He studies me again for a moment. "You sing."

"Hey, how'd you know?"

He wiggles his fingers in front of his body as if he's playing the piano. "I've got an accompanist's sixth sense."

Before I can ask him what he means or tell him that I also play the lute, Mercedes flings open the double doors that lead into the cafeteria. A deafening roar overtakes us. Talking, laughing, shouting, and singing jumble together over music pumped through speakers in the ceiling. Kids are everywhere. In chairs, on the floor, on top of tables, slouching against the walls, dancing in the corners. I've never seen so many different kinds of people together in one place. From dark-skinned to light-skinned and every shade in between. Brown hair, blond hair, blue hair, no hair. Earrings, nose rings, pierced eyebrows, cheeks, and probably lots of places that I can't see. Three girls in a little huddle are even wearing fairy wings. I want to stand quietly in the doorway for a long time getting used to it all, but Ari comes back to my side, grabs my wrist, and drags me to the lunch line.

With my tray full of fruit and salad I push into the seating area. Ari and Mercedes hang back, surveying the scene. "Hey!" I point to an empty bench on one side of a long table in the center of the room. "Here's a free space big enough for us." I hurry over to plunk my tray down before someone else gets the seats, then I turn around and wave my hand over my head to make sure Ari and Mercedes see me. "Over here!" I call. They both stay absolutely still, staring at me with wide, intense eyes. "What?" I ask, and jerk around to see what I've done wrong. Am I stepping in a big puddle of spilled milk? Is the table covered with something disgusting? Did I accidentally pee my pants and not notice?

"Uh, can I help you?" the pretty girl sitting across from my tray says, although she doesn't really sound like she wants to help me at all.

"With what?" I ask.

"Look, bee-yatch," the girl says, shaking her head so that her long shiny black hair moves like a curtain across her shoulders. She stares at me with cold, calculating eyes—green and almond-shaped, like a cat's.

I look carefully all around. "I don't see anything," I tell her, and the guy sitting on her right starts to laugh so hard that orange soda sprays from his mouth.

"Jesus, Timber," the girl says to the guy, and shoves him hard on the shoulder. Then she wipes tiny drops of his soda off her bare arm while muttering, "Disgusting," to the three girls on her left.

"Who the hell is this nancy at our table?" one of the girls asks while all three of them stare at me. The girls seem a lot less happy to see me than the guy who is grinning so fiercely that I think of a wolf.

"I'm Zephyr," I say. "Not Nancy. Who are you?" But they must not have heard me over the din in the room because nobody answers.

By then Ari is right behind me. He touches the back of my arm and stands on his tiptoes to say firmly into my ear, "Not here, Zeph."

"Oh." I pick up my tray and smile at them. "Sorry." The wolf boy leans on his elbows and smirks. I think he'll lick his lips as he watches me walk backward, bowing and repeating, "Sorry, sorry, so sorry," until his intense gray-blue eyes make my skin itch and burn.

I join Ari and Mercedes huddled in a corner far away from my mistake. They both writhe on the floor, screaming with laughter as they recount over and over again what just happened.

Mercedes sits up tall and arranges her face in the exact look of near horror that the girl at the table gave me. "Uh, can I help you?" she says in a dead-on impersonation.

"With what?" Ari asks breathily, hand pressed against his chest, big eyes blinking in a way that I'm guessing is supposed to be me.

"Look beeee-yatch," Mercedes spits, wagging her head.

Ari pretends to look all around, up and down, under the table, inside his shirt, then straight back at Mercedes as if challenging her. "I don't see anything," he deadpans. "And my name's not Nancy!" They howl with laughter before playing the entire scene again.

No matter how many times they go over it, I have no idea what I did, or why it was so terrible, or so terribly funny, anyway. All I can think about is the boy called Timber who looked as though he wanted to devour me. I shiver.

When they've exhausted themselves, Mercedes grabs both my shoulders with her hands and says, "That was off the hinges, Boo! And what's so great is, you don't even know why, do you?"

I shake my head miserably.

"First of all," says Mercedes, "that's where the seniors sit."

"Except for Timber, he's a junior," Ari adds.

"Secondly, two words," says Mercedes. "Bella Dartagnan."

This sounds like the beginning of a healing spell my mother might mutter when someone has a rash.

"She does commercials, TV, and movies," Ari says, and I realize that Bella Dartagnan is the name of the girl with the cat eyes.

"She missed five weeks of school last year because she had a speaking part in some new Disney movie," Mercedes says. "Plus she knows Mary Kate and Ashley."

Those must be the three girls sitting next to her on the bench.

"Not that that's cool," says Ari.

"No, we hate them. But still," says Mercedes.

"And the guy? Timber Lewis Cahill? You remember him, right?"

Ari asks, checking to see just how lame and clueless I am. I shake my head because I've never heard of him.

"He had a boy band when he was twelve," Mercedes says.

"We're talking major-label record deal," Ari adds.

"TLC Boyz," Mercedes says as if I should know.

Ari shimmies his shoulders and sings in falsetto, "Baby want to walk my dog." Then he turns and yells, "Pure crap!" over his shoulder.

"We hate him, too. But still," Mercedes says again.

"And you!" Ari says. "Sauntered right on up to their lunch table, where no mere mortals dare to venture."

A pang of panic darts through my body when he says "no mere mortal." Did I give myself away? Was it that easy to guess? On my first day?

"Oh my God! Oh my God!" Mercedes is up on her knees shouting and I cringe deeply into myself. If they've figured me out, I'm doomed. That'll be it for me. I'll have to leave and never come back.

"What? What?" Ari asks breathlessly.

"Zephyr!" Mercedes points straight at me, her eyes wild.

I am freaking out. I'll have to make a run for it. Get away. Hide in the subway like a rat. But what if I get caught? Where will they take me? What will they do to me?

"What about her?" Ari demands.

"The ELPH camera!" Mercedes yells.

At the mention of the word "elf" I spring to my fingers and toes in a runner's stance. When I hear the word "camera" I scan the room for recording devices, then locate the doors, planning my escape, praying I can outrun whatever surveillance they'll use to track me so I can get home in time to warn my family. We'll have to flee. This is terrible. My mom and dad were right. This was too much for me to handle. I should've never thought I could be normal. Now I've ruined everything.

Just as I push into my feet to take off, I slip on a paper napkin and wind up sprawled on the floor like a squashed bug.

Ari grabs my arm and pulls me up. "Perfect!" he yells. He looks deeply into my eyes. "Zephyr," he says urgently. I squint, turn my head away, afraid of what he'll say. "Do you have an agent?"

I open one eye and peek at both Ari and Mercedes, who are inches from my nose. "Huh?" I ask, trying desperately to figure a way out of this mess. This is the time when knowing how to lie would come in handy. Or being able to cast a backward timespell. But since I can't do either, I'm stuck.

"Do you have an agent?" Mercedes repeats.

"An agent?" I ask. "Is that like a lawyer?" Maybe I'll be snatched away to some secret laboratory where I'll be studied like a mouse. My family will come looking for me and then they'll be captured, too. The others in Alverland warned us about this. They didn't want us to move to Brooklyn, but my father insisted and I was thrilled. Now I imagine sitting sadly in a large cage with my little sisters while erdler doctors poke us with needles.

"Yeah, kinda," says Mercedes. "But a lawyer can only negotiate your contracts after you get a gig. An agent helps you get the gig first."

"What's a gig?" I ask, my heart pounding as urgently as a beaver's warning slap against the water. "Is that like a trial?"

"No, that's the audition," Ari says.

"Audition?" I ask, thinking of the black binder. "What's an audition got to do with it?"

Mercedes sits back on her heels and studies me for a moment. "Look," she says slowly, as if I'm very, very stupid. "Casting agents come to this high school looking for new talent all the time. It's part of the reason everyone wants to go here." They both look at me to see if I comprehend what she's saying. I nod, but I'm unsure what this has to do with my family not being human, because I'm picturing a police raid in Alverland. My aunts, uncles, cousins, and grandparents rounded up like stray dogs and hustled into the back of unmarked vans.

"Last week," Ari tells me, "the ad agency that's working on a new camera campaign announced that they're going to cast the lead for their new Web ads from this school."

"This camera is called an ELPH, because it's small and cute, you know, like an elf," Mercedes says.

I shake my head, annoyed by the stereotype. Where did these erdlers ever get the idea that all elves are small and cute and slave away in Santa's workshop? The small mischievous ones are the brownies or pixies or magical dwarves of fairy tales, not elves. Not real elves anyway, who are tall, strong, great hunters and healers. Just another race, more or less. Except for the whole magic thing and the fact that we live for hundreds of years. But still, we put our pants on one leg at a time just like everybody else.

"So the idea is," Ari continues, "they'll film a cute, perky girl and then digitally shrink her so she looks small next to the camera. Then they'll put those ads up on the Web and maybe, if they do well, eventually on TV. Do you get it?"

I shake my head. "I have no idea what you're talking about," I admit, still confused and scared.

Mercedes huffs, annoyed with me. "Listen," she says. "Bella Dartagnan gets cast in every freakin' part that comes through this school. I don't know what it is, if her agent has some kind of secret power or something. But seriously, she gets everything and we're sick of it."

"Hey," Ari says to Mercedes. "I thought you were going to audition for the ELPH thing."

Mercedes waves him away. "I audition for everything, but you know

I won't get it. I never do. Zephyr, though, she could whoop Bella's butt into Tuesday."

"That's true," Ari adds, looking at me. "You would be the perfect competition for this ELPH thing."

I wrack my brain trying to put it all together. "Why me?" I ask.

"Because," Mercedes explains, "you totally fit the description that the agency wants."

"You're pretty and perky. And you just have this quality. I don't know what it is," Ari says. "You're not . . . ," he searches for the right words, "a normal, average girl." I gasp at the insult but Ari looks at me puzzled. "That's a compliment, Zephyr."

"Yeah, Ari's right," says Mercedes. "You're sort of elfin." My mouth drops open. "But not in a bad way."

"Why would being an elf be bad?" I demand, incensed.

"I don't know." Mercedes shrugs. "I meant it as a compliment. Like, you know, you're nice and sweet but also maybe kind of mischievous or something."

Then it hits me. Ari and Mercedes actually think I'm just another kid like them, unlike when my cousins and I would go into Ironweed, the tiny erdler town near my home. The local kids there know we're from Alverland and they torment us. They call us hippies and freaks, say that we're inbred, pagan communists. Our parents tell us to ignore them and to be nice so that someday they'll see what kind and loving creatures we are. But here, for the first time outside of Alverland, being a little bit different is a good thing. The heavy weight in my chest lifts. I breathe deeply and a huge smile takes over my face. "So, will you do it?" Ari asks.

"We'll totally help you," Mercedes promises.

I pick myself up off the floor and say, "Sure. What do you want me to do?"

"Audition," Mercedes says.

"For what?" I ask.

"Is there something wrong with her?" Mercedes asks Ari.

"For the camera ad," Ari tells me.

Even though I still don't know what that means, I say, "Yes!" because at this point I'd do anything to keep Ari and Mercedes as my friends. They whoop and slap hands. I sit back and smile because finally things are going according to My Plan for Life in Brooklyn.

When my first day of school is (finally) over, I'm so exhausted that I could fall into a hundred-year-sleep, but of course I can't because I still have to get home. As I'm standing with my head against my locker, trying to muster enough energy to leave, I feel a tap on my shoulder. I turn to see the wolf-boy from earlier in the cafeteria grinning at me.

We stand nearly eye-to-eye, but he's about an inch taller than I am. His hair is thick and dark, falling messily but perfectly around his face. His eyes are a deep-set gray with flecks of vivid blue. And his smile is dazzling, like cut quartz shimmering in the sun.

"I didn't get a chance to properly introduce myself earlier," he says, slick as fresh dew on the morning grass.

"Your name's Timber, right?" I ask.

"Yeah, like a tree. TIM-BER!" he shouts, and pretends to fall over. I laugh at his unexpected goofiness. He stands up tall again and extends his hand to me like a branch reaching toward the sun. "So, it's nice to officially meet you."

I hesitate, remembering what Mercedes told me about being too nice and holding my own so I stop smiling and I say, "I don't think your friends liked me."

"Who, Bella?" he says as he withdraws his hand and rakes his fingers through his hair.

"And Mary, Kate, and Ashley."

Timber fills up the hallway with his laughter. "Oh my God, you're so right. Chelsea, Zoe, and Tara would crap themselves if they heard you call them that." Then he leans in close to me. "But, of course, they'd be secretly flattered, you know."

I don't know at all, but I'm not going to tell him that. "Well, anyway, my name's not Nancy."

Again he cracks up, shaking his head and grinning at me. "Obviously," he says. "So what is it?"

"Zephyr. Zephyr Addler." This time I hold out my hand.

"That's a great name." He hangs on to my hand for a few seconds too long.

"Thank you. I like yours, too." And it's true, I do. Timber is the kind of name someone in Alverland would have. "But I have to go now." I pull back my warm and tingly hand.

He falls into step beside me as I head down the hall. "You live in Brooklyn?"

"Yes," I say, then hesitate again because for the life of me I can't remember how to get home. What train am I supposed to take? Where is the subway station? Am I going to have to rely on the kindness of strangers to get me where I want to go . . . again?

"My mom lives in Brooklyn," Timber says. "But my dad's uptown. East Side, so you know."

"Why do they live in different houses?" I ask. Then I remember that erdler families split up a lot, which is very rare for elves. "I mean, which place will you go today?"

"Probably my mom's. Closer."

We pass a tangle of kids hanging out on a bench, passing around little machines with headphones and singing three different songs all at once.

One of the girls looks at us and jams her elbow into another girl's side. That girl smacks one of the guys on the leg. They all stop singing and stare, but Timber ignores them.

"What 'hood are you in?" he asks me.

"Hood?"

"Neighborhood."

I try to remember the name of the area we live in. Something about a park or a hill or a slope. We push through the big green doors at the end of the hall and just as I'm about to admit that I don't know where I live, I see Ari and Mercedes on the steps outside. I run and fling my arms around both of them.

"Do you know my friends?" I ask Timber.

He hangs back by the doors. "Uh, no."

"Ari Mendelbaum," Ari says from his perch on the stoop. His voice is different than I remember. More hard-edged and deep now. "We're in the same improv class."

Timber shrugs. "Yeah. There are a lot of people in that class."

"I sit in front of you," Ari tells him. "We were paired up last week for the tug-of-war exercise."

"And this is Mercedes," I quickly interject.

Mercedes lifts her hand in a weak wave. "How's it going?" she says. We all look away from one another awkwardly.

Timber moves first. "Okay, so, yeah. See you around, Zephyr." He jogs down the stairs with his fist in the air. "Rock on," he yells without looking back at us.

"That wasn't very nice," I say. "The way he just left like that."

Ari and Mercedes look at each other and groan. "Such a jackass," Ari says.

Mercedes stands up, then she bumps down the steps exactly as Timber did with her fist above her head. "Rock on," she bellows in a deep voice, just like him. Ari cracks up and so do I because, hey, at least it's not me she's impersonating this time. Now all I have to do is find my way home, and with my friends by my side I feel like I could do anything.

chapter 3

MY SECOND DAY of school goes better. I think I'm start-
ing to figure this whole erdler thing out. I got there without a problem,
found all my classes, aced a botany quiz, and managed not to cause a riot
in the cafeteria by upsetting the delicate balance of who can sit where.

After school Ari and Mercedes decide to escort me all the way
home.

"We have so much work to do, Boo," Mercedes says as we wait on
the crowded subway platform. A sour wind picks up and blows my hair
around as the next train approaches with a roar.

"That ELPH audition is only two weeks away so we've got to start
now," Ari yells over the noise.

I don't argue because I'm glad for the company on the train. It still
feels strange to me to be whooshed around the city in a metal box full
of vacant-eyed people. I learned pretty quickly to stare at the adver-
tisements overhead instead of smiling and saying hello to everyone
around me. But today, I hang on a pole and listen to Ari and Mercedes
plot how to turn me into a superstar.

I don't mention that I'm having second thoughts, though. I'd like to try acting, but I'm terrified that I'll make a fool of myself in front of Bella and her evil minions if I audition and that's not what I need right now. On the other hand, I'm so happy to be with my new friends that I go along with Ari and Mercedes, nodding my head as they make plans to transform me into the next ELPH elf.

As we get closer to my stop, I start getting nervous. "You know, you guys, my family's a little bit weird," I tell Ari and Mercedes.

"Whose isn't?" Ari says.

Three seats have opened up, so we sit side by side, swaying to the *clickety-clack* rhythm of the train.

"You ain't seen nothing, *chica*, until you meet my twin sisters and my crazy *abuela*," says Mercedes.

"But my family is a little bit, um," I search for the right word to describe us. "Traditional," I say.

"You mean like religious?" Ari asks.

I shake my head. "No, I mean my mom and my older sister are really focused on being at home and taking care of everyone. They don't understand why I go to school."

"I got an aunt like that," Mercedes tells us. "She's real old school. Keeps her kids home and teaches them there. Makes my cousins wear dresses. I think she's a Jehovah's Witness or something."

"It's been hard for the rest of my family to get used to Brooklyn," I say. "So don't be surprised if they seem out of place."

"That's the great thing about living here," Ari says. "You can be anything you want to be and nobody cares."

I lean back against the hard orange seat and smile. "That's exactly why I love it. Where I'm from everybody is the same and if you're different, nobody gets it."

"Yeah, well, welcome to New York, baby," Ari says as the train emerges from an underground tunnel and climbs up an elevated track.

He points out the window to a green statue far away in the harbor beyond the graffitied buildings and the highway choked with cars. I squint until I see that he's pointing to the Statue of Liberty, torch raised for all the newcomers like me.

"It's good to be here," I say.

After two more stops I stand up.

"You live in the Slope?" Ari asks.

"I have no idea," I say.

"If you get off here, then you do," he tells me. "And so do I, which must mean we're practically neighbors."

We run up the stairs and I realize that my neighborhood is finally becoming familiar to me. I recognize the Pavilion Movie Theater on the corner and the Connecticut Muffin coffee shop across the street, where I've already imagined my first erdler date. First we'll see a movie, then, holding hands, we'll walk over to the coffee shop to discuss the film while sipping something hot and sweet. I've got the plan, now I just need the guy.

"Let's cut through the park," Ari says, pointing to the stone wall surrounding acres of grass and trees.

I'm so happy when we get inside the park that I want to run down the grassy hill into the big open meadow, kick dandelion fluff, or dance on the clover. I want to shimmy up the big maple tree in front of us to sit where a red-tailed hawk has perched high in the swaying branches, surrounded by slowly fading fall leaves. The only thing that would make this better is to have my imaginary date boy to share it with. We could roll down hills, jump in ponds, and chase squirrels through the open fields. But of course that's the kind of thing we'd do in Alverland, not in Brooklyn, where nature isn't something you're a part of, but something set aside for picnics and kite flying. Still, I feel so rejuvenated by the green space around me that I start to hum.

Ari joins in, singing the words so familiar to me, "Cast a spell of beauty, cast a spell of love, join me in the meadow, fly with me like the dove." He has a lovely mellow voice with just enough gravel to give it a satisfying edge.

I harmonize with him on the chorus, "Through the sky, through the sky, fly with me through the sky."

He smiles broadly after the last note. "You like that song?"

"Of course," I say with a laugh.

"What do you mean, 'of course'?" Ari asks. "Most people don't know Drake Addler's music. I thought it was only goths like me."

"What's a goth?" I ask.

"Me," Ari says, opening his arms for me to take a good look at him, but I'm not sure what I'm supposed to see.

"Is goth your religion?" I ask, because my dad has told us that erdlers take their belief systems very seriously and sometimes have wars over who's right.

Ari laughs. "No, I'm a Jew through and through."

"I've read about Jewish people and the horrible things that happened to them," I say. "Are you really religious?"

"Nah," Ari tells me. "Just a regular New York Jew. No pork—"

"Except bacon at a diner," Mercedes says and Ari laughs.

"Synagogue during Passover. Cheesy bar mitzvah with a god-awful DJ when I was thirteen. Stuff like that," he adds.

"So a goth Jew is one who does only some of the religious stuff?" I ask.

Mercedes rolls her eyes at me for the umpteenth time today. "Girl, you really are out there, aren't you?"

"Out where?"

She snorts, then laughs fully. "But it's impossible not to like you."

"Thanks," I say. "I think."

"Don't mention it," she adds dryly.

"Goth is how I dress, Zephyr. This style," Ari says as he motions up and down to his entirely black wardrobe. "Because I don't want to be just another jerk in Gap jeans and an Abercrombie shirt. Really, though. How can you not know what goth is but you do know Drake Addler's music?"

"Ari," I say, laughing hard, happy to be the one who knows something this time. "Drake Addler is my dad."

Ari freezes in the middle of the path. He shakes his head from side to side slowly and pushes his hair back to expose his broad forehead. I see that beneath all his unruly hair, he has brown eyes with long lashes like a deer. "Drake Addler is your father?" he asks me.

"Yeah," I say. "Remember? Zephyr Addler, that's me."

Mercedes doubles over laughing so hard I think that she'll fall down. "Look at him!" She points to Ari. "Boy's going to dookey in his pants."

"Are you for real?" Ari demands. "You're not just yanking my chain?"

"Yes, I'm for real, Ari. Drake's my dad. We just moved here a couple of weeks ago so he could play with his new band and record another album and go on tour. He couldn't do all those things in Michigan and he didn't want to be away from us so much anymore."

Ari walks in little circles, hands still in his hair. "Drake Addler is your dad," he repeats over and over again and I continue to say "yes" each time he does. Suddenly he drops to a park bench. "I can't go to your house." Then he pops up. "I so badly want to go to your house!" he exclaims. He plops down on the bench again. "But I can't meet your dad." He's up again, pacing. "Oh my God, do you know how long I've wanted to meet him? I've been to his concerts. Snuck in when he played Irving Plaza last year. Made my mom drive me all the way to the Berkshires for an outdoor festival last summer. I have a bunch of links to his music on my Facebook page."

"Ari," I say gently and put my hands on his shoulders. "Relax. Stop. He's just my dad. He's nothing all that special. Believe me."

"Nothing special?" Mercedes says, wiping the tears of laughter from her eyes. "This boy would follow your daddy around like a sick little puppy if he could."

Ari nods his head rather pathetically.

"Look," I say. "He's not even home. He's on the road right now. I think he's up in Vermont or New Hampshire or something until the weekend."

Ari takes a deep breath.

"Son, you best start kissing booty," Mercedes says to Ari.

"What's that mean?" I ask.

"Sucking up, you know, getting on your good side," Mercedes explains. "So he can meet your daddy."

"You can meet him anytime you want," I tell Ari. "And you don't have to kiss my boots."

"Honey," Mercedes says to me with a snort. "We gotta teach you how to talk."

When we come out of the park, I spot the tall pine tree obscuring the front of our house. I think the tree is the reason my parents moved us to this place. Passing beneath its branches and seeing birds, like the hawk circling high above me now, reminds everyone of our real house in the woods of Alverland. But, as soon as I open the front door, I realize bringing Ari and Mercedes here was a mistake.

My sister Poppy has built a nest of blankets and pillows on top of the bookshelves in the living room. She loves birds and doesn't understand why she's not allowed to climb trees in the park to sing with her feathered friends. From her perch, she's reading aloud from a big, leather-bound Audubon guide, practicing different bird calls. Below her on the floor, my brother Bramble is working on some healing incantations for a bunny with a broken leg, a one-eyed cat, and the three lame sparrows that he brought home in the first few days that we lived here. My mom had to put a limit on the number of ailing animals he can bring in the house because she realized we'd be living in a petting zoo if he was left to his own devices. Both Poppy and Bramble are wearing tunics and leggings with several amulets around their necks, but my youngest sister, Persimmon, who is only two years old, is running buck naked from room to room with a half-eaten apple in her grubby hands, while singing at the top of her lungs. My older brother Grove is on the road with my dad, but my older sister Willow is nowhere to be seen and I don't blame her. After being around erdlers all day, I see how weird my family really is.

Just as I'm about to push Ari and Mercedes back out the door, my mom races down the stairs in an old brown tunic and a soft green hat, phone pressed to her ear, in the middle of a conversation. She carries Persimmon's tunic and shouts, "Yes, yes!" into the phone. "I certainly have experience with warts and other skin ailments."

Behind me, Mercedes says, "Warts?" and Ari shushes her.

"There are some amazing herbs that can clear that right up," Mom says.

"My mom's a naturopath," I quickly explain to Ari and Mercedes, leaving out the part about elves being great healers and my mom being one of the best.

"That's so cool," Ari says.

I realize I can't turn back now. "Come on," I say as I pull them through the chaos of the living room toward the kitchen. "I'm hungry, aren't you?"

We carefully step over the cardboard boxes holding Bramble's animals as Persimmon dodges between Ari's legs. Poppy catches sight of us and leans over the edge of her nest, sticking the giant book in my path and letting out the ear-piercing shriek of an angry blue jay. "Who are you?" she shouts at Mercedes and Ari, making them both jump.

I push the book out of my face. "Cut it out, Poppy!"

"Shhhhh!" my mother hisses with her hand pressed over the mouthpiece of the phone. She wrestles Persimmon to the ground and stuffs her into her clothes while Persimmon flops like a fish just plucked from a stream. Percy accidentally kicks the side of the sparrows' box, which sends the birds into a flightless frenzy, desperately flapping their little bandaged wings. They chirp fiercely as Poppy tries to soothe them with an imitation of a mother sparrow cooing to her young.

"Persimmon!" Bramble wails, but our little sister has squirmed away and dodged beneath the dining room table, where her stash of handmade baby dolls are arranged for a tea party.

My mother retreats to a semiquiet corner to finish her conversation while I quickly cross my pinky over my ring finger and my pointer over my middle finger, then loop them in front of my mouth and point at Poppy before she has a chance to bug us again. I've just done the ol' five-second silence hex—perfect for nosy little sisters. With Poppy momentarily on mute, I pull Ari and Mercedes into the relative calm of the kitchen.

"Sorry," I say. "Things are hectic around here sometimes."

Ari's eyes are wide and blinking with disbelief. "My God. I thought Mercedes's house was crazy."

I grab the first thing I find on the counter. "Dried boysenberries," I offer, and shove a bowl of shriveled fruit at them.

"Poison berries!" Mercedes nearly shouts, waving the snack away.

"No, *boysen*berries," I say.

"What the heck is a *boy*senberry?" Mercedes asks.

"It's just a berry. A fruit," I say, staring at the little wrinkly orbs in the bowl and wondering if even our food is strange.

"Like a raisin." Ari pops one in his mouth. "Only gross." He spits it into his hand. Mercedes laughs as I give Ari a napkin.

"How many people live here?" Mercedes asks.

"Six kids, plus my mom and dad, and the animals. How many people are in your family?"

"I have two younger sisters," Mercedes tells me. "Plus my grandparents live in the apartment next to ours so they're always at our place."

"That's how it is where we're from. I miss my grandmother so much."

Mercedes rolls her eyes. "Just more people to get up in your business," she says, but somehow I don't believe she means it.

"How about you?" I ask Ari. "How many brothers and sisters do you have?"

"None," he says.

"None?" I'm as incredulous about his family as he is about mine. "What do you mean none?"

"I'm an only child."

Such a thing is unheard of in Alverland. "That's so sad," I say. "Aren't you lonely?"

"Heck no," says Ari. "It's great. No competition. I get whatever I want."

"Wow," I say, considering the possibility of life without all my brothers and sisters.

"Do you have anything normal to eat, that doesn't taste like that?" Mercedes asks, pointing to the boysenberries.

I grab three pears and a bowl of almonds from the counter. "Do you like goat's milk?" Ari visibly blanches and Mercedes twists her face into a look of disgust.

"What are you guys? Health nuts?" Mercedes asks.

"Do you have any coffee?" asks Ari.

"Iced tea?" I offer, and thankfully they both accept. I don't mention that it's made from slippery elm bark and hawthorne leaves. "Come on," I say, pouring each of them a glass. "There's a back staircase. We can go up to my room where it's quiet."

Just then my mom pushes through the kitchen door, calling, "Zephyr!" She nearly bumps into us. "Oh, there you are." She wraps her arms around me and starts mauling me as if I'm some little kid who's been lost in the woods for three days. "How was your day? Did you get lost this time? Were people nicer to you? Did you have any trouble? Do you still want to go back? Aunt Flora called today, Briar misses you. And who's this?"

I peel myself away from her, embarrassed by all the elfin affection. My mom's going to have to tone it down now that we're not in Alverland anymore. I introduce Ari and Mercedes and my mother exclaims, "You made friends!" as if I'm a total idiot who would never manage to hold a conversation, let alone befriend another person.

Ari holds out his hand. "Nice to meet you, Mrs. Addler. I'm a huge fan of your husband's work."

Instead of shaking his hand like a normal person, my mom pulls Ari into a hug. "Oh, that's so very kind of you. Drake will be so delighted to hear that. You'll have to come back and spend some time with us when he's home." Ari blushes crimson. Mercedes giggles behind her hand. "And please call me Aurora."

"Mom," I say. "Come on. Let him go. Not everybody hugs everybody else around here."

She releases him. "Oh, right. Sorry. I get carried away." At that moment a yowl erupts from the living room and my mom bolts back out the kitchen door. I catch a glimpse of Poppy sprawled on the floor in the middle of Bramble's empty boxes. The bunny is limping across the room and the cat is clawing its way up the side of the bookshelf to Poppy's abandoned nest, where one of the sparrows has managed to reach.

"Is everybody where you're from like this?" Ari asks.

"Like what?" I ask, panic-stricken because I knew this was a mistake. Now my new friends will run screaming for the door or, worse, they'll get suspicious about who we really are.

"Let's just put it this way," Mercedes says. "I don't know anybody else who has bunnies, birds, and naked babies running around, who all dress alike and drink goat's milk. It's like you're in some kind of weird cult or something."

"Shut up, Mercy," Ari says. "That's just rude. I could say the same about your house."

"We don't drink goat's milk," Mercedes says with a snort.

"No, but you eat tamales wrapped in banana leaves and sausage made out of blood and drink coconut water."

"Are you insulting my Puerto Rican heritage?" Mercedes asks, sticking her hip out to one side and cocking her head toward her shoulder.

"No, I could say the same thing about my family eating gefilte fish and drinking Manischewitz. All I'm saying is, every family's a little bit weird. Besides, this is cool. This is Drake Addler's house," Ari says with a big silly grin.

Mercedes laughs. "You're whipped already, boy."

I hear my mom coming toward the kitchen again so I grab Ari and Mercedes to make a break for the back stairs. They don't need any more evidence that we're not like other families.

In my room, we find Willow slumped in the windowseat, hugging a pillow and staring into the blue sky. Even though it's nearly four o'clock, she's still in her white sleeping tunic with her hair pulled back in a long messy braid that brushes her waist. She's been like this since we arrived in Brooklyn. All she does is sigh and mope around, missing her boyfriend, Ash. Some days I feel bad for her. She's too old to go to high school here, not that she'd want to anyway, and she doesn't want to try an erdler college. What she wants is to be back in Alverland with Ash and her friends. Even though I miss Alverland, especially my cousin Briar, who's my best friend, I don't want to go back. There's too much to do and see and experience here. But Willow would rather everything stayed the same. I nudge her. "Hey, will you go in Mom's room, please?"

She glances up at us and stares at Ari and Mercedes as if she can't quite figure out what they're doing here. Reluctantly, I introduce everyone. "This is my older sister," I tell Ari and Mercy. "And these are my friends," I tell Willow. Her eyes get misty at the mention of friends.

"Aunt Flora called today," she says.

"Mom told me," I say.

"Briar wanted to talk to you."

"Sorry I missed her."

"Ash was there." She sniffs and wipes a hankie under her nose. "He walked all the way to Ironweed so we could talk."

"You must've been so happy to hear his voice," I say, but she lets out a little sob. "Oh, Willow," I say, and rub her shoulder. I hate to see her so lonely so I say, "You can stay in here with us, if you want." But Willow shakes her head, grabs a pillow, and shuffles out of the room. "She misses her boyfriend," I say to Ari and Mercedes.

"Dang, it's like *Little House on the Prairie*, walking ten miles for a phone," says Mercedes.

"Is she okay?" Ari asks quietly.

"Looks like she needs Prozac," Mercedes mutters.

"Who's Prozac?" I ask.

"What, not who," Mercedes says. "They're happy pills."

"Really!" I say. "Do you have some?"

"No," she snorts. "Do I look like I need medication?"

"Adderall, maybe," Ari says.

"Shut up," Mercedes says and pushes him.

"Willow is fine," I say. "She doesn't really like Brooklyn, that's all."

"How can you not like Brooklyn?" Mercedes asks.

"I don't know," I say. "I love it here!"

"Maybe she's homesick," Ari points out, and I know he's right, but I'm tired of Willow getting all the attention because she's sad. "She's like some gorgeous, pouting goddess," Ari says. "Between the two of you, you could have half of Brooklyn on their knees."

"Really?" I ask. "In Alverland, Willow and I are nothing special, but ever since we moved here, people stare at us and tell us that we're beautiful all the time. She hates it."

"You like it?" Mercedes asks me.

I shrug. "Not really, but you know, there are worse things people could say."

"Why aren't you dressed like the rest of your family?" Ari asks. "They all have those cool long shirt things with all those necklaces. Your dad dresses like that, too. I thought it was just some kind of costume for the band, but it's for real, isn't it?"

"They're called tunics and I didn't wear mine because I wanted to look normal."

"You think that looks normal?" Mercedes points to my decidedly dorky pleated skirt and sweater vest.

I shrug helplessly.

"Let's look in her closet." Ari opens the double doors next to my bed. I plop to the floor and munch on almonds as they rummage through my clothes.

"Why'd Timber walk you out of school yesterday?" Mercedes asks as she scoots hanger after hanger of my new erdler clothes across my closet bar.

"I don't know," I say. "He just stopped by to properly introduce himself."

Ari narrows his eyes. "Yeah, right. Suddenly he's the BAPAHS Welcome Wagon."

"What's BAPAHS?" I ask.

Mercedes gives me the look of exasperation and amusement that I'm growing accustomed to. "That's where you go to school, Boo. Brooklyn Academy of Performing Arts High School."

"So what's a welcome wagon?"

"Never mind," says Ari. "I'm just saying, Timber isn't known for being Mr. Friendly."

"Unless he wants to hit dem skins," Mercedes says. Then before I have to ask, she turns to me and says, "That doesn't mean playing the drums, Zephyr. It means, you know, getting with you."

"You mean like boyfriend and girlfriend?" I ask as a blush creeps up my neck into my cheeks. Will he be at the movie and coffee shop with me someday?

"Bella is his girlfriend," Mercedes says. "But that doesn't stop him from messing around."

Before I can ask for a more detailed explanation, Ari lets out a shriek from the very back of my closet. I'm afraid he's come face-to-face with one of Bramble's blind mice or three-legged squirrels, but he emerges with an armload of my Alverland clothes. "Jackpot!" he yells, and tosses tunics, leggings, and boots onto my bed. "Look at this, Mercy!" He holds up my favorite robin's-egg-blue tunic with indigo and brown embroidery around the neckline and sleeves.

"Dang!" Mercedes says, fingering the soft linen. "That's fine, girl. Where'd you get this?"

"My grandmother made it," I tell them.

"Put it on! Put it on!" Ari says.

"Fashion show," Mercedes sings and shoves the tunic at me.

I hold it in my hands and shake my head. I know how erdlers act when they see us in our Alverland clothes. Anytime we leave our village in the woods to go into Ironweed for supplies, we get stared at, yelled at, called names. "Oh, I get it," I say coldly, understanding for the first time what Mercedes has been trying to teach me. This is where I have to hold my own and protect myself. "You're trying to convince me to wear something stupid so you guys can laugh your heads off when I show up at school looking like a freak." I crumple the tunic in my hands and toss it to the floor. I'd truly convinced myself that Ari and Mercedes might be my friends, but obviously, like everything else I've thought I understood here, I'm wrong.

"Zeph!" Ari says. "We're totally serious. This is amazing. I bet you look like a freakin' goddess in this thing."

Mercedes says, "My aunt Nina would kill for this."

"Nobody has anything like it," Ari adds.

"Exactly," I say.

They both nod. "That's just it," Ari tells me. "This is the kind of thing everyone at our school would die for. To have their very own style. We all try to be so original, but look at us, we're just copying somebody else in the end. But this! This is hot."

"No it's not, really," I tell them. "It's very lightweight. My grandmother wove it out of linen from the flax we grow."

They both shake their heads and chuckle. "Timber would be slobbering all over you if you showed up dressed like this," Mercedes says.

I shiver at the mention of Timber. "Really?" Maybe they aren't trying to trick me.

"Really," Ari says resolutely.

A little bell rings and I look around the room, confused. Did I set an alarm? Is someone ringing our doorbell downstairs? The dinging continues as Ari rummages through his messenger bag. "My BlackBerry's pinging," he mumbles, and I wonder if he's a little bit crazy. I mean, first off, blackberries aren't in season and second, unless he knows some magic that I don't, blackberries don't make noise. But then he holds up a small machine and stares at its tiny screen. "Hey, check it out!" he says to Mercedes. "Bella's blogging."

"Move over," Mercedes says, grabbing the thingy from him.

I squirm in beside her so I can see what they're looking at. "Oh wow!" I say. "It's like a little, tiny computer!"

Ari's mouth hangs open. "Are you telling me that you've never seen a BlackBerry?"

"This thing?" I ask, to make sure he's not really talking about the fruit.

Mercedes asks, "What about a Palm Pilot or a Treo or an iPhone?"

I just shrug.

"Do you even own a computer?" Ari asks.

Once again my face burns with embarrassment. I'm starting to think I'll go through the rest of my life here looking like I have permanent sunburn. "I've seen computers," I tell them. "Sometimes we went to the library in the town nearby to use them."

"Whoa," Ari says. "It's like you're Amish but you're not."

I look away from the BlackBerry and stare out the window like Willow. Blackberries, boysenberries—everything I understand is so different from what's here.

Ari comes to stand next to me. "Hey, so what, Zephyr. It's no big deal. Actually, computers are a huge pain in the ass. Mercedes doesn't have one either."

"Shut up, *pandejo*. That's not true. My parents both have laptops."

"Yeah, but you don't personally have one."

"I've seen a freakin' PDA before," Mercedes says.

Ari sighs. "Jeez, Mercedes, I'm trying to make her feel better, you nimrod. Get it?"

"Oh, I get it all right, *pinche pito de pitufo*. Make the Puerto Rican girl seem like a bass-ackward loser so the new girl doesn't think she's all alone. My family didn't just row over from the islands, you know. Both my parents are lawyers."

"God, Mercy, don't get all ACLU on me."

"Are you guys really fighting?" I ask. My breath gets short and my head spins. We don't speak to each other like this in Alverland unless someone is extremely angry, and then watch out because the spells start to fly and someone is going to end up looking like a toad.

Mercedes is the first to stop. She punches Ari on the arm, then smiles broadly. "Nah," she says. "Just giving each other a hard time. Let's see what our little enemies have to say today."

Ari holds up the small screen so all of us can look at once. "Whenever Bella and her clique start blogging, I get pinged."

"Most people just have a MySpace or Friendster page with a blog, but Bella has to be *special*," Mercedes says in a whiny voice. "She has her own Web site. I heard her daddy hired the same company that designed Britney Spears's Web site. Which is, you know, totally gross because Britney is such a ho dog and a has-been."

"And of course Bella has a blog, because who doesn't have their own blog these days? I swear my cat could have his own blog," says Ari.

Bella's pretty face stares out at us from the screen while soft music plays in the background. Next to her picture is something she wrote, which I read through quickly.

BAPAHS is the coolest school on earth! We just found out that in two weeks the O'Donnell Casting Agency is holding auditions for a new ELPH camera Web ad at our school. I can't wait to audition for

**this part. I've done a few TV commercials and had
a few small speaking roles on TV and in movies, but
I would love the opportunity to work in Web-based
advertising.**

"What a load of crap!" Mercedes says. "If you want the real story, you have to go to the secret blog." They both grin.

"There's a hotspot," Ari explains. "If you click this picture of Bella's stupid dog in the corner . . ."

"Which is appropriate because it's a female dog, if you know what I mean," Mercedes adds.

Ari navigates the blinking dot on the screen until it touches the little fluffy white dog's face. "You find a secret link." Ari clicks and a new blank page with a white box in the center opens up. "And voilà, here's the secret blog."

"Or so they think," says Mercedes.

"Someone leaked the password on another blog called I-Hate-Bella," Ari says. "And the password is . . ." He pauses dramatically then bellows, *"Belladonna!"* as he types.

"How stupid and self-centered is it to call *yourself* beautiful lady?" says Mercedes.

"That's what 'belladonna' means in Italian," Ari explains.

"Belladonna is also the name of a plant," I tell them. "My mom uses it for sore throats or sprains but you have to be careful because it's poisonous. The berries are really sweet but they can kill you." Ari and Mercedes both stare at me like they're interested so I continue. "It's also called deadly nightshade or devil's cherries," I tell them with a half laugh. Now they look at each other with their mouths hanging open.

"Dang, that's sick," says Ari.

"That girl is messed up, calling herself the devil's cherry," Mercedes adds.

We all turn our attention back to the screen, which has changed again. Now it's full of pictures of Bella and her friends from school. In some pictures, the girls are all holding brown bottles or smoking cigarettes. In others they look really tired, draped over furniture, half-asleep. Then sometimes they look almost crazy, jumping around, sticking out their tongues, dancing. There are also a few pictures of Timber. When I see his smile, I get fluttery inside.

"Everybody reads it," Ari tells me.

"They put up pictures of themselves partying and say rude stuff about other people at school," Mercedes says.

"Do Bella and her friends know everyone reads it?" I ask. Mercedes and Ari both shake their heads and snicker. "They don't know that you read it?" I say, eyes wide. "Isn't that snooping?"

"Oh puh-leeeeze!" says Ari. "Don't be so naïve. They're probably the ones who leaked the password in the first place. And anyway, if Bella was smart she could go check out her user stats on her Web hoster and find out who's been on her blog."

"But they act all innocent so they can be like, 'Oh we have this exclusive, private blog where we can say any snarky thing about anybody we want!' But no one else can say, 'I saw what you said on your blog,' because they'll be like, 'What are you doing reading my private blog?' Like anybody cares anyway," Mercedes says.

"But you guys care," I say, totally confused.

"Only because it's so funny to see what they're bitching about and then make fun of them for being such jerks," Mercedes snaps.

Now I read Bella's entry in the secret blog.

> **My agent called O'Donnell, the casting agent running the ELPH audition. He says the audition at school is definite. Why am I paying that a-hole agent if he can't get me an exclusive? It's not like**

it's even a real commercial. Some dumb Web thing.
Yet, once again I have to go through the whole stupid audition with every loser at school, then I get
the part. Why can't they just skip a few steps and
give me the part to begin with?
And speaking of losers at school! OMG who's that
new nancy w/ urkel pants pulled up to her pits?
Another grubworm with no fraz. Can't wait to get out
of this place and move to LA!

Below that are comments from her friends. It's easy to see who said
what because each comment has a picture of the girl who wrote it. I recognize them from the cafeteria. One has short black hair, a hoop through
her eyebrow, and bright red lips. That's ZoEzOe. LadyBug has straight
blond hair that brushes her bare shoulders. CH3L-C has red hair, a nose
ring, and a scowl on her face. And BELLA is the girl with those mean
cat eyes.

—Gag. That outfit was so velveeta.
Posted by: ZoEzOe

—U mean the yatch in the caf the other day who said
'My name's not Nancy'? Um der.
Posted by: LadyBug

—TLC thought it wuz hilar . . . nearly popped a head
vein laughing.
Posted by: CH3L-C

—Thought Bella would hi-ya his A.
Posted by: ZoEzOe

—As if.
Posted by: BELLA

"You know they're talking about you, right?" Mercedes asks me.
"Really?" I try to read it again, but I'm completely confused by all the
unfamiliar words and weird abbreviations. "What's it mean?"

"It's hard to understand at first because they use a lot of their own slang," Ari explains.

"'Yatch' is their word for bitch, from bee-yatch. And a 'nancy' is a nice girl," Mercedes explains.

"Are you a nancy, too?" I ask her.

"Hell no. 'Nancy' means a dorky nice girl, which I'm not."

"But how can someone be a *yatch* and a *nancy* at the same time?" I ask, confused.

"Good question," Ari says. "But then again, we're not dealing with the brightest bulbs in the pack."

Mercedes points to the screen. "Zoe calls you Velveeta which is their word for cheesy."

"What's cheesy?" I ask.

"You know, tacky, nasty, cheap, tasteless," Ari explains.

"And, dang girl!" Mercedes says. "Bella calls you a 'grubworm with no fraz.' Translation, a lowlife with no style. Mmm, that's gotta hurt."

She's right, it does hurt and my eyes sting from holding back the tears. "Why are they being so mean to me? They don't even know me. Just because I put my tray down in the wrong place yesterday? That's so unfair."

"But, Zephyr, don't you see?" Ari asks. He and Mercedes stare at me with little smirks. "Right here they talk about Timber."

"TLC," Mercedes says, pointing to Chelsea's comment.

"Chelsea knows that it bugged Bella when Timber laughed about what happened in the cafeteria," Ari says. "Chelsea's always rubbing it in when something annoys Bella. Sometimes I wonder if Chelsea even actually likes Bella."

"Right," says Mercedes. "And then Zoe says she thought Bella would kick Timber's ass for laughing, but Bella acts like it didn't bother her."

"Only it did," says Ari. "Because if it truly didn't bother her, then she wouldn't bother to write about you, but she did, so you got under her skin."

He and Mercedes laugh meanly, but I don't think any of this is funny.

"Now let's check out BellaHater!" Mercedes says.

"This is awesome." Ari makes a new screen appear. "A few months ago, somebody started this I-Hate-Bella blog, only nobody knows who does it."

"But everybody has a theory," says Mercedes.

"Every time Bella posts on her blog, BellaHater puts up some hilarious response," says Ari.

"I think it's the fairy girls," says Mercedes.

"No way," says Ari. "They're clueless."

"Jilly—she's the head fairy girl, you know, those girls who always wear wings?— hates Bella," Mercedes points out.

"So do a lot of people," says Ari.

The new screen is filled with awful pictures of Bella that have been changed. Her teeth are blacked out of her smile. In some she has horns on her head or a mustache. I giggle, because it is funny to see her looking so ridiculous, but then I feel bad for laughing at something that's so unkind.

"I don't know how she does it, but sometimes BellaHater gets pictures of Bella when she's messed up," says Mercedes.

"What do you mean, messed up?" I ask. "Like her hair is messy?"

"No, as in she's had a few too many," says Ari.

"A few too many what?" I ask.

Ari and Mercedes look at each other and sigh.

"Moving on!" says Mercedes.

She reads the day's entry aloud to us:

So apparently, Bella thinks the ELPH audition should be handed to her on a silver platter, like everything else in her life. Well, the smella's the fella, Bella, and I know b.s. when I catch a whiff of it. Would someone please kick her butt this time?

"That's going to be you, Zephyr," Ari says.

"What's going to be me?" I ask.

"The person who kicks Bella's butt," says Mercedes.

I gasp. "I can't do that! I can't fight someone." They have no idea how gentle elves are. I couldn't kick someone if I wanted to.

"No, no, no," says Ari. "Kick her butt means beat her at the audition. That's what you're going to do."

"With our help," Mercedes adds.

I squirm, uncomfortably. I should tell them that I'm having misgivings about the whole thing, but before I can figure out how to say it, Ari says, "Listen *hombres*, sorry I can't stick around for more dastardly plotting to end the evil reign of Bella." He clicks the BlackBerry off and stashes it inside his bag. "But I have rehearsal."

"For what?" I ask.

"My band," he says with a small shrug.

"Yeah, I should get out of here, too," Mercedes says. "My *abuela* hates it when I come home past five." She gathers her things.

"Yeah, I guess I have some homework and stuff to do," I mumble, trying to seem as busy as they are.

As they walk out of my room, I see them grin at each other. "This is going to be fun," Ari says.

"Oh yeah." Mercedes rubs her hands together. "Total blast."

chapter 4

THE NEXT DAY the fairy girls eye me when I walk through the green BAPAHS doors and I get the sneaking suspicion that I've been duped into wearing my Alverland clothes to school. Why oh why did I trust Ari and Mercedes when they said that a long, handmade tunic and deerskin boots would be cool in a place like New York City? Even the weird girls who wear fake wings over their strappy tank tops and flouncy skirts are looking at me like I'm the freak! I wish I could be like my dad—proud and confident when he's onstage in his elf clothes. Then again, this isn't a stage and I'm not playing to my adoring fans. I'm back at BAPAHS, where evil lurks in the form of Bella Dartagnan, who already called me a "nancy with no fraz."

The fairies are in a huddle, gossamer wings flittering as they whisper together and glance over their slender shoulders at me. I know I'm going to have to make a move, either back outside past all the kids on the steps leading up to the school or forward, deeper into the jaws of the BAPAHS beast. Before I can make up my mind which way to go, the big green doors open behind me. A warm breeze ruffles my tunic, reminding me how ridiculous I must look next to everyone in their soft worn jeans, funky tops, and little flat slipper shoes. A guy and a girl pass me, holding hands. "Hey, cool dress," the guy says nonchalantly over his shoulder. The girl glances at me and nods. "Nice," she says, and they go along their way, leaving me in a puddle of gratitude and relief.

Okay, I think, maybe this wasn't such a bad idea after all. Maybe Ari and Mercedes were being honest. Plus, there are no clothes in the world that I'm more comfortable in than my tunic and boots. This is me. If Ari is goth, then this is who I am. I take a big breath and begin walking down the hall. But . . .

The fairies again. They've spread out, three in a row, and are heading toward me, wings shimmering on their backs. Maybe that couple was being sarcastic, which I've noticed is very popular around here. Every other sentence out of Ari's and Mercedes's mouths is like someone cast an opposite spell on them. So when that couple said "cool dress" and "nice" did they really mean "dorky dress" and "bad"? Are they huddled in a corner, laughing at me, fingers flying over the keys on their blueberries or blackberries or whatever they're called as they post comments about my stupid clothes on their glogs or bogs?

"Hey," says the fairy leader. That must be Jilly. The three of them stand in front of me now. The queen fairy is shorter than I am and as slender as a sapling. "Can we ask you a question?" The other two girls (in pink wings and yellow) stand slightly behind their fearless leader, peering out as if they're hiding behind a tree.

"Sure." I brace myself for something totally embarrassing.

"Where'd you get that awesome dress?" the fairy queen asks me.

"It's hot," adds Pink Wings.

"Smoking," says Miss Yellow.

"Really?" I ask. "Does that mean you like it?"

"Duh," says Pink.

"Can I touch it?" The queen reaches out and strokes the fabric. "So soft," she tells the others. They reach out, too, and I blush at their attention.

"So pretty," says Pink.

"And you look amazing in it," adds Yellow.

"Very Guinevere," says the queen.

"Totally Guinevere," the others agree.

"Who's Guinevere?" I ask.

"You know, King Arthur's wife," the queen says.

"Lancelot's lover," Pink adds, wiggling her eyebrows.

"We're kind of obsessed with the whole Camelot thing," Yellow Wings explains and all three nod.

"I could never pull off a dress like that, though," the queen says to her friends. "You have to be tall and willowy, like her."

"Oh no," I tell her. "Everyone looks great in these. And they're so comfortable! You can do anything in them. Climb trees. Hike up a mountain. Sleep." The fairies look at one another and twitter. "I mean," I stammer and blush, "if you like to do those sorts of things. Or you can just, you know, wear them to school and hang out or whatever."

"So where'd you get it?" the queen asks me again.

I'm not sure how to answer. If I tell them that my grandmother made it will they think I'm a weirdo who can't afford to buy real clothes? But I can't lie. "Michigan," I say.

"Michigan?" The queen blinks and frowns. "Where's that? Lower East Side? Williamsburg? Is it a boutique or a chain?"

"The real Michigan," I say. "The state. That's where I'm from. I just moved here." Before they can ask me anything else about my clothes I quickly add, "My name is Zephyr. What's yours?"

"I'm Jilly," says the queen. "This is Rienna and Darby."

"It's so nice to meet you," I say. "I noticed you yesterday in the cafeteria with your wings and everything and I wondered who you were and . . ." I stop because I realize that I'm gushing.

The doors behind me open again. A rush of warm air circulates through the hall, ruffling papers attached to the bulletin boards on the walls. The fairies watch whoever is coming, then they bite their lips and elbow one another. I glance over my shoulder and squint into the streaming sunlight. I can just make out the silhouette of a guy taking off his sunglasses and running his fingers through his hair as he steps into the hallway. My stomach clenches and buzzes as if I swallowed a beehive.

It's the wolf-boy, Timber. He sees me and flashes that gorgeous smile full of teeth. Bees burst from their hive in my belly. They buzz through my tingling arms and legs then I turn to honey, sweet and gooey, as he walks toward me. I hear the fairies suck in air and giggle behind their hands.

"Hey, Zephyr," says Timber, slow and easy.

"Erp," I squeak like a mutant mouse and before I can make something intelligible come out of my stupid mouth, Bella, the queen bee, floats through the open doors. She is followed by her three drones. They walk in step, as if music follows them everywhere.

"Timb," Bella says without even so much as a glance at me. Her eyes are obscured behind giant white sunglasses and her hair falls softly in waves over her shoulders. She is looking down at her phone, busy punching numbers. "I need a frappucino," she commands, and he falls in step with her, down the hall and away.

I'm left facing the fairies, who stare at me with eyebrows raised. "What?" I cringe.

"You know him?" Jilly asks.

"We met the other day," I half explain with an apologetic shrug. "That's all."

Rienna rolls her eyes and snorts. "I've known Timber since preschool. He came to my tenth birthday party and we held hands at the seventh-grade spring fling dance." Then a bell rings, making me jump. The fairies gather their bags. "And still," Rienna says over her shoulder, "he never says hello to me." The three scurry off into the rush of people flooding through the hallway.

"Bye," I call hopefully after them. "See you later?" But they don't turn around.

I find my first class, New Music Ensemble, and pick a seat in the back. Two girls and one guy look up briefly from their conversation. I offer them a weak smile, but they ignore me and go back to talking. I'm not looking forward to this class. I wanted to join one of the chamber music quartets, but none of them needed a lute player. The only ensemble that had space in it was this one, where we'll "explore contemporary vocal-ization," whatever that means. I'm already embarrassed by how bad I'm going to be. They'll probably make me rap and I'll look like the biggest moron that ever walked the face of the planet! Rapping in an elfin tunic—what would Mercedes say? "Off the hinges!"—sarcastically, of course.

Someone slips into the seat beside me. I feel the person leaning in close, "Ready to vocalize?" he asks. I peer out of the corner of my eye, then do a big dorky double take when I realize that Timber is sitting right next to me.

"Oh hi!" I say, my voice as high and chirpy as a nuthatch. I can just imagine Mercedes shaking her head and telling me to tone it down, girl, tone it down. "You're in here, too?" I ask stupidly.

"Nope," he says. "I'm out there." He points to the hallway. "This is my clone." He points to himself.

"Right. Duh." I snort, which is even more embarrassing. "Obviously you're in here."

Timber leans back in his chair and stretches his legs from under the small desk. He rests his hands across his belly. "Yeah, I'm kind of a musical loser," he says. "All I can do is sing and pick out a few songs on the piano, so there's not much choice for me at this school outside of voice ensembles. It's not like I'm some kind of viola virtuoso who takes private master classes all day."

"But I heard you were in a band when you were a kid, so you must be really talented," I say, then stop abruptly, because again with the gushing. What's wrong with me? "Not like I'd know," I add quickly. "I mean, I'd never even heard of your band until someone else told me about it."

The people around us snicker and Timber's face goes through several contortions as I blather. First he's smiling, then he scrunches up his mouth as if he's in pain, then he squints at me as if he's puzzled, finally he laughs in disbelief. "I have no idea what to make of you," he says, shaking his head.

"What do you mean?" My cheeks begin to warm. "I'm just talking. You can ignore me."

"Not easy to do," he says, then leans in close to me again. "Especially in that dress."

Now my face really burns. I stare down at my clothes, mortified by how ludicrous I must seem—the bizarre new girl nattering away in her strange clothes.

"What do you call this?" He reaches out and plucks my sleeve between his forefinger and thumb. I can feel his skin graze mine and I get goose bumps up and down my arms.

"A muumuu," someone says as she walks past us. I look up to see Bella's red-haired drone drop into the seat on the other side of Timber.

"Hey, Chelsea," Timber says, quickly leaning far away from me.

She stares icily at me for a moment before turning her attention to Timber. "They were popular in the seventies. Our grandmas wore them."

Before I even realize what my body is doing, my hand curls into a fist, raises to my lips, and the words "flotsam, jetsam, tantrum" are on the tip of my tongue. But I stop myself. Instead of unleashing a temporary babbling spell that would make her ramble about any thought that entered her head for the next five minutes, I press my fist against my lips and swallow my words. Back in Alverland, if one of my friends were teasing me (although elves are rarely that unkind), I would smack her with this little spell just for kicks. And she'd retaliate, casting a counterspell as quickly as she could. It's a game, a harmless one that's tolerated by our parents because it sharpens our skills. But here, I have to be careful not to expose myself. The only weapons I have now are words, without the magic.

"It's a tunic," I tell her sharply. "And my grandmother wove it for me from flax that she grows."

"Oh, really?" Chelsea feigns disbelief. "And I thought it was Prada."

"It's cooler than Prada," Timber says. "I hate that crap. So boring."

"You like it fine when Bella's in it," Chelsea says.

Timber shrugs with a little smirk on his face. The people around us mutter and laugh, but then our instructor walks in, singing a major scale in his booming alto voice, and everyone snaps to attention. I do the same, happy to lose myself in music, when who I am and what I'm wearing fades as I become a part of a song.

"She called it a muumuu," I tell Ari and Mercedes. We're out in the courtyard behind the school instead of in the cafeteria because it's such a gorgeous day. Ari and Mercedes spent the first fifteen minutes of lunch explaining to me where each group sits, what tables are safe, and when I should come out here. Before school and during lunch is fine. During or after school means you're a druggie. Except for Bella, of course, because no rules apply to her. And when she's out here, she always sits at the table in the middle.

"Which one was it?" Ari asks. We sneak a peek at Bella's foursome in their usual spot center stage. I immediately notice that Timber isn't with them and my stomach sinks. I haven't mentioned to Ari and Mercedes that he liked my tunic or made a point to sit next to me during ensemble.

"The redhead with the nose ring and that tiny little skirt," I tell them.

"Chelsea. Such a skank," Mercedes says. "They're all like Bella's freakin' lap dogs." Mercedes holds her hands like paws in front of her chest and starts sniffing around, wagging her head, and whimpering. "Anything I can do, Bella? What do you need, Bella? Want me to sniff your butt, Bella?"

As Mercedes is doing her doggy impression, Jilly, the queen fairy, walks by. "Oh hey, Zephyr," she says. "How's it going?"

"Great," I tell her. "But I'm worried that I made Rienna mad this morning."

"Don't worry about it," Jilly says with a wave of her hand. "Poor Rienna has been crushing on that guy since she was in preschool. She'll get over it."

"What guy?" Mercedes asks, but I ignore her question.

"Where are Rienna and Darby?" I ask Jilly.

"I don't know," she says, craning her neck. "I was just looking for them."

"You want to sit with us?" I scoot over to make room between Ari and me.

Jilly looks blankly at Mercedes and Ari, who look blankly back at her. "No thanks," she says. "I'm sure I'll find my girls."

"See you later," I call after her.

Ari and Mercedes stare at each other, then they look at me. "You and Tinkerbell best friends now?" Mercedes asks. "Because the fairies sit over there with the other drama turds."

Before I can answer or point out that Mercedes does drama, a guy named Zack who was my lab partner in biology this morning waves to me from a table full of boys on the other side of the courtyard. "Hey Zephyr, come here," he calls out. "These guys don't believe that you know how to skin a deer."

"What are you doing talking to Zack Wheeler? He's a total skoner." Ari says.

"A what?" I ask.

"Skater and a stoner," Mercedes explains.

"Do you really hunt?" one of the guys with Zack yells.

"My grandfather taught all of us," I call back.

"Seriously?" Ari guffaws. "I thought you were a veggie."

"A what?" I ask for the second time in ten seconds.

He points to my plate of salad, fruit, and cheese. "A vegetarian. That you don't eat meat."

"Oh no," I clarify. "We eat meat, but usually on special occasions and then only meat that we kill and dress ourselves."

"Holy crap!" Mercedes yells. "We best be locking up the cats and dogs when Zephyr comes to visit." She pretends to load and cock a shotgun. "Happy Easter, everybody!" Then she fires and makes a strangled dog howl.

Neither Ari nor I laugh. "Actually," I tell her coolly, "we use bows and arrows that we make ourselves. It's a tradition that goes back a long, long time."

"Dang," Mercedes mutters, shaking her head. "I knew you were from the sticks, but I didn't realize you were some kind of NRA redneck."

"Jesus, Mercy," Ari says with disgust. "You need to learn when to shut it."

"What?" Mercedes demands.

"Obviously Zephyr's not some NRA redneck, as you so delicately put it," he says. "They don't even use guns. And her family's hunted for generations. Big deal. It's a cultural thing. Why are you being so judgmental?"

"Maybe you should step off, Ari," Mercedes says angrily. "And go sit with Zephyr and all her new best buddies before you go getting up in my face for making a joke."

Ari puts his hands on his hips and stares Mercedes down. "Is that what this is about, Mercy?"

"What?" she asks.

"Are we jealous that Zephyr made some new friends today?" he asks in a baby voice.

"No, I'm not jealous," Mercedes mocks him.

"You guys," I plead. My stomach clenches into a small hard knot. "Stop. Okay? I've been looking forward to seeing you all day. I don't want to sit with anyone else. I want to sit with you."

As quickly as Mercedes went dark and cloudy, her face brightens into a big silly grin. "Dang, this girl is so 'We Are the World'!" She grabs my hand and Ari's and lifts them above our heads, swaying back and forth, singing, "We are the world. We are the children."

"All right, all right, Jacko," Ari says with a forgiving laugh. "Put the eighties back in their coffin."

Mercedes drops our hands. "Oh hey, I almost forgot." She pulls a flyer out of her backpack. "Check it out." She lays the paper in the center of our small circle. "After school everyone who's interested in the ELPH audition has to go to this info meeting with Mr. O'Donnell, the casting agent. Can you do that, Zeph?"

I pick up the paper with the details and nod. "Sure," I say. "Are you going to be there?" A bell rings, and as usual, I jump like a startled bunny. I cannot get used to my day being controlled by some invisible buzzer.

Mercedes gathers her things and stands up. "Yeah, I'll be there, but a little late. I have a costume fitting."

"What is it this time?" Ari asks.

"Witch number three in *Macbeth*," Mercedes says with a quick roll of her eyes. Then she hunches her back, rubs her hands together, and croaks, "Fair is foul, and foul is fair: Hover through the fog and filthy air." She points to the table where Bella and her posse still sit as if they have no place important to go. Mercedes continues her witchy recitation. "'Double, double toil and trouble. Fire burn and cauldron bubble. Scale of dragon; tooth of wolf; Witches' mummy; maw and gulf, of the ravin'd salt-sea shark; Root of hemlock digg'd i' the dark; Liver of blaspheming Jew . . . ' Hey, that's you, Ari!" she says, becoming Mercedes again. "Come here and give me your liver, boy!" Ari scrambles to his feet as Mercedes chases him around a table and through the courtyard. "I'm casting me a spell. Gonna turn those girls into dogs for real!"

Oh right, I think to myself while I watch their silly erdler interpretation of the dark arts. I tend to forget that here witches are old scary women on broomsticks who stir big black cauldrons while elves are three feet tall and live in some little wizard twerp's closet under the stairs. If only casting spells were so easy, I think as I shove the flyer in my bag.

After school, I'm the first one in the room for the ELPH audition meeting. I think I must be in the wrong place until a man comes in carrying a briefcase. "Great look," he says, then studies me for a moment before he exclaims, "See, this is why I love running auditions at this school. You kids totally embrace the characters. Although . . ."—and here he drops his voice and leans in closer to me as he opens his briefcase—"I have to say that this is probably a bit fancy for an elf, don't you think?" He points to the intricate embroidery covering the neckline and cuffs of my tunic. "I mean, elves are simple creatures. Mischievous little wood sprites."

"Oh really?" I ask, trying to keep from laughing. Before he can start in on the Keebler Elves and Snap, Crackle, and Pop, girls stream through the open door. I see Rienna (the pink fairy) and lift my hand to wave to her, but she turns away quickly so I find a seat off to the side by myself. I put my bag on an empty chair beside me for Mercedes.

As the man hands around packets of information and chats with some of the girls who give him head shots and résumés, I see Bella enter the room. I notice that she's changed clothes since lunch today and now wears a short, fitted green dress with flowing sleeves. She's added a brown sash around her waist and a simple silver necklace with a leaf pendant. Right behind her is Chelsea. Everyone shrinks back and pales as those two girls stride across the room.

"Hi, Mr. O'Donnell." Bella lays her hand on the man's arm.

"Bella!" he exclaims. She steps in for a kiss on the cheek. "I was hoping you'd make it. I spoke with Suzy at your agency and she said she'd courier over your portfolio."

"Oh good," says Bella with a toss of her hair. "I didn't have any left at home. I've been so busy with requests, lately."

"This is a great look, by the way," the man tells her. "See girls," he addresses the rest of us. "You could learn something here. Dress the part, girls, and dress the part correctly." His eyes land on me but he points to Bella as if I should be taking cues on elfin behavior and style from a mean erdler girl like her.

Instantly, I'm incensed. What is it with these erdlers and their silly stereotypes about who we are? Telling *me* I should look more like

Bella—what a joke! My teeth grind together, my eyes narrow, everything in the room goes fuzzy, and I feel fire shooting up inside my belly. I bet if he knew there was a real elf in this room, he'd sweat right through his shirt he'd be so nervous. Which gives me an idea. I bring my hands together over my mouth and nose and breathe the heat of my body into my palms, then release it out toward that stupid troll who doesn't know the difference between an elf and an elephant. It doesn't take long for Mr. O'Donnell's cheeks to turn pink, then red, and tiny beads of perspiration to prickle across his top lip and forehead. He sticks a finger into the collar of his shirt and tugs to loosen his tie.

"Whew." He takes off his suit jacket. "Did it suddenly get to be like a hundred degrees in here? Doesn't this place have air-conditioning?" I can see sweat rings forming under his arms and I'm giddy with delight, at first.

Bella and Chelsea saunter away from the suddenly sweaty man and head straight for me. I shrink back, afraid that I've been caught in the act of hexing. Why did I do it? But apparently I'm wrong, because Bella is smiling at me.

"Hi, Zephyr," she says sweetly and I'm shocked that she knows my name. "Anybody sitting here?" She lifts my bag from the chair beside me and sits down before I can say that I'm saving the seat for Mercedes. Chelsea slinks away. "By the way . . ." Bella leans closer to me and says, "I'm completely mad about what you're wearing!"

"You're mad?" I ask, my heart racing. "I didn't mean to make anyone angry."

"Not that kind of mad," she says with a little laugh. "Mad in a good way. Like crazy. You know, the Mad Hatter, mad about you, mad for chocolate. Like that."

"Oh, well, thanks," I sputter, because I'm so caught off guard by how nice Bella Dartagnan is being.

"It looks handmade," she says. "Really special."

"My grandmother made it, so I guess it is kind of special," I say, and smile, thinking that maybe Bella isn't as bad as Ari and Mercedes said.

"It's been the talk of every fashion victim today so you know that tomorrow a hundred girls are going to show up trying to dress exactly like you." She rolls her eyes and shrugs. "But what can you do? Show an ounce of originality in this place and pretty soon even the janitors will be copying you. I gave up trying a long time ago because I got so sick of all the little Bella clones running around. Now I just show up in any old thing that's comfortable. Jeans, flip-flops, a T-shirt, whatever."

When she says this, I feel silly for being so overdressed and I wish I could wear jeans and a T-shirt, too, but then I'd be copying Bella, which is exactly what she doesn't like. "Sheesh," I mutter half to myself. "It's easier where I'm from. Everyone just wears the same thing."

"Oh God, how awful," says Bella. "You had to wear a uniform?" Before I can explain, she's on to a different topic. "Have you done an audition before?" she asks me while flipping through her info packet.

"No," I admit.

"You picked a great first one. This guy, Mr. O'Donnell, is a total sweetheart. So easygoing and nice. I've worked with him a bunch. Some of the casting agents that show up here are such assholes."

Now I feel even worse for giving Mr. O'Donnell a heat wave. What a stupid, stupid thing to do in front of all these people! I could get myself in so much trouble. I also feel bad for assuming that Bella is evil and that she doesn't like me. My parents have always told us that people who are unkind are usually just uninformed and intimidated by what they don't understand. Not that Bella would ever be intimidated by me, but maybe the other day when she was so mean, it was because she didn't know me. Plus I did take her by surprise when I plopped my tray down in front of her and made her boyfriend laugh. I don't really know what it feels like to be confronted by an outsider. So maybe my parents are right—if I'm kind to her and show her my true self, she will be kind to me and show me her true self.

"My friends told me that you're a super-successful actress. I bet you've worked really hard at it," I say.

Bella watches me for a few seconds as if uncertain, but then she says, "You're right, I do work hard. Most people around here don't understand that. They think I get all my acting gigs by magic." I snort a little laugh when she says this because, believe me, if magic worked like that, I wouldn't be sitting in this audition either. "But the truth is," Bella continues, "I've been working my butt off since I was six years old."

As I listen to Bella, I kind of like her. My dad says that erlders are different than elves because they have all kinds of different personalities rolled up into one. He says you have to get to know the whole person before you decide what they're really like, but they'll only show you one side at a time. So maybe how she acted in the cafeteria and on her blog is only one side of her and really she's very nice.

"Do you want to be famous someday?" I ask.

She blinks at me a few times without answering and I wonder if that was the wrong question to ask. Maybe she's already famous? But then she looks away from me, back down to the packet on her lap, and says, "I just love acting. I don't care about fame."

Mr. O'Donnell is in the front of the room ready to start. Poor guy has nearly soaked through his shirt. "You girls hot?" he asks, pushing up his sleeves and mopping his brow with a soggy tissue. Several girls giggle and I feel terrible for what I've done. I try to think of a way to remedy the situation without getting myself in a deeper mess but then the door opens and Mercedes bounds into the room.

"Sorry I'm late," she says to him. "I had a costume fit— Yikes!" She jumps back when she realizes how sopping wet he is.

"No problem. Just take a seat." He motions to the chairs, flinging droplets of sweat across the girls in front of him. They all flinch and cower, clearly grossed out. Oh dear, I've created such a disaster. I can't do a drying spell because that would be too suspicious, plus I can't think of one anyway. I could probably stop him from sweating, but I just can't quite remember the counterspell to the heat wave I put on him. I have to try something, so I cup my hand around my mouth and curl my tongue into the shape of a straw, then try to suck the heat back into my own body.

Mercedes sees me and grins but then stops abruptly when she sees that Bella is sitting beside me. She knits her eyebrows together as if to ask me what's going on. I just shrug helplessly as she finds the only empty seat on the other side of the room. When I look back at Mr. O'Donnell, he's shivering. He picks up his suit jacket and puts it on.

"Okay," he says, his teeth chattering. "Let's get started." He wraps his arms around himself and rubs his shoulders. "Man, it's cold all of the sudden, isn't it? Did that A/C kick in or what?"

Uh-oh, too strong. I've made things worse and now I'm getting hot.

"Mr. O'Donnell, are you okay?" Bella asks. "You don't look so good."

"You know, I don't feel so good. I must be coming down with a cold or the flu or something. I might have to postpone this."

"Here, let me help you." I hop up and walk over to him. I place my hand on his arm then lead him to a chair. I concentrate on evening out his temperature with mine while we're touching. I'm not good enough at casting spells yet to get it right from across the room. "Is that better?" I ask, putting my face close to his so that my breath will enter his mouth and nose and get both of us back to normal.

"Hmm, yeah," he says after a few seconds. "That is better. Maybe I just needed to sit down for a minute."

I pat his arm and smile, relieved.

"What's your name?" he asks me.

"Zephyr," I tell him. "Zephyr Addler."

"Thanks, Zephyr," he says, then stands. "Now, let's get started."

I walk back to my seat and notice Bella staring at me with her jaw clenched. "Clever," she leans over and whispers to me. "He certainly won't forget you now." She has a smile on her face, but her words do not sound friendly.

"Is that a bad thing?" I whisper back to her, but she's turned her attention to Mr. O'Donnell. I try to catch Mercedes's eye, but she's also focused on him, as is everyone else in the room. I decide to do the same thing.

As I listen to him describe the audition process, I realize that there's so much more to performing than I thought. Bella's right, it's hard work, and I'm afraid that I'm going to make the biggest fool of myself if I do this. I look over at Mercedes again. She catches my eye and winks this time. She's obviously counting on me. I have the sinking feeling that if I don't come through for her, I'll go back to being that sniveling lost girl that I was on the first day of school. I steal another glance at Bella. She's perfectly poised. There's no way I can compete with her. I hold my face in my hands and wonder how I've managed to get myself into so many messes in such a short time.

chapter 5

ARI AND MERCEDES are waiting for me outside the classroom after the meeting is over, but Bella grabs my arm before I leave the room. "So what'd you think?" she asks. "Are you going through with the audition?"

"I guess so," I say uncertainly. "Can't hurt to try, can it?" I add, hoping to convince myself.

"Unless you totally blow it," she says with one eyebrow arching up. "You don't want to start out on the wrong foot with these casting agents. Once they think you suck, you never get another chance."

"But you said Mr. O'Donnell is so nice."

"Nice, yeah," says Bella. "Stupid, no. He's not going to waste his time on people who can't act."

My stomach churns. "My friends Ari and Mercedes said they'd help me." I point to them.

Bella glances their way, then she says, "Maybe we can run lines together sometime. You know, help each other out."

"Really?" I nearly jump up and down I'm so excited that Bella is offering her help. "That would be so nice of you! And I'm sure you'll like

Mercedes, too. You guys could come over to my house, or maybe we could go to the park . . ."

Bella wrinkles her nose and shakes her head. "Uh, no. I mean the two of us help each other. Three people don't work. Someone always ends up feeling left out." As she says this I see Timber lingering by the door. At first, I think his wolf grin is for me and I start to smile and wave, but then I realize that he's come to get Bella. I quickly look away, flushed and flustered by my mistake. Without saying good-bye, Bella is out the door, arm looped around Timber's waist.

"What was that all about?" Mercedes is by my side.

"You have some secret strategy you aren't telling us?" Ari asks. "Know thine enemy or something?"

"What?" I ask, afraid it's obvious that I'm crushing on Timber.

"Bella!" says Mercedes impatiently. "Why are you suddenly so chummy with her?"

"And what were you guys talking about?" asks Ari.

"She sat next to me," I tell them. "Said maybe we could run lines together. Actually, I think you've misjudged her. She's really very nice."

Ari and Mercedes shake their heads in unison. "Girl, you're bent," Mercedes tells me. "If Bella Dartagnan is being nice to you she's either high or she wants something from you or she's planning something."

"Maybe you just don't know her very well," I point out.

"Right," says Ari. "And in the three days you've been at BAPAHS, you've become soul sisters? You have no idea what you're dealing with, Zeph."

Mr. O'Donnell calls my name. I turn around to see him packing all the other girls' portfolios into his briefcase. "Did you give me your résumé and head shots? I can't find them."

"Er, um, well," I stutter.

"She'll have it for you next time," Ari tells him. "She just moved here so she has to update the résumé and get new pictures."

"That's fine," says Mr. O'Donnell. "But don't forget. You can't audition without them."

"Okay, I won't," I tell him, but truthfully I have no idea how to get those things. This is when I wish I'd studied more magic with my grandmother before we left Alverland. About the only thing I can do is hex people to mess with their appearance and bodily functions. I won't know how to conjure things up or change my own form for another twenty years, especially at the rate I'm going.

Ari nudges my arm. "Don't worry. I've got you covered," he whispers.

Before Mr. O'Donnell leaves I ask, "Are you feeling okay now?"

"Strangest thing, that," he says, shaking his head. "Must have been something I ate, but I feel fine now." He clicks his briefcase closed and heads out the door. "Thanks for asking."

Once he's out of earshot, Mercedes pretends to wave good-bye, then fans her hand under her nose and says, "Smell ya later!"

"You're so immature," Ari says, but we both laugh anyway.

Turns out, Ari totally has a plan for my portfolio, but not one I'm entirely comfortable with. After school he takes pictures of me in the park with his digital camera and now we're in his bedroom, him at the computer and me on the floor between his bed and his desk. His cat, Ari Jr., is curled up on my belly, purring happily as I scratch behind his ears. "You don't understand, Ari. I can't lie," I tell him.

"It's not lying, Zephyr," he says impatiently. "We're just exaggerating a little bit."

But it's impossible to explain that for me, there is no difference. Elves don't lie. We just don't. Honesty is in our nature. As is kindness. And for those elves who go against their intrinsic goodness, there are serious consequences. Or at least I think so. It's never happened since I've been alive, but I've heard that some elves become dark and have to leave Alverland. Sometimes I think parents just made up the idea of Dark Elves to keep kids in line, kind of like the bogeyman, but you never know.

"Look, Zeph." Ari turns toward me. The late afternoon sun streams through the big window behind him, exposing a corridor of dust floating lazily in the still air. It's funny what you can see in the clear, strong light. So far, Brooklyn has felt like one big shadow to me. "I have to write something down on this résumé. You heard the guy, you can't audition without a portfolio."

"What's wrong with this being my first audition?" I stare at stickers of planets and stars on Ari's ceiling and I miss the night sky in Alverland, which is so open that you can see galaxies. Here, you're lucky to catch a fleeting glimpse of the moon and one star through all the blaring city lights.

"But most people start with amateur stuff, not a real audition for a professional gig," Ari explains. "Weren't you ever in a show or school play or onstage with your dad in Michigan? Or is that against your religion there?"

Ari Jr. stretches his front legs, digging his claws into my belly, then hops off and struts around the room. I roll to my side and prop my head on my hand. "Where do you think I came from?" I ask Ari, slightly amused. "It's not like we don't put on plays or sing or have fun there."

"I don't know," he answers. "I've Googled your dad like a million times trying to figure out where you guys are really from, but it's kind of a mystery, which is cool."

"What's Googling?" I ask, imagining some kind of fancy, high-powered binoculars.

"Jeez, and you wonder why I think you grew up in a hole in the ground. Come here, I'll show you." He picks up his laptop and flops down on his bed, where we can sit side by side on top of his messy covers. After typing in some words, a screen comes up with the word "GOOGLE" in colorful letters across the top of the page. He keys my dad's name into a little box, then a huge list appears with "Drake Addler" highlighted in bright blue over and over. "You can click on any of these Web pages and read about your dad," he tells me.

"Whoa," I say. "That's so weird. How does the computer know so much about my dad?"

"Because he's kind of famous," says Ari.

I bump him with my elbow. "No, he's not. You're teasing me again."

"Yeah, Zeph, he is." Ari turns toward me and flaps his arms around as he talks superfast about my dad. "I mean not like totally famous. I wouldn't like him if he were. But he's got a huge underground following. I'm talking humungous, which is so much cooler than being popular because your record label paid a zillion dollars for your CD to be on an iTunes download list."

"Why do you have to go underground to follow him?" I ask.

"I mean secret."

"But it's all over the computer." I point to the screen.

Ari drags his fingers through his hair. "Okay, not secret, but not mainstream. You know, he's on an indie label and he still tours by van and plays small clubs but he has a lot of fans."

"Really?" I ask.

"Yes, really." Ari drops back against the wall behind the bed as if explaining all of that exhausted him. "And I want to be just like him. My career, I mean." He repositions the computer on his lap. "Here, check out some of these sites, you'll see what I mean."

I move closer to Ari's side and roll my finger over the little black ball at the bottom of the keyboard (which Ari calls a mouse for some strange reason). I click on a Web site. Up pops my dad on a stage with his guitar strapped across his body. "Wow," I say as I study the picture. He's wearing a short ochre-colored tunic with bright red embroidery that my mom made and soft buckskin pants and boots. His hair has come loose from his normally tidy ponytail and whips across his open mouth as he sings. I look more closely at the picture, trying to find a glimpse of my older brother, Grove. I think I see one of his arms and his foot off to the right side.

"I miss them," I say to Ari and lay my head against his shoulder. "My mom and Willow are great, but I'm really close to my dad."

"God, seriously? I wish my dad would skip town every once in a while. He's always here. The man's never heard of a business trip."

"Mine's gone too much." I realize then that I haven't hugged my dad in over a week. "Every time he calls, he can talk for only a minute. He has no idea what's going on in my life. And he's the only one in my family who gets why I want to be here and go to school and try new things. He would be so excited about the audition."

"But aren't you used to it by now? I mean, isn't he gone all the time?"

"He used to go on the road before we moved, but that was different. Everything was familiar at home and we were with all our family and friends, so having him gone was no big deal. Here, though, when Grove and Dad are gone, it feels like there's a big empty hole in our house."

"Don't fall in!" Ari says with a snicker.

"What?"

"The big hole in your house."

I jab Ari in the side. "You're as funny as a snakebite," I tell him, but I'm laughing.

"Want to hear him sing?" Ari clicks onto another page and my dad's mellifluous, deep voice fills up the room.

"Ugh, I hate this song. It's so dramatic." I stand up on my knees beside Ari and I sing along to "Raven Call," exaggerating my dad's voice. "And the RAVEN, watching SILENTLY, wings beating HUM and THRUM!" I stop singing. "What's 'hum' and 'thrum' anyway? That's so annoying."

"Some people think the hum and thrum means a beating heart," Ari tells me. "That maybe your dad is referencing Poe."

"What's a poe?" I ask, flopping back down beside him.

"As in Edgar Allan. The poet? The guy who wrote 'The Raven' and 'The Tell-Tale Heart'? Tell me you know Edgar Allan Poe!"

"I've heard of him," I say. "But I'm sure my dad hasn't."

"Of course he has!" Ari nearly yells, but he's laughing, too.

"It's not like my dad sits around reading poetry, Ari. He's more into, like hunting, and fishing, and telling stories when he's not playing his guitar."

"I don't care what you say, Zeph, your dad definitely knows Poe because your dad is a poet."

"No, he's not." I push Ari. "He's a singer."

Ari buries both hands in his hair, as if I'm driving him crazy. "Have you even listened to his words?"

"Of course," I say. "I've been listening to him all my life."

"No, his songs, Zephyr. His songs! He has such amazing things to say. There are entire Web sites where people discuss the meaning of his lyrics."

"What people?"

"Like this site, DrakeAddict.com." He pulls up a Web site and more pictures of my dad, some old and some new, fill the screen. The soft guitar part from the beginning of his song "West Wind Blowing" plays.

I grab Ari's shoulder and yell, "I love this one!" My dad's voice comes in quietly, humming for a few bars.

"So you do like your dad's music?"

"This is his best song, don't you think?" I ask with a sly smile.

Ari shrugs. "It's okay, I guess."

"Ari!" I slap his arm. "Listen to the words." I sing along. "'The west wind carried you in, tiny flower, you floated on the breeze, growing up tall and sturdy, among the alder trees . . .'" Ari looks at me blankly. I grab one of his pillows and swing at him. "It's about me, you loser!" I yell, but I'm laughing so hard that I keep missing him with the pillow.

"Oh my God, I get it now!" Ari grabs the pillow from me and I collapse back on the bed, as if exhausted. "Zephyr means west wind! It *is* about you. I'm totally going to post that." He starts typing furiously.

"Wait! Stop!" I grab his hand. "I don't want everybody to know that."

"Why not? It's so cool. Your dad wrote a song about you."

"No." I squeeze his hand. "Seriously, please don't. My family is very private."

Ari sighs but he stops typing. He pushes the cancel button and the Web page disappears. Then he leans back against the wall. "Tell me about where you're from. What's it like? Do you miss it?"

I lean back, too. Our shoulders touch. "In some ways it's amazing. So beautiful and quiet. There's hardly anything there, no stores, no cars."

"Whoa," says Ari. "You didn't have a car? How'd you get anywhere?"

"There's a town next to ours called Ironweed where our clan, er, I mean family, keeps a car that we use when we need to bring in supplies. Plus, my dad has his own van that he drives to gigs. But mostly, we walk."

"Do you go to that town a lot?"

"No." I smooth the soft linen of my tunic over my knees, then yank out a tiny brown thread that's come loose from the hem. "The people in Ironweed don't like us."

"Holy crap. I'd shoot myself if I had to stay in the same place all the time. Didn't you get bored?"

"Sort of, I guess, but really there's plenty to do. We study during the day and then we do chores and then we can go do whatever we want. All my brothers and sisters and cousins on my mom's side are there. My dad's whole family is just an hour's walk away, so it's not like we ever get lonely. Plus, we have lots of celebrations. There's always some kind of party or special holiday to plan for or go to. And lots of people from different clans, um, families I mean, get together for those."

As I say this, I think of the fun I'm missing in Alverland—birthdays, full moons, planting festivals, berry picking, bird-call competitions, overnights on hidden uninhabited islands with my cousins and friends from other clans where we practice magic all night, zapping one another with silly spells like uncontrollable laughter or farting hexes. I sigh.

"But you like it here, right?" asks Ari.

"I do. That's the thing, I love it here!" I tell him. "I'm a lot like my dad and my brother Grove. We're a little bit different from everyone else in Alverland because we have dreams that could take us away from that life. That's why we came to New York. So my dad could record a new album and tour with a full band, not just my brother. Plus in New York he can meet record-label people. Maybe get on TV. All the things he wouldn't get to do in Michigan."

"And so you could go to BAPAHS," Ari says.

"Yeah! When he and my mom decided we'd all come to New York for the year, I begged them to let me go to school. My dad is the one who found BAPAHS for me. Even though my mom was really worried and didn't want me to do it, my dad knew I'd love it so he supported me."

"You know, BAPAHS saved my life," Ari says. "Middle school was really rough for me. There were only two other kids in my whole class who liked music. Everybody else was into sports. All I wanted to do was play my piano and write songs and perform. Now I get to do that and it's cool. But it was all right being unhappy, you know? It made me understand the dark side of things. How to be a cynic and find humor in what hurts. That's what a lot of my songs with my band, GGJB, are about."

"I'd like to hear your music sometime." I put my hand in his and I squeeze.

Ari turns his head toward me. "Zephyr," he says slowly. I look up at him and I smile. "Listen, I hope you aren't expecting something . . ."

"Expecting what?"

"You know . . ." He drops my hand. "Something between us."

"You mean like boyfriend and girlfriend?" A flush crawls up my body.

He nods. "Because I don't think . . . you know, you and me, and well . . ."

I curl my knees up tightly to my chest. "Why would you think that, Ari?"

"Well, you've been touching me a lot. You put your head on my shoulder. And then you were holding my hand."

"Sorry!" I'm laughing but I cover my face with a pillow so he can't see how red I've become. I peek over the top of the pillow and try to explain. "We're very affectionate with one another where I come from." I realize that up until now I've spent every day of my life with the people who love me and know me. We thought nothing of holding hands, or giving each other piggyback rides, or curling up together like puppies or kittens for a nap. And although I'll admit that sometimes that got old and I just wanted something new and different in my life, now I kind of miss it.

"Good," says Ari. "Because I should tell you something. I think that I might be, you know, gay."

I look at him, puzzled. I know I've heard that word before.

"You do know what 'gay' means, don't you?" Ari asks.

I scratch my eyebrow and bite the corner of my mouth. "I think I do, but I'm not really sure."

"Gay is when a guy likes a guy or a girl likes a girl," he says slowly, as if I'm slightly stupid. "Instead of, you know, being straight, when a guy and girl get together."

"Oh right!" I say. "Now I remember."

"Let me guess, you don't have gay people where you're from?" He sounds angry.

"Oh no," I tell him. "We do, we just don't call them something different. People just love each other, it doesn't matter who. Most people get married and have big families, but then there are some people who spend their lives together, two men or two women, and we call them a word that means something like Always Uncles or Always Aunts because they don't have their own kids."

"God," Ari lays back against his pillows as if he's woozy. "That sounds like the coolest place in the whole world. I bet even a goth, gay, Jew boy like me could get along."

"Now you're a goth, *gay*, Jew boy?" I tease.

"That's what my band's name means. GGJB, goth, gay, Jew boy."

"I like it!"

Just then a little screen pops up on Ari's computer. "Hey, cool. It's Mercy. She's IMing me."

I read over his shoulder, but as usual, parts of the message seem like they're in code:

—Is Z there? B's blogging smack about her again. Uh-huh, such a nice girl!

"You see that?" Ari asks then he types back to Mercedes:

—Checking it out now. Back in 5.

"We told you, Zephyr, they're mean, mean, mean." He jumps over to the latest entry on Bella's secret blog:

> **Went to the ELPH aud 2day. Snap. O'Donnell luvs me. Y bother w/ this ruse. Give me the part already! Nobody WTE there. All cactus.**

"What's WTE mean?" I ask Ari.

"We think it means 'worth the effort,' but they change their slang all the time," Ari says. "I don't know what 'cactus' means, though. Hang on." He opens the I-Hate-Bella blog where there are new nasty comments about Bella and her friends.

"Goodness, I feel bad for them!" I say as I skim the horrible things other people are saying. "Who do you think does it?" I ask.

"Some people say it's Timber's ex-girlfriend Tessa. She moved to Jersey last year and lots of people think she does it from there. But I doubt it," says Ari. "She doesn't strike me as the vindictive type. Plus, how would she know what happens at BAPAHS, unless she has a spy?"

"Who then?" I ask.

"Beats me, but I'd like to shake the hand of whoever's behind it."

"That's mean, Ari. Nobody deserves to be hated that much by other people."

"God, Zephyr, you just don't get it, do you? You shouldn't feel sorry for them."

"I know what it feels like to be picked on and hated for no reason, Ari! Every time my cousins and I walked into Ironweed, the people who lived there yelled hateful, stupid things at us. Sometimes the kids would throw rocks and sticks and we'd have to run away into the woods like scared little chipmunks because our parents wouldn't let us fight back. It was awful."

"I got called a faggot every day of junior high," Ari says. "I know what it feels like. But I'm telling you, these girls bring it on themselves." He types in a question:

> —**Anybody have the 411 on 'cactus' from Bella blog 2day?**
> Posted by: gothboi.

We wait for what seems like a full minute, although it was probably a lot quicker, then a message pops up:

> —**Cactus from Sept 15 BELLA / LadyBug exchange:**
> > —**Anybody in calculus?**
> > Posted by: LadyBug
> >
> > —**F*ing wasteland.**
> > Posted by: BELLA
> >
> > —**Sahara Dessert?**
> > Posted by: LadyBug
> >
> > —**"Desert" you moron. Me and a bunch of cactus.**
> > Posted by: BELLA
> >
> > —**Cactus! F*ing hilar. LOL**
> > Posted by: LadyBug
>
> Posted by: BellaHater

"Oh, now I get it," says Ari. He thanks BellaHater, whoever that is, and clicks back onto Bella's blog.

"I don't understand any of this," I admit, but then again, I can't stop reading Bella's entry either.

> **That yatchy nanc kissed A at the aud. Just give O'Donnell a b.j. already.**
> **And OMG! What was that thing she wore? Looked like it was made out of a bedspread.**

Below that, we read the comments:

> —**Fo' real! C calls it muumuu.**
> Posted by: ZoEzOe

—LOL! A muumuu! FNO she's MooMoo.
Posted by: BELLA

—TLC liked it better than Prada.
Posted by: CH3L-C

—C u'r a slag & MooMoo will fall flat on her fat ass. ELPH is mine. End-o-story.
Posted by: BELLA

When I'm done reading, my heart races and my palms are sweaty.

"Do you understand what they're saying?" Ari asks me.

"They're making fun of my tunic."

"Yep and they've given you one of their illustrious nicknames. 'FNO'—from now on—you will be known as 'MooMoo' to them."

"They're going to call me that?" I ask, horrified at the thought of walking through school while being lowed at like a cow.

"Not to your face," Ari says. "Only behind your back, which is how they do everything."

I skim the entry again, understanding it better this time. "And Bella thinks I'm no competition, right?" I ask.

"Right again."

I'm furious. It's the exact same feeling I used to get walking down the dusty street in Ironweed, trying to ignore the taunts hurled at us from erdlers in their cars. "Burn in Hell, Satan Worshipers!" "Go back to the commune!" "We don't want your cult here!" So many times, my cousins and I planned the hexes we'd like to cast on those people, making their hair fall out in clumps, giving them all diarrhea for forty days, turning them into goats if our magic ever got strong enough. But our parents always told us no. That's not what our magic's for. It would be wasted on revenge. And we'd do ourselves harm in the end because if you cast spells only for evil, you can make yourself sick or lose your powers for a while or worst of all, you have to leave Alverland forever because your heart becomes dark.

I never thought anything could make me feel that bad, but this is a thousand times worse because Bella pretended to be nice and she *lied*, saying she'd help me. I want nothing more than to plague those mean girls with the Curse of Wrinkled Butts, Contagious Belching, Bloody Tears, and Swollen Tongues. I want their noses to grow long and twist into their mouths. Their ears to blow up like cauliflower and their hair to turn to straw. And at this very moment, if I knew how to send a spell through the wires of a computer, I'd zap them with everything I've got.

"So?" says Ari. "Still feel sorry for them?"

"No." I grind my teeth until my jaw aches.

"You wanna kick some Bella butt? Waste her at the one thing that's actually important to her?"

"What's that?" I ask, thinking for a minute that he means Timber.

"The audition," he says simply.

"I don't know, Ari." I shake my head. "How could I beat her? She's a professional and I'm just . . . me. What if I end up making a total fool of myself?"

"Look," Ari says. "Mercedes and I are really good at this. I can make a résumé that would convince anyone to hire you and Mercy's a great actress who could totally coach you . . ."

"If she's a great actress, why isn't she trying out?"

"Mercedes will have her chance someday," Ari says. "But she and I both know this isn't the time. The description of what the casting agents are looking for just doesn't fit her. See, that's the thing, Zeph. The biz, I mean TV and movies and stuff, is not just about talent or experience. These agents are always looking for something different. Something new. Something they've never seen before. You're new. You're gorgeous. You've got this quality, I don't know what it is, but I'm telling you, you've got IT. Now, you just have to want it."

I consider all this. I'm not sure I believe him, but it feels pretty good to have someone think I'm special, and not in a weird way. Plus, this is what I came for, to perform. Not to mention that I could get even with Bella.

"Or," he says, leaning away from me, "you can just be MooMoo at the mercy of Bella like everyone else around here."

That hurts. I look at him squarely. "All right, let's write my résumé."

"You don't think it's lying anymore?" Ari teases me.

"I want that ELPH part," I say coldly, imagining how furious Bella will be if I get the part and she doesn't.

"Yahoo!" Ari hollers. He dashes a note quickly to Mercedes:

—Now Z's p.o.'d!

She writes back:

—Let's kick some A!!!!!!

"Let's," I say, and vow to myself that I'll do whatever is necessary to make sure that I beat Bella at her own game.

chapter 6

I'M STILL SHAKING with anger as I walk home from Ari's house through the park, so I cool myself off by casting silly spells. First I whip up a tiny leaf tornado beside the path. A group of kids playing nearby stop and stare at the spinning leaves, then run screaming toward their nannies who sit chatting on a bench. I didn't mean to frighten them, so I flick my fingers at the leaves, and they float gently to the ground. The kids run back to the pile and poke it with sticks. A hawk flies above me. Seems like every time I'm in the park, I see this same bird, which is sort of comforting. Maybe its nest is nearby. I point to the hawk, trying to catch it in my power, but it soars higher beyond my reach. I settle for a yellow butterfly, instead, and bring it fluttering in a zigzag pattern toward me. I land it on my nose to stare cross-eyed at its wiggly antennae and long curled proboscis.

Kids do this kind of thing all the time in Alverland. Altering nature is the first way we use our magic and learn the consequences of using our powers for the wrong reasons. There's always some ornery group of elf kids who dare one another to cast wicked spells on birds and frogs, at least until their magic dries up for a few hours, and leaves them with coughs and runny noses. I let the butterfly go and with it some of my fury about Bella's blog. Even though I don't feel as mad anymore, I'm still totally confused. I wish I could talk to my dad. I just don't understand the erdler world. People act one way in front of you and then call you something horrible behind your back. Why? What good does that do?

I come out of the park and see the big pine tree in front of our house. It still feels funny to call this place our house. It's not *our* house. *Our* house is in Alverland, in the middle of a grove of tall maple trees that we tap for syrup, next to the stream where I learned to fish for trout, not far from a tangled patch of black raspberries that we pick every summer and cook into jam for the winter. Now syrup comes in a glass bottle with a picture of a tree on the label, and trout is something dead on a Styrofoam tray with no head or tail, and we've eaten almost every jar of homemade jam that we brought with us because it tastes so much like home that we can't keep our spoons out of it. This house is a strange place with its locking doors and shuttered windows and tiny patch of green in the back that we own but do not share.

I open our front door and trudge through the dark, gloomy living room. "Hello?" I call, hoping that my mom or Willow will answer because I need to talk, but there's no answer.

I find my mom in the sunny kitchen humming one of Dad's songs as she chops up vegetables. That's a good sign. She hums when she's happy. In Alverland, she was always humming, but I haven't heard her pretty singing voice much since we've been in Brooklyn.

"Hi, Zephyr," she says when I walk in. She stops what she's doing and wraps me in a hug. "How was your day?"

I hop up on the counter beside her. "I just don't understand erdlers," I say, swiping a carrot from the cutting board.

"Why not?" She goes back to deseeding a cucumber.

"I can't figure them out." I wave my carrot around. "Are they nice? Are they mean? Seems like they're both, all the time, at the same time."

"I think that would be exhausting." She slices open a juicy tomato.

"Exactly!" I say. "I don't know how they keep track of who they like and who they dislike and who they're friends with and who they hate, especially because it keeps changing all the time. I mean, one minute Bella is sitting next to me offering to help me and the next minute she's telling everyone that I'm going to fall flat on my face!"

"Who's Bella?" Mom asks. "Did I meet her the other day?"

"No that was Mercedes and Ari. They're my friends. But see, it's weird. How can Mercedes and Ari be so nice to me, someone they hardly know, but then hate Bella so much that they want to make her miserable?"

"That doesn't sound very nice," says Mom. "Are those the kind of erdler friends you want?"

"I think they're all that way. And what worries me most," I continue, "is whether my friendship with Ari and Mercedes is real or if I'm just a convenient way for them to get at Bella. What if Bella beats me at the audition? Will Ari and Mercedes like me anymore?"

"What audition?" Mom asks.

"Because if that happens," I say, ignoring her question, "then I'll be back where I started on the first day of school when I cried like a stupid baby in the middle of the hallway."

"You cried?" Mom looks stricken at the thought of me upset, like she might cry, too.

"Yeah, but it was okay because then I met Mercedes and Ari and I wasn't alone anymore."

"I don't know, Zephyr," she says. "This all sounds very complicated and—" As she says this the phone rings. Without finishing her thought, she answers, as if she's been waiting for the call. "Yes! Yes!" she says, and I can tell by the tone of her voice that it's about her naturopath business. She hands me the knife and points to the veggies on the counter.

I cut a big hunk off the tomato and sprinkle some salt on it before popping it in my mouth. As I chew, I try to puzzle through why Bella makes Mercedes and Ari, the fairy girls, and all the people on the BellaHater blog hate her so much. Wouldn't it be easier if she was just nice to everyone? But the weirder thing is, if all those people hate her so much, why do they spend so much time thinking about her, talking about her, plotting revenge against her? Then I realize, I'm standing here thinking about her right now, too! Aargh! I have to stop.

On the windowsill in front of me, I notice an envelope with Aunt Flora's handwriting. That must be why Mom is so cheery. Suddenly I miss Alverland terribly. Especially my cousin Briar, whose love and friendship I've never had to question. I look out the open window over the sink and see that Poppy, Bramble, and Persimmon are in the garden building another bunny hutch out of scraps of wood. Up until now, that was my life in Alverland—happily building bunny hutches with my brothers and sisters and cousins and friends, never having to worry about who liked me and why. Poppy looks up and sees me staring at them.

"Zephyr's home!" she shouts, and they all run into the kitchen. They surround my legs and Persimmon reaches her arms up to me. I pop her on my hip and hand her a slice of cucumber.

"Come outside with us!" Poppy says.

Bramble wraps his arms around my thighs. "I missed you," he coos up at me. I pat his head.

"Here Fephyr." Persimmon shoves the cucumber in my mouth.

"Come on. Help us," Poppy begs and yanks on my tunic.

Bramble tugs at my free hand. "Come outside."

"Help Fephyr," Persimmon says, pointing out the window.

"No, not right now," I tell them, and set Percy on the floor.

"But why?" Poppy whines. "We need your help. We haven't seen you all day. Did you go to school? Are your friends with you? Do they want to help us?"

I wish Mom would get off the phone so I can talk to her some more about Bella, Mercedes, and Ari. I want to tell her about the audition and ask her if it was okay to let Ari write a résumé for me. But she's still blathering into the phone about primrose oil and black cohosh.

Persimmon whimpers up at me. "Help, Fephyr, help!"

"I need to talk to Mom," I say, annoyed.

"You never play with us anymore," Poppy shouts.

Mom glares at us and waves her arms frantically, shooing us out the back door, which makes Persimmon cry. I scoop her up and pull Bramble and Poppy outside with us. Mom slams the door behind us and we all jump, then Percy wails.

"Why is she mad at us?" Poppy cries.

"She's just busy." I rub Persimmon's back to calm her down.

"She's always busy," Bramble mumbles. He picks up a hammer and bangs uselessly on a rock.

"It's hard for her with Dad and Grove gone," I say.

"Daddy?" Percy says excitedly and looks around.

"He's not here," I tell her. This sets her tears off again. "Where's Willow?" I ask, more annoyed now that I'm the one taking care of the little ones by myself when I've got my own problems to deal with.

"All she does is hug her pillow," Poppy says.

"She's sad," Bramble adds.

I squint up at the top floor of the house. The hawk perches on the roof peak above the open windows and wispy clouds float by. "You're right," I tell Poppy. "All Willow does is stare at the trees with her pillow in her arms thinking about Ash." And this is annoying, because sure,

I'd like to have a boyfriend, too, but at least I'm making an effort to have a life here. I pick up a wood chip and fling it up toward our bedroom window while shouting, "Willow! Hey, Willow!" Poppy joins me. "Willow!" we both yell and throw our wood chips. The hawk spreads its wings and takes flight above the trees. Then Bramble and Persimmon start jumping around, throwing wood chips and yelling, too. "Willow!" we all scream at the top of our lungs. "Willow!"

For some weird reason the hawk swoops down and lands on the top of our fence to screech at us. "Look! Look!" Bramble yells excitedly. He starts climbing up the fence to get a closer look. "Do you think its nest is up there?"

Before Bramble gets very far, the back door flies open and my mom is yelling at us, "What are you doing? Have you lost your minds?" The hawk flaps its wings and lifts off into the air again.

"You scared it away!" Bramble yells at my mom.

"I cannot run a business with you howling like a bunch of wild coyotes when I'm on the phone," Mom shouts. We all start talking at once to protest, but then she zaps us. I feel it in my throat, a deep itchy tingling and my tongue goes numb. We're all mute. No sounds come from our open mouths. We stare at her—this crazy, shouting woman who used to be our calm, happy mother. She slams the door and we can see her through the kitchen window, pacing furiously while talking on the phone again.

Bramble has dropped down from the fence. He, Poppy, and I blink at one another. Our mother has never hexed us before. Never. Only the worst, most impatient elfin mothers hex their children. I look down at Persimmon. She wails silently, bewildered by what has happened and where her little voice has gone. My stomach is tight and my head hurts. I want to scream but I can't.

Just then, Willow pops her head out the upstairs window. "What's going on?" she asks sleepily. "Why'd you wake me up?" I'm so angry right then that I pick up a rock and fling it at her. "Hey!" she shouts and ducks back into the window. The rock bounces off the side of the house. Willow peeks out again. "Why'd you do that?"

Poppy must feel the same as me because she picks up a handful of pebbles and hurls them toward the sky. They rain back down on us, pelting our heads and shoulders.

"What's going on?" Willow demands. I pick up another rock and aim it toward her. Before I can throw it, she zaps it and turns it into a fistful of sand that sprinkles through my fingers to the ground.

I drop the sand and point to a sparrow flying past the window, toward a tree. I redirect the bird straight toward Willow's long hair ruffling in the breeze. The bird flaps frantically, fighting against the force of my magic. I see Bramble out of the corner of my eye. He waves his arms and jumps up and down, pointing toward the bird, but his magic is not powerful enough to stop me. Willow, though, is quick and sharp. "Wither Arm!" she shouts, sending my arm flopping uselessly by my side. The bird cartwheels in the air then swoops away and disappears into the branches of a tall oak tree.

I try to yell at Willow, to tell her that I'm sick of her not helping and that her stupid moping is making everyone else miserable, too, but my voice is still gone. So I run toward the house. I fling the door open with my one good arm (the other flaps like a broken wing beside me) and I charge through the kitchen, past my mom, and up the back stairs. I hear the others close behind me.

Willow is waiting for us at the top of the steps. "Zephyr, what's wrong with you?" she asks. "You're acting like a lunatic."

I move my mouth, but no words come out. Then Bramble tackles me from behind. I'm on the floor, Bramble on top of me. I wrench around and see his mouth opening and shutting, opening and shutting, and I imagine that he's silently yelling at me about the bird. I'm powerless then without my voice while one arm lays like a dead fish on the floor and the other is pinned to my side by Bramble's strong little legs. Poppy darts out from the stairwell to my rescue. She flings herself at Bramble, knocking him off my back, and they land in a heap on the rug. Willow rushes to them. "What in the name of Mother Earth is going on with you guys?" she shouts.

Now I'm peeved at Bramble, the little toad, for tackling me. I zing a hiccupping hex at him, but in all the confusion of arms and legs with Willow trying to separate Poppy and Bramble, my hex hits all three of them and they are instantly seized by tiny squeaking convulsions, "Hic! Hic! Hic!" I try not to, but I laugh because it's so funny to see them all hiccupping in unison. And wouldn't it figure that that's when my voice comes back so they all hear me. My magic must be getting weak, though, from all the spell casting, plus I'm out practice, because the hex lasts only a few seconds, then all three of them are glaring at me as I snicker meanly from my place on the floor.

"No, no!" I squeal, because my voice is faint. I skitter backward across the rug. "I didn't mean it."

Poppy is as mad as a cornered skunk. It's almost funny to watch her try to summon some kind of spell to get me back. She lifts up on her toes and raises her arms above her head, then she yells, "Poop!" with all her fury as she flings her arms toward me. But her magic is so puny that in the tense seconds following her mighty attempt to zap me with a horrid hex only an itty-bitty squeaky fart escapes from my butt. Then we all lose it. Even Willow. We are all on the floor rolling, clutching our sides, and howling with laughter until our eyes are full of tears and we can barely breathe.

The only thing that stops us from laughing until we're sick is my mom, who storms up the stairs yelling, "What in the stars is wrong with you kids!" She stands over us with her hands on her hips, then suddenly asks, "Where's Persimmon?" Each of us pops upright. We look around.

"Percy?" we say. "Percy, where are you?"

"Where'd you go?"

"She's not here."

"Where is she?"

"Come out."

"Come on, Persimmon, no hiding now," Mom says firmly, but our sister doesn't reappear.

We comb the upstairs, each of us sure that she followed us up the steps. But she's not in her room, not under her bed or anyone else's bed, not in any of the closets, or hiding in the bathtub, or squatting behind a chair. We fan out. Willow and I go to the first floor, my mother is on the second floor, while Poppy and Bramble continue looking on the top floor. We all call to her, our pleas going from gentle coaxing to angry demands that she show herself. We meet up in the kitchen after five minutes of fruitless searching and then we begin to panic.

"When's the last time you saw her?" my mother asks.

"Outside," we tell her. "But then she came upstairs."

"Are you sure?"

"I don't know," I say. "I went first. Bramble, did you see her?"

"I followed you," he says and turns to Poppy. "Did you?"

"I thought she was behind me," Poppy says, but my mom is already out the back door, not interested in our excuses. We run behind her.

The garden is tiny and with the five of us scouring every square inch, it doesn't take long to realize that Persimmon's not here either.

"Where is she?" Poppy crumbles to a little quivering heap on the ground. Bramble's chin quivers and soon he's sobbing, too. My eyes fill with tears because I know this is all my fault. I should have been more mature. More responsible and helpful instead of so self-centered, focused only on my stupid problems at school and how much Willow is bugging me.

My mother stands motionless in the center of the garden. She closes her eyes and then slowly lifts her arms. Soon, the air is still, the breeze is gone, the leaves above us no longer flutter, and the birds are quiet. We wait. My mother raises her head to the sky, her arms are above her now. We feel her, inside of us, pulling at us, bringing us toward her, drawing us back into her heart. Her magic is so strong that it almost hurts and we wince, whimper, moan a little, but we stay put so her power can go through us to our lost baby sister. My mother strains, calls all her children. Somewhere Grove must feel the tug of her, too. We each add our own yearning for Persimmon, making the force of our family undeniable, and then we hear her. A distant cry from behind our garden.

We run to the fence, shouting her name. "Persimmon! Persimmon!" Bramble is the first to pull the ivy and honeysuckle away from the fence. He sees a hole at the bottom and tunnels down like a groundhog. The rest of us claw at the vines as my mother scrambles to the top of the fence. She hops over and disappears.

Willow runs for a ladder leaning against the house. We prop it against the fence and each clamber to the top. I go last. Ahead of me, Willow and Poppy hop over a row of our neighbor's peony bushes, then run up a stone walk after my mother and Bramble. They swing open the cellar doors against the back of a stranger's house.

"Stay there, Zephyr," my mother commands over her shoulder and I plant myself on top of the fence, ready to pull everyone back home to safety. *Please let her be okay. Please let her be okay,* I say over and over again in my mind.

Persimmon's wails are louder now and the owner of the house comes out her back door, frightened by the sudden intrusion of five tunicked strangers tumbling out of her cellar. My mother emerges from the dark steps with Persimmon tucked up against her body.

"What on earth . . . ?" the neighbor woman says.

"My baby," says Mom, then buries her face into Percy's soft hair. "She must have wandered into your yard and . . ."

"But how? Why?" the woman sputters and looks from my mother and my siblings to me on the fence.

"There's a hole under the fence," Bramble says, and points to the back of her yard.

"We live over there. My name is Poppy!" my sister adds brightly. "And she's Persimmon."

"Is she okay?" the woman asks, softened by Poppy's and Bramble's sweetness.

My mother lifts Persimmon up and gazes at her tearstained face. "Yes," she says softly. "She's okay. Just frightened."

"Oh dear," says the woman. "Poor little thing. How could she have gotten down in my cellar . . . ?"

Mom hands Percy to Willow. Poppy and Bramble follow them back toward the fence.

"I'm so very very sorry," Mom says to the woman. "She doesn't normally do this kind of thing. We just moved here and . . ."

I don't hear the rest of the explanation my mother is concocting, surely leaving out the part where my entire family was hexing one another like a bunch of uncivilized trolls running rampant in the woods. Willow hands the little ones to me and I carry them down the ladder, one by one, into our garden.

Soon, my mother and Willow are back over the fence and we are all inside, huddled together on the floor of the kitchen. Persimmon is asleep against my mother's chest with the rest of us draped over her.

No one talks. We are all shaky and exhausted from casting spells and losing Percy. Plus, I'm absolutely sick to my stomach. This whole thing is my fault and everything in Brooklyn—at school and at home—is going wrong. Nothing is how it should be and no amount of new experience—performing, making friends, or getting a boyfriend—is worth this. For the first time since we moved here I want to be back in Alverland where things make sense, where my family is normal and together and everyone is nice again. Where I don't have to worry about who my friends are, whether my sister will ever be happy again, how long my dad and brother will be gone, or when my mom will freak out next and turn us all into stone.

I'm the first to sniffle then sneeze. My head feels buzzy and my eyes are tired. I've only ever exhausted my magic once before, when I was eight years old, trying to make a mischievous raven tell me where it hid my favorite silver amulet. Bramble coughs next, then Poppy sniffles, too.

"See, this is what happens," my mother says quietly. "Your magic is a powerful force and you have to use it for good." But then Mom sneezes. We all look up into her face. Her eyes are as wide with surprise as ours are.

"You, too, Mommy," Poppy says. "You hexed us."

"Oh dear," says Mom. "That's right. I did, didn't I?"

"You did?" Willow asks, her eyes wide and worried.

"Yes and she yelled, too," Bramble says. "So now she has a cold."

Willow and I exchange slight smiles. We know that our mother couldn't possibly have exhausted her magic from one little hex on us. She's far too powerful for that. But it's cute that Bramble and Poppy think so.

"I'm sorry," Mom says, wrapping her arms around us and squeezing. "I lost my temper with you guys. Just like an erdler mother."

"But why?" Poppy asks.

"It's hard here, Pop, with your dad and Grove gone. I have to take care of you guys and I also have to work so we'll have enough money to pay for this house and food and lights and water."

"We have to pay for water?" Bramble asks, amazed.

Mom nods. "We have to pay for everything here," she explains.

"Even air?" Poppy asks, looking around suspiciously as if it's costing her something to breathe.

Mom laughs. "No, not air, but just about everything else it seems like."

"I don't like it here," Bramble is the first to say, burrowing deep into my mother's side.

"Me either," says Poppy. "When can we go back to Alverland?"

Willow searches my mother's face hopefully. I also watch my mother's expression carefully, trying to detect her true feelings. Does she hate it here as much as Poppy, Bramble, and Willow? Could it really be that we'll leave? Even though I'm miserable today, I feel my heart sinking at the prospect of leaving Brooklyn. I would never see Ari and Mercedes again. Never know if I could beat Bella at the audition. Never again see Timber grinning at me. And worst of all, I'd never know if I could truly be a performer beyond the pageants and festivals in Alverland. If I have what it takes to make it in the erdler world. I don't want to be just an ordinary elf like everyone else except my dad.

My mom's face gives nothing away. I have no idea what she's thinking until she says, "I got a letter from Aunt Flora today. Would you like me to read it to you?"

We all say yes and I scramble up to get it from the windowsill.

"There's one for you, too, from Briar," Mom says when I hand it to her. She slips a sheet of folded yellow paper from the envelope. My name is written in Briar's bubbly script. I settle back down next to my mom, with Briar's letter folded in my lap. We all listen to Mom read.

Dearest ones,

It's a quarter moon and the woods are quiet. The end-of-summer storms have passed without much damage. Now the geese are migrating down from the Great Lakes to warmer shores. They carry crisp, cool fall air on their wings that's already painting the tips of maple leaves orange.

We're getting ready for the Acorn Festival, which won't be the same without Willow and Zephyr in the lute band or Poppy and Bramble in the chorus. And of course we'll all miss Aunt Aurora's acorn mush fritters.

"I love that festival," Poppy says.

"I learned how to make an acorn whistle last year," says Bramble.

My mom reaches out to stroke his hair, then she continues:

All is well here. Cedar, Cliff, and Jay brought home an eight-point buck last week and the younger boys have been setting rabbit traps. We should have plenty of smoked meat for the winter. Plus the gardens are producing lots of corn, beans, squash, tomatoes, pumpkins, and potatoes.

Grandma has gone off on one of her mushroom hunts again. You know how she is, there's no telling when she'll return. The last time she came home empty-handed and tired. Hopefully she'll do better this time.

Nothing much else to report except that we're missing you all something fierce. Love, Flora

"I miss Aunt Flora," Poppy says.

"I miss Grandma Fawna," Bramble adds.

"I miss everyone," says Willow.

As my brother and sisters reminisce about everyone in Alverland, I silently read Briar's letter.

Dear Zephyr,

How are you? Is Brooklyn amazing? Do you have an erdler boyfriend yet? Have you seen a movie in a movie theater? I bet you've made hundreds of new friends.

I'm so jealous I wish I was there with you. Alverland is Boring Boring Boring! I miss you.

Love, Briar

"Do you want to read Briar's letter to us?" Mom asks.

"No." I fold the letter.

"What'd she say?" Willow asks.

I don't want my family to hear all the silly hopes and dreams that Briar and I had for Brooklyn. None of which are coming true. Boyfriends, movies, one hundred friends. Ha! "She just said she misses us," I say.

"Well, we miss her, too," says Mom, then she sighs. She hugs each of us and rubs circles on Percy's sleeping back. "Just wait until your father gets home." She's softened back into our elfin mom again. "Things will get better when he comes back tomorrow."

chapter 7

THE NEXT MORNING is Saturday. When I wake up and walk sleepily downstairs, I hear my father singing. At first, I assume my mom is playing one of his CDs, but then I realize that there are no drums, bass, or guitars so I hurry through the house, following his voice to the kitchen. I find him, sitting at the table with a mug of steaming tea in his hands. When he sees me, his green eyes open wide and he belts out the words to my song: "The west wind carried you in, tiny flower, you floated on the breeze, growing up tall and sturdy, among the alder trees . . . " He opens his arms and I run to him.

Hugging my dad is like hugging a tall and sturdy tree. Immediately, I feel relieved, as if I've found a nice cozy patch of the forest where no rain can fall on me. But also, I feel kind of goofy for acting like I'm seven years old. I pull back to look at Dad. His hair is neatly tucked into its usual long blond braid down his back and, like me, he's wearing a soft white sleeping tunic. "When did you get home?" I ask.

"Late," he says. "Or early. Depending on how you look at it."

"You don't look tired."

"That's the magic of your mother's bugbane and lady slipper tea." He brings his cup to his lips.

I stick my tongue out because I hate that stinky herbal brew they swear by. "Why don't you guys just drink coffee, like the erdlers?"

"I do sometimes when I'm on the road," he tells me, then he peers closely at me and asks warily, "Have you been drinking coffee?"

"No," I say with a shrug. "I could. My friends all drink it, but I haven't tried it. Yet."

"Yet?" Dad repeats and shakes his head. "Well, all I can tell you is that your mother's tea is far superior to anything out of Starbucks. In fact, any Starbucks worth its salt would pay top dollar for what your mother brews."

"Salt?" I ask. "Don't you mean any Starbucks worth its sugar?"

"Or maybe worth its beans, Miss Wise Acre," he says, and we both laugh. I like that my dad is not afraid to make fun of himself.

"Where's Mom?" I ask, surprised that she's not down here with him.

"Sleeping in." He holds his finger to his lips.

I nod and say quietly, "Yeah, I think we exhaust her."

Dad's eyes crinkle happily. "You'd exhaust me, that's for sure." He pushes out a chair for me with his foot. "So Zeph, how are things? How's school going? Do you like it? I want to hear everything."

"Oh, Dad!" I say and fall into the chair. "You would not believe these erdlers!"

He throws his head back and laughs long and loud. "Try me, Zeph. Grove and I have been riding around in a van with a bunch of them for the past two weeks."

"They're so complicated!" I complain. "One minute they're happy. Then they're sad. First they're nice. Then they're mean."

"You catch on quick," says Dad. "But that doesn't surprise me." He leans forward and winks. "Because you're just like me."

I grin at him, so happy that someone finally understands me. Then, right as I'm about to launch into the whole story of Bella and the audition, I hear squeals of "Daddy! Daddy! Daddy!" and the pounding of feet coming down the hall. In an instant, the little ones are charging into the kitchen. This is when being an only child like Ari doesn't sound half bad. Lucky Ari never has to share his dad with annoying little brothers and sisters, I think, as my dad scoops Poppy, Bramble, and Persimmon into his enormous hug, and my chance to vent goes straight out the window.

Later, when everyone is awake and assembled in the kitchen, my dad puts his arm around my mother's waist and says, "Hey, you guys, we have some good news."

"Are we going home?" Poppy asks.

"Back to Alverland?" Bramble adds, smiling big.

My stomach clenches. My mom smiles up at my dad. I wonder if she told him about how badly we behaved yesterday, then how homesick everyone was when she read Flora's letter. Maybe they've decided it would be better to take us back to Alverland. No matter what I thought yesterday, I realize now that I don't want to leave Brooklyn.

"No, no, nothing like that," says Mom.

"Actually, the good news is one of our songs charted," says Dad.

I open my eyes. No one says anything. Probably because none of us knows what that means.

"On Billboard," Grove adds from the countertop beside the sink, where he sits munching on a green apple.

"Which means it's being played on radio stations all over the country," says Dad.

"I like the radio," Bramble says, looking up from his bowl of Mom's homemade blueberry granola.

Grove hops down from the counter to stand beside Dad. "Plus, it's going to be on a TV show on a channel called Fox."

"I like foxes," says Bramble.

Poppy stops braiding Persimmon's hair to ask, "Does this mean we can get a TV?"

"What's a TV?" asks Bramble.

"We're not getting a television," Mom says.

"This is exactly what we wanted to happen," says Dad. "It means that coming here and getting more exposure and going out on the road with a band is paying off."

"That's great!" I nearly yell. "So we're staying in Brooklyn?"

"Of course we're staying in Brooklyn," Dad says, confused.

"Hurray!" I jump up and down. Persimmon and Poppy look at me and laugh, then they start jumping, too.

"Where else would we go?" asks Dad.

"Home!" Willow shouts. Persimmon, Poppy, and I stop jumping and everyone stares at Willow. She grips the edge of the table. Her knuckles are white and her cheeks are flushed. "To Alverland. Where we belong."

"Honey," Dad says. "This is just temporary. For a year. Until we get more exposure."

"*We?*" Willow shouts. "You mean *you*, Dad. Not us. You're not here. You don't know."

"I do know," Dad says, taking a step toward her with his arms out. But Willow turns and runs out of the kitchen, her long hair whipping behind her. She charges up the stairs, then slams a door.

Dad turns to Mom. "Do you see now?" she asks him.

"What's going on?" Grove asks me quietly.

"She hasn't been very happy," I whisper to him.

"Obviously," he says with a little snort. "She's acting like an erdler."

I can't help but snicker at the thought of Willow, the most elfy elf I know, being human.

"You know what we need?" my dad booms. We all look up at him. "We need to get out of this house! We need fresh air in our lungs, open skies above our heads, and grass beneath our feet. Let's explore this park across the street that I've heard so much about."

When he says this, it makes perfect sense because we're hardly ever in our house in Alverland. Only to eat and sleep, and then sometimes we just stay outside for those things anyway. "That's probably what we needed the last couple of days," I tell him, "when we were all stuffed in here together getting on one another's nerves."

"Were you really on one another's nerves?" Dad asks.

"It's hard to get out with them all," Mom snaps.

Everyone is quiet and watchful of our mother, who rarely talks like that. Even my dad looks a little taken aback by her tone, but then he reaches out and massages her shoulders.

"Yes, it would be hard to take all you little weasels to a strange new place," he says.

"Hey, I'm not a weasel," says Bramble.

Dad reaches down to tickle Bramble's belly until Bramble is a wiggly, giggly mess on the floor. "But now that we're all together . . ." Dad lifts Bramble onto his shoulders.

"I'm going to climb a tree!" Poppy yells, hanging on my dad's arm.

"I want to build a fort," Bramble says from on top of Dad.

"Pick berries!" Persimmon adds, tugging at the hem of Dad's tunic.

"Well." Dad chuckles. "I don't know that we can do all that, but we can have a nice long walk, then find a good place to lie down under the open sky and enjoy some of your mother's cooking."

"Even Willow?" Poppy asks.

"Yes," says Dad. "Even Willow."

While Grove and I help Mom and Dad pack a picnic, the phone rings. We all assume it's a business call for Mom or maybe Dad's manager, Martin, because those are the only reasons our phone rings. So when Mom says, "Flora? Is everything okay?" we all look up. "I thought she was mushroom hunting again."

"Who?" Poppy asks, tugging on Mom's tunic.

"Shhh," Mom hisses.

"Grandma Fawna?" I ask Willow, who shrugs.

Mom listens with her eyebrows furrowed. "When did she leave?"

"Who?" Poppy asks Dad.

"Probably one of the dogs," he says while slicing bread for sandwiches.

"My dog?" Bramble asks.

"Do dogs mushroom hunt?" Poppy asks.

"Hush," Willow tells them as we strain to listen to the conversation.

"What do you mean when you say tired?" Mom asks. "Run down? How bad?" She listens. "Sick or just sleepy?" Then she says "Uh-huh" a lot and hangs up.

We all stare at her. "Well?" asks Willow.

"Flora's worried because Grandma came back very tired from mushroom hunting earlier this week and now she's gone again." Mom busies herself washing apples. "She's been gone only a few days. I'm sure it's nothing."

"But you said 'sick,'" Willow says.

"Exhausted more likely," says Mom.

"But isn't that strange?" Willow asks.

"You know how Grandma Fawna is," Dad says. "Always off doing something mysterious. Who knows how far she went for the perfect magical mushroom?"

"That's right," says Mom. Despite her casual tone, my mom frowns as she wraps sandwiches in a checkered cloth. When the phone rings a few moments later, she grabs it and says, "Flora, is that you?" Her eyes open wide. "Oh, sorry." She holds the phone out to me. "It's for you." My brothers and sisters stare.

"Hello?" I ask, confused.

"Hey Zeph, it's Ari." He's talking fast. "What are you doing today? Mercy and I think we should go over the script and maybe add a few more things to your résumé. Plus, we were thinking of going into the city later to look for something for Mercedes to wear to the audition, and you should come with us to help her because your clothes are perfect so you'll have good ideas, you know?"

He pauses just long enough for me to say, "My dad just got back in town—"

"Oh my God!" Ari shouts in my ear. "Is he there? In your house?"

I laugh. "Of course he is, Ari. Where else would he be?"

"Drake Addler is in your house," Ari states as emphatically as a newscaster.

"We're going to the park for a picnic," I tell him.

"Drake Addler goes on picnics," he says, and sounds almost dreamy.

As Ari babbles on about the best place in the park for a picnic, I cover the mouthpiece of the phone so that he can't hear me. "Can Ari and Mercedes come with us?" I ask my parents.

My dad looks at my mom with his eyebrows up. "Those are her new friends from school," Mom fills him in.

"Ah, the coffee drinkers," he says. My mom looks perplexed but I giggle. "It's fine by me, I'd like to meet them," he adds.

"Sure," says Mom. "We'll pack extra food."

"Do you and Mercedes want to come with us?" I ask Ari, which is the only thing that shuts him up.

Then, after a beat of silence, he asks in the most serious voice I've ever heard from him, "What time and where?"

My family (including a sulking Willow) sets off an hour later looking like a band of . . . well, a band of woodland elves traveling through the forest. In other words, nothing like true Brooklynites. All of us are in tunics, boots, and hats. Mom and Willow are carrying woven rucksacks packed full of enough food to feed a small village. Dad and Grove have their guitars and blanket rolls slung over their shoulders. Bramble carries his little bow at the ready with a deerskin quiver of arrows strapped across his back. (The tips are blunted, of course, since there is no hunting in this park.) Poppy pulls Persimmon (plus almost all of their rag dolls, penny whistles, and a collection of drums and shakers) in a little wooden wagon. I've got jugs of Mom's homemade sweet red serviceberry tea and wild strawberry juice in my own backpack.

As soon as we enter the greenery of the park, we all relax. Simply hearing birds sing, watching squirrels scamper, and seeing a hawk glide in lazy circles above the trees makes us all feel more at ease. We head down a path toward the road that circles the inside of the park. Since today is Saturday, the road is filled with walkers, runners, bicyclers, people pushing baby carriages, and even a few riding horses. Out of the corner of my eye, I catch sight of a guy jogging without a shirt and I get a tingly, weird feeling as if someone cast a staring spell at me and I can't look away or blink. Then I realize why. It's Timber!

At least I think it's Timber. This guy's legs are long and his shoulders are broad and straight. I can see the outline of muscles on his bare chest and his thighs as he bounds down the road. He has one of those little white pod thingies clipped to his arm with wires going into his ears and he's mouthing the words to the song he's hearing. Suddenly he looks up and I can see his face with those deep, sparkling gray-blue eyes. It *is* Timber! I jump behind a big bush by the side of the road, wishing more than anything that I knew an invisibility spell. It's bad enough that Ari and Mercedes are going to see me with this group of weirdoes known as my family, but I'd die of embarrassment if Timber saw us, too.

I peek out and see him do a double take as my parents step into the road. That's no surprise. In a city where supposedly anything goes, we Addlers manage to look like freaks. Now that I see us in the midst of normal people, in normal clothes, doing normal things like riding bikes, running, and walking dogs, I realize that it's worse than I thought. We are mutants on parade. I had this idea that everything would magically get better when Dad and Grove got back, but now I see that having all of us together creates a whole new set of problems.

Timber slows to a walk with his hands on his hips and stares first at my father, who looks like some prehistoric caveman lost in the urban world. Then he glances at my mom, with her long straw-colored braids and big goofy grin beaming out. Timber's eyes pass over Grove and Bramble (increasingly smaller versions of my dad), Willow (dragging her feet like a waterlogged banshee), then Poppy and Persimmon, who chatter away like crazy squirrels. Luckily, I manage to escape his notice from behind the bush, although I'm sure everyone can hear my heart pounding inside my chest like distant drums and the gulps of my loud, quick breathing. What's wrong with me? I've never felt like this before. Never not wanted to be seen with my family. Finally, Timber has enough. He shakes his head, bewildered—and who can blame him? As I watch him run down the road into the woods, my stomach gurgles, my skin shivers, and my palms are moist with sweat, but I'm relieved. Crisis averted.

Until my father calls my name: "Zeph? Zephyr!"

I cringe. *No! No! Don't turn around, Timber!* I think.

"Which way, Zephyr?" my dad asks. "Hey, where'd she go?"

I step out from behind the bush reluctantly, but lucky for me, Timber is long gone. "That way," I mumble, pointing toward the meadow where we agreed to meet Ari and Mercedes. I stay a few paces behind the most embarrassing family in the whole world, hoping to the high heavens that I don't see anyone else I know today.

The park is already crowded with picnicking families, soccer players, and kite flyers on this warm fall Saturday morning. As we meander down the path circling the baseball fields and two main meadows, I watch people steal glances, then talk and snicker behind their hands at the sight of my bizarro family. My mom and dad, being insane, wave and smile at everyone, calling out "Hey there!" and "Hello!" and "Nice day, isn't it?" as if they've just been released from an asylum. Even though I've gone to school for only a week in Brooklyn, I already know that people here don't talk to strangers unless they have to. But here are my parents, acting like everyone's new best friends. I'm almost relieved to see Ari and Mercedes beneath a large elm tree on the side of a hill. I want nothing more than to get my family off the path and into the shade where they will be less of a spectacle.

Only that doesn't happen because Ari is completely beside himself when he meets my dad. He pops up from his place on the blanket and charges at Dad with his hand out and his mouth running like river rapids. He's talking so loudly that I'm sure more people are staring at us now.

"Oh my God, hello, Mr. Addler. Hello. Or should I call you Drake? Can I call you Drake? It seems like I know you because, you know, I listen to your music all the time. Even before I met Zephyr. I have a bunch of links to your music on my Facebook page. I love your work because it's brilliant. Some of the best music out there today. I'm a musician, too, and I have a band called GGJB. I saw you at Irving Plaza and up in the Berkshires last year. And when I met Zephyr and she said that you're her father . . ."

"You must be Ari!" my dad says with a hearty laugh. He claps Ari on the back, sending him stumbling for a moment, but then he regains his balance and just keeps right on talking.

"What's with that?" I ask Mercedes, pointing to Ari's crazy black floppy hair pulled into a stubby ponytail.

Mercedes gives me a withering look. "I know. And check out the pants."

I look down at Ari's legs. Instead of his usual black jeans and All Star sneakers, he's wearing khaki green cargo pants and a pair of hiking boots.

"Goth boy's gone folky," Mercedes says with a snort.

"Because of my dad?"

"Duh," says Mercedes. "I'm surprised he didn't make his mom sew him one of those long shirt-things y'all wear." Then she shakes her head. "Dang, girl, does your whole family always dress alike?"

I flop down on the blanket beside her and cover my face with my hands. "I've never been this mortified in all my life!" I groan.

"Yeah, that's pretty rough," Mercy says. "You're like the Von Trapps meet the Swiss Family Robinson."

"I've got the most embarrassing family in the entire universe," I moan. "Just look at them!"

"Honey," Mercedes says. "You don't know embarrassing until you've walked down the street with Rico Loveras, my eighth-grade crush, followed by my *abuela* yelling in Spanish to pull down my shirt, pull up my pants, and stop hanging around Dominican boys because in her crazy mind, I'm allowed to date only Puerto Ricans. And even then, not until I'm eighteen."

"But that's just your grandmother," I protest. "My entire family is certifiable. Your family isn't like this."

"You think you're the only person in the whole world to think your family is *loco*? Heck, everybody's family has their own craziness. You act like this is the first time you've ever been embarrassed by them."

"But—" I start to protest. This *is* the first time I've ever been embarrassed by them. In Alverland, my family doesn't seem crazy at all. Then again, as I keep reminding myself, we're not in Alverland anymore. Before I can explain this, Poppy runs over and plops herself between Mercedes and me. Persimmon is right behind her and she plunks down in Mercedes's lap.

"Hi!" Poppy yells. "Do you remember us? We're Zephyr's little sisters!"

"Really?" Mercedes says in a tone that I now recognize as sarcasm.

"Yes, really," Poppy says seriously. She fluffs Mercedes's curls with her fingers. "My name is Poppy and this is Persimmon and you're Mercedes. I like that name. It's pretty. My name is a flower. Are you named after a flower, too?"

"Nope, a car," says Mercedes.

Poppy's eyes are wide. "A car?"

"That and my grandmother," Mercedes says.

"Your grandmother is a car?" Poppy asks, still amazed.

"Duh, Poppy! Of course her grandmother isn't a car!" I say.

Mercedes laughs. "It's okay, Zeph. I have little sisters, too. Remember?"

"Are your sisters named after cars?" Poppy asks, giggling.

"Yeah, Beemer and Caddy," says Mercedes.

"Those are pretty, too," says Poppy kindly.

"She's just like you, Zeph. All nicey nice." Mercedes pokes Poppy in the ribs. "I'm just fooling with you, *mami*! That's not really their names.

Their names are Nellie and Marisol. They're twins about your age. You'd like them. They could be your friends."

Poppy jumps up with her hands pressed over her mouth, barely suppressing wild giggles. Then she runs to my mom with Persimmon following. "Mommy! Mommy! Mercedes says I can be friends with her sisters!"

"Are you really named after a car?" I lean over and ask Mercedes now that my sisters are out of earshot.

"Naw," she says. "Virgin Mary. You know, Our Lady of the Mercies. My grandparents are very Catholic." She touches her forehead, her chest, her left shoulder, and her right shoulder. "At least they like everyone to think they are, but really my *abuela* is back in the bedroom with her little Santeria altar to the spirits with all its candles and beads and statues and fruit. You want to talk about embarrassing? That's embarrassing!"

"I don't think that sounds so bad," I say, thinking of my own grandmother and the little altars she builds from rocks and sticks and berries for all the spirits in the woods.

Mercedes elbows me hard in the side. "Oh my God," she says. "Look who the cat dragged in."

"What cat?" I ask, confused.

She points to the path, a few feet away from our blankets. "It's your boyfriend."

"I don't have a boyfriend." I look to where she's pointing. Immediately my skin goes hot, then cold, then hot again, and my mouth goes dry. There's a tremor in my chest and my stomach climbs up into my throat. Timber is walking straight toward us.

"I thought that must be you," he says with a smile big enough to swallow me in one gulp. "I saw this whole group of people dressed like you back there but I didn't see you."

I can't say anything. Nothing will come out of my mouth. It's as if my mother has hexed me again and I'm mute. I just sit there, staring at him like an idiot. Staring at his bare chest and his long strong legs. I want to shrink. Turn into a little mouse and scurry away into the woods.

Timber drops down on the grass beside me. "Is this your family?" This is awful. The worst thing ever. He'll tell Bella and her horrible friends about us and then they'll say terrible things on their berry blogs. But obviously I can't deny that this is my family since we all look exactly alike. "Yep," I sort of squeak, then I add dumbly, "we're having a picnic."

"Cool," says Timber, nodding. He looks at Mercedes. "How's it going?"

"Hey," she says back, but all the warmth has drained from her voice.

Timber stretches out in the grass. "Man, I just ran around the park twice. Six miles. I'm beat."

Mercedes looks at me and does one of her trademark eye rolls.

"Most guys I know can run around three or four times, but me, I'm a total wuss," Timber says with a laugh. "All I think about the whole time is a big fat Red Bull with chicken wings."

"You don't look like you have trouble exercising," I say, trying to imagine why he'd think of a bull with chicken wings, especially a red one, to help him run. But then after I say this, I blush. "Uh . . . um . . . uh," I stutter and stammer because I sounded like I was checking out his body. Which, of course, I was, but I don't want him to know that.

Timber smiles broadly at me. "Thanks," he says, and props up on his elbow to face me. "It's all in the genes." He pauses. "I only wear Sevens." He waits with a silly smile. "That was a joke. Seven jeans, not human genes."

"Yeah, we got it," Mercedes says, but of course I'm lost as usual.

"Never mind." He shakes his head and almost looks a teeny bit embarrassed. But then he recovers and asks me, "Do you work out?"

"Work out what?" I ask, and both he and Mercedes laugh.

"You're so deadpan, Zephyr. It kills me," Timber says.

"You think she's kidding," Mercedes leans over and tells him.

"I don't know what she is," Timber tells her. "Except funny."

Just then my mom saunters over, carrying a big basket of food. Timber immediately stands up. "Hello, you must be Zephyr's mother. I'm Timber Lewis Cahill, a friend of hers from school." He sticks his hand out.

"Freaking Prince Charming," Mercedes whispers to me.

For some reason, my mother just can't get the whole erdler handshaking thing. Instead of sticking her hand out, too, she opens her arms and wraps Timber in a big, stupid hug. "Welcome," she says kindly. "It's so nice to meet the people Zephyr knows. Please join us. Have some food." She places the basket on the ground in front of us.

"Great!" Timber says. "I'm starving." He sits back down beside me and digs in.

Somehow things actually get better once we start to eat. Ari even drags himself away from worshiping at the feet of my father to join Mercedes, Timber, and me. We all munch on fresh fruit and cut-up veggies, and sandwiches made with hunks of cheese, smoked fish, or venison jerky on my mom's homemade brown bread. Ari, Mercedes, and Timber talk about which classes at school suck and which ones are good. Then Mercedes gets us all cracking up with her impersonation of some of the teachers and other students. Thankfully, no one ever mentions Bella and her friends.

Finally, when we're all stuffed, Ari says, "Anybody want to play Frisbee?" He reaches into his bag and pulls out a flat, orange plastic disc.

"Since when do you play Frisbee?" Mercedes snatches the thing from Ari's hands.

"Since forever." Ari snatches it back.

"Since never," she says, and grabs for it but he holds it out of her reach.

"God, you guys fight worse than me and Bella," Timber says, shaking his head.

Mercedes gives him the look of death. "Only we're not boyfriend and girlfriend, *pendejo*."

"You act like you are," Timber tells her.

I see Mercedes rearing up, gathering a storm of abuse to unleash on Timber's head, so I grab the orange thing from Ari and quickly ask, "What's a Frisbee?"

All three of my friends look at one another then at me.

"Are you serious?" Ari asks.

"She's clueless!" Mercedes shouts happily.

"For real, you don't know?" Timber asks. I shake my head. He tosses his arm loosely around my shoulders. "It's cute the way she's so out of it." He takes the Frisbee from me and waves it in front of his body. Ari runs down the hill, then Timber zings the thing through the air. Ari jumps and catches it. "Come on," Timber says to me. "We'll show you how to play."

"I want to play, too!" Poppy jumps up and follows us.

"No, Poppy," I say. "You can't come."

"Yes, I can," says Poppy.

"They're *my* friends," I tell her.

"Mercedes is my friend, too. She said so."

"She's not, Poppy. She said you could be her sisters' friend. You'll be in the way. Stay here and play with Persimmon."

"No!" Poppy shouts. "I'm coming with you."

"Shhh," I hiss. I don't want Mom and Dad to hear us fighting like erdler kids. "Fine," I tell her. "You can come but you're only watching. Not playing."

We find a nice flat place in the middle of the meadow and spread out in a circle. Ari tosses the Frisbee to Mercedes and she throws it to me. I catch it, but then I have no idea what to do with it. Timber jogs over. "Here," he says. "I'll show you how."

I hand him the Frisbee. "See, you hold it flat like this," he says. "Then you flick your wrist and let it go." He throws it a short distance. Poppy runs after it like a little dog and brings it back. "Thanks!" Timber says to her, but I shoot her an evil look. "Here, you try." He hands it to me.

I hold it flat and flick my wrist like he did, but the thing goes all wobbly and lands nearly at my feet. Poppy runs over and picks it up again. "This is fun!" she yells, and puts it on her head like a hat.

I grab it from her. "Stop it! Go sit over there." I point to the grass behind me.

Poppy folds her arms across her chest and squints. "You're mean, Zephyr," she says, but she stomps away and leaves us alone.

"How do you do it again?" I ask Timber.

"Like this," he says. He stands behind me and puts his arms around my body. I'm warm and my skin prickles as he touches me. I can feel his breath on the back of my head, which makes the little hairs on my neck stand up. He takes my wrist in his hand and lifts my arm, then bends and straightens it like I'm a puppet. My heart is beating so fast that my legs get wobbly and I'm afraid I'll fall down. "You have to swing your whole arm," he tells me as he continues moving it back and forth. "And you step out with this leg." He pushes his knee into the back of mine, making my leg move forward. "Then, at the very end, you flick it." We put all the motions together, Timber behind me guiding my body. I flick my wrist and let go of the Frisbee. It sails through the air, making a long, wide arc straight for Ari. Ari jumps and catches it and we all cheer and clap.

"That was great!" Timber says.

"Poppy!" I yell. "Did you see that? I did it!" I turn around to make sure she saw it, but I can't find her. "Poppy?" She's not in the grass where I told her to sit. "Have you guys seen my sister?"

Timber looks around. "She must be with your mom and dad."

"Mercedes," I call, jogging toward her. "Did you see Poppy go back up the hill?"

Mercedes looks over her shoulder to where my family is sitting. "No. I don't see her up there."

Ari runs over to us, tossing the Frisbee up in the air and catching it. "You looking for Poppy?" he asks and I nod. "I saw her go that way." He points in the opposite direction.

"What! Why didn't you stop her? Why didn't you tell me?" I yell at him.

Ari drops the Frisbee. "I . . . I . . . I," he stammers. "I thought it was okay. You sent her over there."

"Oh no," I moan and feel sick. "She doesn't know her way around. She could be anywhere."

"You want me to get your dad?" Ari asks.

"No!" I say sharply. "We have to find her."

I can't let my parents know that Poppy disappeared. Not after what happened with Persimmon yesterday. If another one of my sisters gets lost, they will yank us out of Brooklyn so fast that I won't even have a chance to wave good-bye.

"She can't be far," says Timber. "Where's she like to go?"

"I bet she wanted to climb a tree," I say. "That's what she does at home when she's upset."

"Ari and Mercedes, you guys go that way," Timber says, pointing toward one edge of the meadow. "And Zephyr and I'll go this way." He points to the other edge. "Those are the closest trees. She has to be in one place or the other."

Ari and Mercedes take off, then Timber and I start running. "Poppy! Poppy!" I call up into the trees. "Where are you? Come on! I'm sorry that I was mean to you."

"Is she good at climbing?" Timber asks. We both look up into the tangle of branches and leaves over our heads.

"She's great," I tell him. "She could be to the top of one these things by now."

Timber laughs a little.

"It's not funny."

"No, no." Timber puts his hand on my shoulder. "I'm not laughing about your sister running off. It's just that, you guys are all so interesting. I don't know girls who've never seen a Frisbee but can climb to the top of a tree. That's all."

"I don't think this is working," I say, shrugging off his touch. "You go that way and I'll go this way."

We split up. I walk into the middle of the trees and close my eyes. I try to conjure up my mother's trick of calling her children back. I concentrate on Poppy, trying to see her and feel her lost, but I've got nothing. Probably because I'm mad at her so my magic won't work right. I have to calm myself down, remember to love her so that she'll want to come back into my heart. "I'm sorry, Poppy," I whisper. "I love you. You're my sister. Please come back." I lift my arms. I hear a hawk screech, a dog bark, people shouting, but nothing from Poppy. Then I hear Timber yelling my name.

"Found her! I found her, Zephyr!"

I run toward his voice and find him standing beneath a big oak tree with his hands on his hips, looking up. I follow his eyes to see Poppy's feet dangling from a large, low branch.

"Oh, blessed Mother Earth and all her creatures great and small!" I yell and throw my arms around Timber's neck. "Thank you! Thank you! Thank you!"

Timber wraps his arms around my back. I squeeze him tighter and he lifts me off the ground a few inches. I look into his face to tell him how relieved I am that he found her, but as soon as our eyes meet I can't speak. He stares hard at me. His eyes are beautiful, like the early evening sky, and I'm a bird soaring. A little grin lurks on his lips. He gently puts me down on the ground then leans toward me with his eyes closed. That's when I remember what Ari told me. That erdler guys and girls don't hug and touch unless they want something to go on between them. But as soon as I'm about to pull away, Timber tugs me just a little bit closer so our noses nearly touch, then he tilts his head to one side and presses his mouth against mine. We kiss and my whole body goes liquid, as if someone has turned me into warm water.

He pulls away slowly and blinks his eyes open. "You're welcome, Zephyr," he says.

I step back and press my fingers against my tingling mouth. I can't believe what just happened. I'm not sure I understand it. But when I look up, I see Ari and Mercedes, peeking out from behind a tree with their mouths hanging open. On the branch just above them sits a beautiful red-tailed hawk. I wonder if the hawk is an omen. Good or bad. I don't know what it could mean.

"Should we get her down?" Timber asks me.

"Huh?" I say, completely forgetting for just a moment about Poppy in the tree. "Oh, right, yeah, my sister." I shake my head to clear my thoughts, but that kiss, that delicious kiss, will not leave my mind. Timber kissed me. I kissed him. We kissed. Right here, beneath the oaks, I kissed an erdler boy! I want to sing and dance. Pluck flowers from the ground. Skip and shout. Tell it to the world. I wish Briar were here.

"Do you want me to do it?" Timber asks, and for a second I think he means kiss me again.

Oh yes, I want to say, but then I realize he means do I want him to get Poppy down.

"I'll do it," I say, quickly pulling myself together. I plant myself below her feet. "Poppy," I call up gently. "Pop, it's Zephyr."

"Go away," she says.

"Aw, Pop. Come on. I'm sorry. I'm really really sorry that I was so mean to you. You can play Frisbee with us now."

"Don't want to." She rustles in the leaves.

"Please. My friends want you to." I look at Timber and Ari and Mercedes, who've come to stand below the tree with us.

"Yeah," says Mercedes. "Come on down. You can be my partner."

"Please, Poppy," I plead. "Mom and Dad are waiting for us." Poppy is silent. Now I'm getting desperate. "I'll tell Mom that you ran off," I threaten Poppy. "And remember how mad she got when Persimmon disappeared yesterday."

"All right," Poppy says with a defeated sigh. "I'll come down, but you better not tell."

"I won't. I promise."

Poppy crawls over the large branch and then shimmies down the trunk. Timber reaches up for her and helps her to the ground. Despite being annoyed with her, I drop down and wrap her in a big hug. "Please don't do that again," I say. "You really scared the daylights out of me."

Poppy hugs me back. "Then be nice," she says.

I pick her up. "I will. I promise. Now let's go."

"You want a piggyback ride?" Timber asks her.

"Yeah!" Poppy yells. Mercedes lifts her onto Timber's back. Although this is really nice of him, I feel kind of jealous.

As we near the hill, I hear my family before I see them. They're making music. Dad and Grove are strumming hard on their guitars while Mom plays the flute. Even Willow has joined in the beautiful four-part harmony. Bramble has a penny whistle and Persimmon dances around in just her underpants, rattling a shaker full of dried beans. They're singing an old elf song called "The Craggy Rocks of My Heart."

I love this song. It reminds me of Grandma Fawna and late nights around full moon bonfires with all my cousins. Part of me wishes that I'd brought my lute so that I could run up the hill and join right in. But what would Ari, Mercedes, and Timber think? I'm certain their families don't do strange things like this. Of course, Ari is thrilled. He's the first to reach the blankets and plunk himself down near Dad and Grove. Even Mercedes seems to think it's okay because she shrugs, then ambles over to listen.

Timber is the only one who stops. He sets Poppy down and she races to the wagon to grab a tambourine. I stand beside Timber, trying to think up excuses for why my family is so odd, certain that he's regretting our kiss now. But he turns to me and says, "I thought I recognized your dad. He's that singer, isn't he? Drake something?"

"Addler," I say.

"Yeah, now it all makes sense," he says, nodding at me. "The clothes. This whole thing. I get it."

"What thing?"

"It's your dad's schtick. This whole out-in-the-woods, hippy trippy kind of vibe. It's brilliant. The folkies love him, the goths think he's cool, and he can really rock, so he's got good crossover potential."

I have no idea what any of that means, but just to keep up the conversation I say, "One of his songs charted, but I don't know where."

"Really?" Timber asks, clearly impressed.

"I guess so," I say. "Something about a billboard and then he's going to be in a show about foxes."

"What?" Timber says, laughing.

My cheeks grow warm. "I don't know," I mumble. "I guess the song gets played on lots of radio stations and now on TV or something."

Timber shakes his head, but he's also smiling. "God, Zeph," he says. "Your family is so cool!"

Wow, I think, as he joins the others. That's the second most shocking thing that's happened today.

chapter 8

THE MINUTE I walk up the school steps on Monday morning, I get dizzy and woozy. My head feels like a balloon floating above my body held by a thin string. The whole rest of the weekend all I could think about was the moment I would see Timber again. And now that it's almost here, I'm freaking out!

I've been dying to talk to someone about what happened under the trees, but only Ari and Mercedes know. I couldn't tell my mom and dad because first of all, weird. And second, even if it wasn't weird to talk to your mom and dad about the first guy you kissed, I don't know how they'd feel about me kissing an erdler instead of an elf. I definitely can't tell Poppy, because she'd just blab it all over the place until even the pigeons would be discussing it. Normally, I'd talk to my cousin Briar, but obviously she's not here. Or Willow, but she's so miserable without her boyfriend that telling her I kissed a guy would be cruel. I thought about talking to Grove, but then I felt weird because really I want to talk to a girl, plus he's never had a girlfriend, so what would he know. I begged my mom and dad to let me hang out with Ari and Mercedes on Sunday so we could work on the audition (and talk about Timber, of course), but they said no. They wanted family time. As if hanging out in the park all day Saturday from ten in the morning until dark wasn't enough?

So now, after a torturous forty-eight hours, it's finally Monday morning and I'm about to walk into school, where I know at some point I'll see Timber. And yet, for some reason, I just can't seem to open these big green doors in front of me.

"What are you waiting for, your handmaiden?" a voice says behind me. I turn around to see that awful pixie lady bustling up the steps, barking at me. "Overprivileged little princesses. Can't even open doors for yourself. Or do you think it's automatic? Wait till I tell the gals in the office about this one." She pushes past me and swings the door open, bumping me off the top step in the process.

At first, I'm so shocked that I can't think of anything to say. But then I'm mad enough to stomp through the door, ready to zap her. She's disappeared, though. Maybe she really is a pixie and she scurried off to a mouse hole where she belongs with the other rodents.

I'm left standing alone right inside the doors. I scan the hallway for signs of Timber or, worse, Bella and her underlings. What will happen when I see Bella today? Did Timber tell her that we kissed? Did they break up? Is he my boyfriend now? The truth is, I don't know how erdlers do this whole boyfriend/girlfriend thing. In Alverland there are strict rules about who can date (only people from different clans) and when you can meet (at festivals and celebrations when all the clans get together). Also, an elf would never secretly kiss someone if they were already dating another person! I have no idea if what happened in the park with Timber was typical erdler stuff. Who knows what they do! Maybe they go around kissing anyone they take a fancy to, which frankly I'm not into. And it worries me a little bit that I kissed someone else's boyfriend. Maybe that's just the nicey-nice elf in me talking.

Because another part of me is really excited about it. I wanted so badly to ask Timber all of those questions at the picnic, but I couldn't with my family around. It was maddening! I had to sit beside him wondering what was going on in his mind while he was singing with my family, then trading stories with Dad and Grove about being on the road with a band. Maybe today I can steal him away for a little bit and ask him what all of this means.

Since I don't see anyone I know in the hall, I head for the courtyard. Luckily, the first person I see that I know is Mercedes. She's sitting at a table in the sun with her headphones on, finishing her geometry homework. I plunk down in the chair beside her.

"Hola, chica!" she says, taking off her earphones. "Oh, don't we look nice today. Getting dressed up for someone?" she asks with a knowing grin.

I look down self-consciously at my dark green tunic with deep pink roses embroidered around the hems. It's true, I wore this on purpose because it fits a little bit more snug than some of my others and the color makes my eyes sparkle. I even put on my three favorite amulets: a hawk's feather for luck, a clam shell for laughter, and a sachet of dried lavender for love.

Mercedes leans in close. "Did he call?"

I shake my head no.

"Figures." She snorts. "Men! Always pigs."

"But he doesn't have my phone number," I tell her.

She gives me the look with an eyebrow up and her lips crinkled to the side that means I'm being really dumb. "He could find it. Or he could have asked you for it. But he didn't."

My heart sinks and lands like a rock in the bottom of my belly. "But why did he . . . you know? The kiss. Is that, uh, normal?"

"For him it is," she says.

"Is that good?"

"What do you think?"

"I don't know what to think!"

"Do you have ensemble with him today?"

I nod. My heart buoys back into my chest and starts thumping like a rabbit being chased by a fox. "What should I do?"

"Listen." She grips my arm. "You play it cool, Zephyr. Act like nothing ever happened. He's the one who kissed you, right?"

"Right."

"Let him bring it up."

"But what if I see Bella?" I whisper, glancing around to make sure she's nowhere near.

"Who cares about her? After all the smack she talked about you? Don't you get it yet? She's evil, Zephyr. Pure evil!"

"But I don't want to be mean," I say.

Mercedes slaps my leg. "You gotta get over that right now, *mija.*"

The bell rings. I jump. Nothing new.

"Find me at lunch," Mercedes says, shoving her book and tablet back into her bag. "Can't wait to hear what happens."

My legs are so wobbly on my way to ensemble that I'm afraid I'll fall down in the middle of the hallway. My eyes dart everywhere, checking the faces of every kid who passes me, hoping and then fearing that I'll see Timber on my way to class. Everybody else rushes by, but I can't decide what to do. Should I go slowly, maybe stop in the bathroom and check on how I look so that I'll get to the room after him? Then I can see if he saves me a seat. Or should I go fast so that I'll get there before him and save him a seat? What if I save him a seat but he doesn't sit in it? What if he saves me a seat, but I get there too late and someone sits in it and then he thinks that I didn't want to sit next to him?

Oh for thunder's sake I've got to get a grip! Where is Mercedes when I need her?

I pull over to the side of the hallway and lean against the wall to gather myself. Mercedes said to act like nothing happened. How can I possibly act like that? Elves are no good at hiding our emotions. That's one of the drawbacks of elfin honesty in the erdler world.

I guess I'm going to have act like an erdler. I look out at the swarm of kids passing by me. First of all, most of them frown instead of smile. I wipe the goofy grin off my face and replace it with a scowl. Also, a lot of them stomp around, full of attitude, instead of bouncing along happily like I do. I start walking again, but this time I drag my feet. Most of them look down at their feet or up over everyone's heads, instead of into the faces of the people they pass. I drop my eyes to ground. I also notice that instead of saying "Hi!" like a chirpy little bird when they see someone they know, these kids just nod and toss out a quick, deep "Hey" or "What up." That's what I'll do when I see Timber.

I round the corner toward my classroom, trudging along, glowering like a grouchy ogre. I'm working so hard on my erdler act that I don't see who's coming down the hall from the other direction until we both reach the doorway of our class at the same exact time. "Hey, Zeph!" Timber says brightly.

The minute I look up into his gorgeous eyes and hear his happy voice, my mouth blossoms into a huge, silly grin and I nearly sing, "Oh hi, Timber!" like the biggest possible goob in the universe. What happened to the nod? The grunting "hey" noise I was going to make? The frown?

"You okay? You looked like you were sick or something the way you were walking."

"No," I say with an embarrassed laugh as we enter the room. "I'm fine."

I scan the seats. There are only two empty chairs and of course who's sitting between them? Bella's mangy lap dog who called me MooMoo. But Timber nods to her. "Hey, Chelsea," he says.

"What up," she says back, then looks at me and raises one eyebrow but doesn't speak.

I look down at the ground and my cheeks grow warm. Does she know that something's going on between Timber and me? Is it obvious by the way he said hello to me? Or what if nothing is actually going on between us and there's nothing for her to know? Timber takes the seat on Chelsea's left side. I have no choice but to slip into the other chair on her right.

"How was your weekend?" Chelsea asks him.

I stare hard at the top of my desk, straining to hear his answer over the other kids chatting.

"Boring. Bella was upstate with her dad, so I just hung out." Timber says nonchalantly. "So you know, nothing special."

When I hear him say this, I feel like someone punched me in the stomach. Then threw me off a bridge. Then ran over me with a truck. I want to die. Shrivel up and blow away like a little dried leaf. *Nothing special?* My eyes sting and my nose suddenly runs. He said his weekend was nothing special. I turn away and press my face into the sleeve of my tunic. My beautiful, stupid tunic. The one I wore for no reason except to look like a fool.

I drag myself through the next three classes (looking like an erdler now without even trying) just marking time until lunch, when I can fall into Ari's and Mercedes's laps and fully lose it. I walk slowly, head down, trying not to cry when once again, I hear my name. Only this time when I look up, it's Bella. I swear to the high heavens, I'm so surprised that my heart actually stops and I can feel my entire body go numb.

"I've been looking for you," she says.

I'm sure there is terror in my eyes. Why is she looking for me? To kick the crap out of me for kissing her boyfriend, who thinks kissing me was nothing special? Wow, this day is not turning out how I'd hoped.

"So listen." Bella stands close to me. "You want to run lines today? I totally didn't rehearse at all over the weekend." She reaches out and lifts the hawk's feather from my chest. "Cool. Is it real?"

I'm flabbergasted! I don't know what to do so I stammer, "Are you serious?"

"Of course I'm serious." She drops the feather. "I thought we were going to work on the audition together."

"But you said . . . I mean on the . . . you don't even . . . " That's when I get it, finally. I can't say anything about the blog or the fact that Bella doesn't actually like me. It's a secret and if I let her know that I know then she'll change the password and everybody will hate me because everyone loves to read it.

"What?" She lifts her chin and flips her hair over her shoulder.

"Nothing," I mutter.

"So when's your study hall? Who teaches it?" she asks.

"Last period," I tell her, still entirely bewildered. "Ms. Crane."

"No problem," she says. "I'll bail on my calc class and come find you. We can probably use one of the studios upstairs."

"But, but . . . ," I say. I didn't actually mean to agree to anything.

"Don't worry. Ms. Crane will totally let you out if I ask her." A funny little electronic song plays and Bella snaps open her phone. "Gotta go," she whispers to me, then says, "What up," into the phone as she turns and saunters away.

I hurry off to the cafeteria. I need Ari and Mercedes. I don't understand a single thing that has happened to me today. I always thought the erdler world would be so much simpler than the elf world. I mean, it's not as if mushrooms can talk here and people can make themselves disappear. It's not as if anyone uses magic. Life inside the walls of this tiny erdler school is so much more complex than in the whole of Alverland. But I guess that's the thing. If you don't have special powers you have to find other ways to get what you want. And for erdlers, that means confusing your enemies, then stabbing them in the back when they least expect it.

I'm almost running by the time I get to the cafeteria and I nearly knock over the three fairy girls as they come out the doors.

"Zephyr! Oh my God." Jilly, the fairy queen, pulls me into their tight little circle. I notice they're all wearing long silk shirts with flowing sleeves, sort of like tunics. Jilly's is bright blue, Rienna's is white, and Darby's is salmon-colored. Of course, they have their wings on, too.

"We totally read what they wrote," Jilly says in a low, serious voice.

"Who?" I ask, distracted by looking over their heads for Ari and Mercedes.

"You know who," Rienna says, staring hard at me. "On the blog," she whispers.

A pang of fear goes through me. "About what?" I ask. "This weekend?"

"Huh?" asks Darby. "What happened over the weekend?"

"I heard Bella got arrested at a rave in Redhook," Rienna says.

"No, no. I'm talking about what they said about Zephyr's clothes and the audition," Jilly says, then turns to me. "Tell me you've read it."

"Oh just that," I say, relieved.

Rienna's eyes open wide. "Wow," she says, turning first to Jilly then Darby. "She doesn't even care. How's that possible?" Then she looks at me suspiciously. "Why don't you care?"

"No it's not that . . ."

"You're absolutely right," says Jilly. "I wouldn't care either."

Darby laughs. "Get a grip, Jilly. Last year when Bella called you a goth lesbo vampire slut, you totally stopped wearing black and we all got wings."

"First of all, that doesn't even make sense," says Jilly. "How can you be a lesbo and a slut?"

"A lesbian can be slutty," Darby argues.

"Whatever," says Jilly. "But second, I didn't stop being goth because of Bella."

"Yeah right," says Rienna.

"She just happened to say that right after we read *A Midsummer Night's Dream* and I was ready for a change. The whole goth look is so over anyway," Jilly insists.

"It's not over," says Darby.

"Then why aren't *you* all gothed out anymore?" Jilly asks.

I don't want to get involved in their weird argument about when they became fairies, so I wave to them and slip out of the circle into the cafeteria. I quickly spot Mercedes and Ari hunched over Ari's BlackBerry. I jog over to them and drop down on the floor. "You guys will never guess what happened now!" I moan.

"This is so cool, Zephyr. Check it out," Ari says without even looking up at me.

Mercedes is wiggling all around, smacking me on the arm, she's so excited. I peer over her shoulder, certain that whatever's on that itty-bitty screen is something terrible about me. "Ari's band posted their song 'Not Like You' on YouTube like a month ago and then it started getting hits and today it got a featured video spot! Isn't that slamming?" Mercy says.

"What?" I'm really confused now.

"His song is a featured video!" she repeats.

"Oh," I say, because obviously this is important. But actually I had no idea a regular person could even make a video or why you'd hang it on a tube so other people can hit it or why any of that is so exciting and how all of this relates to the BlackBerry. I squint at the screen anyway and can just make out Ari playing the piano. "That's you," I say, amazed.

"Of course it's me," he says. "It's my song."

"I can't really hear it," I say over the noise in the cafeteria. "But I'm sure it's good."

"You don't know what it is, do you?" Ari asks.

"Honestly, no," I admit.

"Your dad's on YouTube, Zephyr," Ari says by way of explanation.

"He's on there?" I ask, pointing.

"Everybody's on here, Zephyr!" Ari snaps.

"Am I?" I ask.

Ari and Mercedes both stare at me, then look at each other. "This isn't about you!" Mercedes tells me with no patience left in her voice.

I feel terrible. I don't want Ari to think I'm not excited for him, even if I don't get it. "That's great, Ari!" I say. "Can I see it?"

He looks up and smiles. "Sure," he says. "I'll start it over."

Before he can hand the BlackBerry to me, the pixie stomps by. "Put it away, son," she barks. "Or it's mine."

"No problem." Ari quickly stashes the BlackBerry in his bag.

"What was that all about?" I ask, watching the pixie bumping through a crowd of kids, throwing elbows and ignoring any protests.

"Not allowed," Ari says. "Because God forbid any of us use technology that the teachers don't understand."

Actually, I'm glad he had to put it away. "So you guys . . . ," I say, hoping to turn the attention to me.

"Featured spot!" Mercedes says to Ari. "That's cold. GGJB's gonna get like a million hits."

"Not a million," Ari says, but I can tell by his little grin that he hopes it's true.

"Simon, Randy, and Paula are gonna call you. They'll be begging you, 'Ari Mendelbaum, please come on *American Idol.*'"

Ari shakes his head. "I don't know, though," he says. "Maybe I should've posted something else. Did you see some of those comments? People were saying, 'You suck,' and 'Give me a razor so I can slit my wrist.'"

"People said that?" I ask.

"Like two a-holes said that," Mercedes says. "And they're probably just jealous because they posted something that didn't get featured. Anyway, everyone else was saying it's great and they loved it. Plus, who cares. You've got a featured video, which means it's definitely good."

The bell rings, sending everyone in a frenzy to gather their garbage and pick up their bags. I stand and follow Ari and Mercedes out the doors. My stomach gnaws at me since I didn't eat, but then again, I don't know if I could eat, I'm so upside down today. "What are you guys doing after school?" I ask.

"I have to get together with my band," Ari says, without looking at us. "We have to strategize how to make this whole YouTube thing work for us."

"And I have to babysit," says Mercedes. "Can you believe that dookie? My *abuela* is going to the botanica for a coral shell reading, then she'll come home with more of her crazy Santeria stuff and start burning a hundred candles to all the saints, praying for my poor lost soul. She always tries to get me to go with her, but I say no way! Then I get stuck taking care of Nellie and Marisol, the spawns of *el Diablo* himself. I'm just handing them a big bag of Cheetos, turning on Noggin, and telling them not to bother me unless one of them is bleeding!"

"Okay, but I sort of have something to tell you."

"Call me later!" Mercedes says as she bops down the hall, waving good-bye.

I don't wave back. My whole body feels heavy and slow. I turn and drag myself down the hall for the second half of this very long day.

Finally it's the last class of the day. At first, I'm so relieved that my day is almost over that I fall into my study hall seat and sigh. I open my copy of *The Age of Innocence* for English class, but then I remember that Bella said she was going to come get me and I can't concentrate. Why on earth does she want to practice with me? And why didn't I say no? I know why . . . because I'm an elf. And elves are nice. We just are. It's in our blood. When everyone is equally nice, you don't have to worry about it. With erdlers though, everything is different. Maybe Bella didn't mean what she wrote on her blog about me. Or maybe if you're an erdler you can say mean things about other people and still be friends. Look at how Ari and Mercedes talk to each other sometimes, and they're best friends.

Before I can puzzle through all of this confusing stuff, the door opens and Bella comes in. Ms. Crane's eyes widen and she smiles as if a celebrity just walked into the room. She leans forward, expectantly, as Bella whispers to her. When Bella points toward me, Ms. Crane slumps back in her chair. She nods, but all the enthusiasm has drained from her body. Bella seems to have that effect on people. Then just like that, I'm walking down an empty hall with Bella.

"Why did Ms. Crane let me out?" I ask.

Bella flicks her hand. "Whatever. She owes me big-time. I passed her lame CD to my agent because he reps a couple of singers she likes. I only did it because I totally screwed up a midterm in her Government class. Can you imagine?" She looks at me and pretends to gag. "A high school history teacher making a CD of her sad sack songs? She's like thirty years old."

"My dad is forty-two and he's a singer."

"Whatever, every teacher here is a wannabe."

"A wannabe?" I ask as we pass each classroom filled with students. "Sounds like a furry little marsupial."

Bella laughs. "Are you joking? That's funny. Tell me you're joking."

"I guess so," I lie.

"'Marsupial,'" she says, chuckling to herself. "That's a great word." She turns down the main hall and heads for the big green doors.

"I thought we were going to rehearse," I say, suddenly wary of where she's taking me.

Bella takes her big white sunglasses from the top of her head and covers her eyes. "I need a frappuccino."

"But are we allowed to leave?" I ask.

When Bella looks at me I see my reflection in the dark lenses of her glasses. I look like a scared little elf. One that was too afraid to go to Ironweed, one that cried on the first day of erdler school, one that didn't want to make up a résumé so I'd have a shot at winning the ELPH part. But that's not me. I'm a Brooklyn girl—well, a Brooklyn *elf*—now and I won't let Bella intimidate me. If she wants to play this little two-faced game, I'll play along. What was it that Ari said? Know thine enemy. Well, Bella, let's get to know each other.

"You don't have to come," she says, but her voice drips with scorn.

My stomach growls. "I did skip lunch."

"Lunch is for fatties," Bella tells me.

We're at the doors. She's pushing them open. I have to decide. Stay or go. "Just one question," I say. "What's a frappuccino?"

A frappuccino, it turns out, is the best thing ever invented by erdlers! "This is so yummy!" I tell Bella for the hundredth time as we walk back from Starbucks, sucking up that half-frozen, sweet, creamy goodness. "I could drink ten of these!"

"God, you're already hyper enough. If you drank ten of those somebody would have to peel you off the ceiling."

"I'm hyper?"

"Oh my God! You're like so perky all the time!" Bella bounces her head and says in a high squeaky voice.

My mouth goes from moist and sweet to dry and sticky. "I don't mean to be," I say. "I didn't know it was a bad thing."

"Why would it be a bad thing?" she asks, but I think I detect a little smirk playing at the corners of her mouth.

"Just the way you said it," I mumble.

"You can *be* that way." She steps into the intersection, ignoring the flashing red DON'T WALK sign. A white delivery truck blares its horn and swerves around us, but Bella doesn't seem to notice, or care. "As long as you don't act that way at the audition."

"Why not?" I ask, determined to get as much out of her as possible.

"Oh." Bella shakes her head sadly as we reach the other side of the street. "I keep forgetting, you've never done this before. Seriously, Zephyr. If you act like a spaz, Mr. O'Donnell will totally think you're an amateur."

I poke my straw down into the slush at the bottom of my cup and try not to grin. All I have to do is keep walking and talking and I'll get her to tell me everything about an audition. "Thanks for letting me know."

"I thought your friends, what are their names, that girl and that guy, were supposed to help you."

"Ari helped me with my résumé, but his band got hit by a u-tube or something exciting like that so he's busy," I tell her.

Bella scrunches up her face. "Got hit by a u-tube?"

"Yeah, isn't that what it's called?" I try to remember. "U-tube or something? His band made a video and got a feature."

Bella slows her walk and squeezes my forearm. "You mean he got a featured video on YouTube?"

"Yeah! That's what I said." I smile, triumphant. She lets go of me.

"What's his band called?"

"GGJB," I tell her.

"Never heard of them. What kind of music do they play?"

"I've never heard them either, but he says it's goth, gay Jew boy music."

Bella chokes and nearly spits out her frappuccino. "Goth, gay, Jew boy?"

I'm not sure why it's funny but I'm feeling so zippy from the frappuccino right now that I giggle. "I think that's what he called it."

"So he's gay? He's not that girl's boyfriend?"

"Mercedes?" I ask. "That's what I thought at first, too, but no. They're just friends because she's only allowed to date Puerto Rican boys."

Bella snorts a disbelieving laugh. "Why?"

"Well, I guess her grandmother came over on a boat and she's really religious."

"Oh my God, she's racist," Bella says.

"Not racist," I tell her. "It's called something else. She keeps an altar in her bedroom with candles and fruit and other offerings to the spirits."

"Voodoo?" Bella asks, her eyes wide.

"No, I think it's called Santeria."

Bella shrugs. "Same thing."

We turn a corner and walk beneath a fortress of scaffolding up the side of a building. I move closer to Bella so we can squeeze past three guys in hard hats who stop hauling bricks to ogle us.

"Hey sugar, what's your name?" the tallest guy asks me.

"Um," I say, but Bella yanks my arm.

"Ignore them." She pushes past. "N.W.T.E."

"N.W.T.E.?"

"Not Worth the Effort." We step back into the sunshine, leaving the brick haulers hooting and laughing behind us.

"So what else do you know about Mercedes?" she asks.

"Not much," I say, still trying to figure out what just happened, and how to steer the conversation back to the audition.

"Really? I thought you were friends."

"We are!" I tell her. "But she can't help me today because her grandmother is going to have a sea shell reading and buy some candles, so Mercedes has to babysit her twin sisters, who she calls the spawn of *el Diablo*." I laugh because I love the way Mercedes says it.

Bella nods, slowly taking it all in. "What about you, Zephyr?" she asks. "What kind of religion does your family practice?"

"We don't really have a religion."

"You must believe in something or are you an atheist?"

"Well, I guess you could say that we believe in nature," I tell her, simplifying things.

"Where are you from?" She cocks her head nearly to her shoulder.

"Just a little town in the upper peninsula of Michigan," I say, because I have to be careful here. Everyone's worst fear in Alverland is to be discovered.

"What's it called?"

"Nothing you've ever heard of. It's really really tiny and most of the people there are from the same clans, er um, families."

Bella bumps me. "Watch out. Dog doo." She points to a smear on the sidewalk.

"Gross!" I step around.

"Are your parents related?" Bella asks.

I watch the ground more closely. "Sort of. My mom's great-grand-mother and my dad's great-grandfather were brother and sister, so somehow that makes them related but from a long long time ago so it's okay."

"Sounds like a very interesting place," says Bella.

"Oh, it is!" I tell her. "I love it there. I mean, not that I want to go back or anything, because I'm totally in love with Brooklyn. New York's the best place ever, but I do miss Alverland."

She whips her head around to face me.

"That's what it's called?" she asks. "Alverland?"

I'm flustered. I shouldn't have told her the name. "Um, well yeah, but you wouldn't find it on a map or anything like that."

"Oh, please," she says, looking away. "Every place is on Google Maps now." We've made it back to school and she swings open the green doors. "You still want to practice?" she asks.

"Absolutely," I say. As we head upstairs to find an empty studio, I rub my temples.

"I'm kind of regretting that frappie thing. What's it called again?"

"Alverland must be the only place on earth without a Starbucks," she says with a snort.

The buzzy feeling in my head has turned into a dull ache behind my eyes. "My head is starting to hurt."

"Oh believe me," says Bella. "There are worse letdowns than caffeine." She peeks in the windows of the small practice studios. "You'll be back for more soon enough." We find an empty room and throw our bags down. "Oh, look at that. We've got only ten minutes left until the bell," she says.

Even though my head is throbbing, I sit on the edge of a desk and ask, "Can you give me a few quick tips?"

Bella positions herself in front of me. "Of course. I said I'd help you, didn't I?"

I have to admit that in some ways Bella is very kind, and she's very pretty. I see why people like her, or like to hate her anyway. If she's your friend she'll probably do a lot for you—like take you out for a frappe-whatsi-whosit, or pull you away from N.W.T.E. brickhaulers, or stop you from stepping in dog poop. And if she's not your friend, you probably want her to be and maybe you get jealous that she's not.

"Mostly you want to be really calm and say your words slowly and clearly because you tend to talk fast," Bella tells me. "Don't do a lot of movement with your arms or your head. Just keep your body super still. Almost kind of stiff, but not stiff in a bad way. Stiff in a professional way. You know what I mean?"

I shake my head. "No, I really don't."

"Okay, watch." Bella stands up very straight and tall and presses her arms to her sides. "The new ELPH camera is so easy, it must be magic," she says in a flat, clear voice.

"Don't you want to sound a little more enthusiastic?" I ask.

"Sure, if you want everyone to know you've never done an audition before."

"No, I mean, it's just that I'd think if someone wants to sell something, they'd want more excitement."

"Oh, right," says Bella. "Well, see, the thing is at an audition, they just want to hear your voice and see what you look like. Later, they'll give you directions about how to sound and how to act if you get the part. So at first, it's like a blank slate. They want nothing. You stand still and say the words. Get it?"

"Okay," I say. "I can do that."

"You try," says Bella.

I jump down and stand up straight. I hold my arms against my sides like Bella told me and I say very clearly and slowly, exaggerating each word. "The new ELPH camera is so easy it must be magic."

"But you're smiling," she points out.

"No smiling?" I ask.

"Remember," she says. "Blank slate."

I nod and try again, this time keeping my face as empty of expression as I can, which isn't hard since my head is aching. "The new ELPH camera is so easy it must be magic," I say loudly but without any gusto at all.

"Yes," says Bella with a big smile. "That was perfect."

The bell rings. This day is finally over. I don't know whether it's been good or bad or just plain weird.

"Do you want to practice again before the audition?" I ask Bella.

"I'm kind of busy," she says. "But I think you've totally got it. Don't even worry about it. The worst thing you can do is overpractice because then it becomes stale."

"Thank you so much for helping me," I say, following her to the door. It worked! I got her to tell me what she knew. Then I feel a huge pang of guilt as I remember my kiss with Timber. Would she be so nice to me if she knew? For a brief moment, I consider telling her, but I don't know how I'd say it. And anyway, Timber is the one who should tell her. Then again, since it was nothing special, I guess she'll never know. "Well, thanks again! That was really super nice of you," I tell her, and I mean it.

She pauses and looks back over her shoulder. "My pleasure," she says with a smile before she slips through the door.

chapter 9

MY CAFFEINE HEADACHE has finally gone away and now I'm starving. I find one of my Mom's homemade granola bars that I stashed inside my locker and I start to devour it. While I'm scarfing it down, Mercedes's aunt, Ms. Sanchez, stops by. "Hi, Zephyr," she says. "I've been hoping to catch up with you. I sent you an e-mail to stop by my office but I hadn't heard back from you."

"An e-mail?" I ask, kind of embarrassed. "I'm sorry, I don't have a computer at home."

"You can use the school's computers, you know. That's what they're here for," she tells me.

I swallow the last of the granola bar, then ask, amazed, "There are computers here?"

"Of course," she says with a kind laugh. "Every student has a school e-mail address and when you're a junior you even get your own laptop." My mouth must have dropped open because she smiles and says, "Really!" Then she gently takes hold of my wrist. "Come on, I'll show you the computer lab."

We walk past classrooms and studios full of after-school clubs and kids rehearsing for upcoming performances. I'm jealous and can't wait for my first audition. "Why did you want to see me?" I ask Ms. Sanchez.

"Just to check in. Is everything going okay?"

"I guess so," I say, not sure what you're supposed to tell a guidance counselor. I mean, should I mention that I kissed Timber but he acts like it was no big deal? Probably not.

"I heard you're going to audition for the ELPH camera ad."

"Yeah, I'm excited. Bella was helping me today."

"Excellent!" Ms. Sanchez says. She pats me on the back. "You're making a lot of friends quickly and getting involved. That's what I like to see."

"Thanks," I say, feeling pretty good about myself.

We get to the student lab, which is a room behind the library with at least fifty computers. Students fill about half the seats. I can't believe it. I've never seen this many computers before in my life. The library in Ironweed has just three and compared to these sleek, shiny machines, they look like they were built by ape people during the Paleolithic era.

"Hi, Kenji," Ms. Sanchez says to the guy sitting at the computer in the front of the room. "Can you please show a new student how to log on to her school e-mail account?"

He removes his earphones and looks up from his screen, where cartoon people run around blowing up things. I have to keep myself from staring because this guy, like everyone here, looks so different from what I'm used to. He's got thick, black shiny hair buzzed short on the sides but long on the top with the ends dyed bright blue so that it flops over his head like the soft wing of a tropical bird. His cheekbones and chin are sharp, as if his face were chiseled out of a smooth piece of wood. Except for his lips, which are full and soft and round. I think of Timber's lips on mine and I look away. My cheeks get hot and probably as red as a cardinal's tail.

"This is Zephyr Addler," Ms. Sanchez tells Kenji.

His eyes stay on me for a moment, then he says, "So you're Zephyr."
I nod, uncertain what that means.

"This is a bit new to her," Ms. Sanchez says. "So you might need to spend some time explaining things." Now I'm even more embarrassed. Not only am I blushing over Timber but now Kenji knows that I'm a complete computer moron.

"No prob," Kenji says, then nods to the chair beside him.

After half an hour, I tell Kenji, "You're very patient." He's shown me how to use e-mail, instant messaging, and the Web. "And you explain things so well. I thought computers were frustrating before this."

"Nah," he says. "It's all easy once you know the basics. And you're a quick study."

"I still don't understand about blogs, though," I admit.

"You mean how to set one up?" he asks.

"Why would I need to set one up?"

"Anybody can have one."

"Do you?"

"Sure."

"What's it called?" I ask.

"Samurai Son," he says as he types. "That's also my IM name and my gaming handle. But anyway, I doubt you'd think my blog is interesting unless you're into gaming."

I look at his screen. It's filled with weird cartoon people with huge eyes in warrior costumes. "Did you do the drawings?"

"Yeah. It's *anime*, Japanimation style," he says, pointing to the characters. "I'm really into manga." When I hesitate, he quickly adds, "Japanese comic books."

"I've never seen a Japanese comic book," I admit, probably sounding even dumber than I feel.

He shrugs. "Not everybody has." He closes his blog and clicks back onto the screen where the cartoon people are blowing things up. "You all set now?"

"I think so," I tell him.

"If you have trouble or think of any other questions, just ask." He puts his headphones on and returns to his game.

I sit down at an empty computer and quickly log on. First I check my school e-mail account. There are twenty announcements about upcoming auditions and performances. I want to go to every single one of them, but I have to get through this ELPH audition first. Next I try instant messaging. First I try Ari, but an automatic message pops up that reads, "2 Busy 4 U. Try me l8er." I figure he must still be rehearsing with GGJB. I try Mercedes, but she's offline, probably busy with the spawn of *el Diablo*. I'm about to log off when I get an idea. Maybe I could instant message Timber. Kenji showed me the school address book online where people list their e-mail addresses and IM names. After a few tries, I find it and look up Timber.

As soon as I type TLC94 into the "To" box, I get nervous. What am I going to say? An even better question is why am I bothering to say anything? Mercedes told me to let him make the first move, but what if he doesn't? Or what if he's waiting for me to make the first move? Plus, just because he told Chelsea that the weekend was nothing special doesn't mean he really feels that way, right? I mean, Chelsea is Bella's friend and if he doesn't want Bella to know about what happened, then of course he's going to keep it a secret from Chelsea. If nothing else, I need to tell him that I don't want to do something hurtful. Bella was nice to me today and it's not very elfin of me to kiss her boyfriend behind her back. I hunt and peck on the keyboard and write this message:

—Hi Timber. Zephyr here. Are you there?

I wait, my heart pounding and my palms prickly with sweat. After a few seconds, a box pops up.

—What up, Z. Cool 2 get yer message. What r u doin?
—I'm in the computer lab at school. Where are you?
—Coffee shop. "Studying" ha-ha. Not really, tho.

I type "Are you having a frappie drink at Starbucks?" with my heart racing. Could he be with Bella? I send the message.

—LOL! U crack me up.

As always, I have no idea what I've said that's funny. The odd thing is that having this computer screen between us makes me feel bold so I type in, "Why is that funny?"

We trade messages quickly.

—1) I don't like Starbucks and 2) real men don't drink frap-puccino.
—What do real men drink?
—U'd have to ask a real man, ; []

I giggle quietly. This is fun. Then I type in "Okay, I'll ask my dad." After I send my message, the screen stays still for a moment and I wonder if I said something wrong. Did I make him mad? I thought we were having fun. Being goofy. Teasing each other. He's the one who started it. Oh, come on, come on, come on! I stare at the screen wishing another message would pop up and wondering if something is wrong with this stupid machine. Did my message get lost in the sky? Then, suddenly, there's his answer.

—Yer dad's cool. I like yer family. The park was a blast.

I'm so relieved that I nearly fall out of my chair. Plus, I'm excited. I read the message again. *The park was a blast.* A blast means that it was *something* special. Not *nothing special*. So he did have a good time. I peck out my response:

> —I had fun, too! My family thinks you're fantastic. Anyone
> who can sing is okay in their world. And you can really
> sing!

I send this, then I wish I hadn't. I'm gushing again. Being too nicey
nice. Not at all taking Mercedes's advice. And I sound like a little kid.
Not cool. I don't know the abbreviations and slang words they use or
how to add all those little funny smiley faces to the end of the message.
He must think I'm a total and complete idiot so before he can respond,
I send another message, this one sarcastic.

> —Guess that ensemble class paid off for you.

But then, this pops up:

> —Very funny. I cd sing b4 ensemble, ya know? I did have a
> record deal back in the day.

I'm afraid that I've hurt his feelings. This is the problem with typing
instead of talking. He can't see my face or hear my tone. I guess that's
when a little winking head bouncing at the end of my message would
come in handy.

> —Oops, sorry. I was trying to be sarcastic. Guess it didn't
> work.
> —Sarcasm from u? Nah, doesn't work cuz the thing I like
> about u is that yer real.

My heart does a little dance in my chest. He likes something about
me! I want to stand up on my chair and yell Yippee! Of course, I don't.
Even I know that that would be the wrong thing to do in a computer lab.
But then I remember the reason I sent him a message in the first place.
I'm not sure how to say it, so I just type what I'm thinking.

> —I feel bad about what happened in the park.
> —Y?

It takes me a second to realize that he means "why." I try to sum up how I feel, but it's hard. So instead, I ask, "Does Bella know?" A few seconds later this comes back:

—About what?

Is he being dense or does he not remember kissing me? Maybe what I'm supposed to do is play this game. Dance around the subject. Act like I don't get it or wait for him to bring it up. Maybe if I were an erdler, I'd know how to do that. But I'm not. Besides, that's what he said he likes about me. So, here goes:

—Does she know that you kissed me? Maybe kissing me was not something special for you. But it was for me. Maybe you kiss everyone. Maybe it wasn't *that* kind of kiss. Maybe I'm making a big deal out of nothing. But still, I feel bad because Bella has been nice to me and I like you and I don't want to hurt her feelings or stop being your friend.

It seems like forever that I wait for his response. My stomach ties itself in knots and I realize that I'm gripping the edges of the keyboard. Finally, he answers:

—Don't worry about Bella. What she doesn't know won't hurt her. And, u r still my friend. Gotta go. L8r!

He signs off. I stare at the screen, even more confused than before. He's still my friend? If what happened in the park is nothing special and I'm just his friend then why do I feel like crap? As I'm puzzling through this another little IM window pops up. Eagerly I read, hoping it's from Ari or Mercedes. But this is what I see from Samurai Son.

—Thought u might like to know they're talking sh*t about u and yer friends again.

I look up over my computer at Kenji. Seems strange that he would send me a message when he's sitting ten feet away. But he doesn't look at me, so I hit reply and type in "Who?" This comes back:

—U know who.

—No I don't.

—U'v never seen the blog?

—How do you know about that?

—Duh. Everybody knows. Probably even yer grandma reads it.

—My grandmother doesn't have a computer and I don't know how to find the blog.

The next box that pops up has just a blue link. I type in "Thanks" send it back to Kenji then click the link to open Bella's Web site. I can't quite remember how to find the secret blog, but I know I have to click on some hidden button. I move my mouse around, clicking randomly until I hit the white dog in the top right corner. A box appears and I type in *belladonna*, the password that Ari told me. The blog opens. I hunch closer to the computer and begin reading.

OMG! Took MooMoo to Starbucks for a frap to get the 411 on her. First of all, she'd never had coffee. F*ing hilarious. Can you believe it? And get this: she's from some kind of commune in the woods. A cult sounds like. Everybody dresses the same. Some weird religion. Her parents are cousins!

And, that guy Ari she hangs with: total homo. (Not that it matters, right? My cousin is gay and like my best friend.) But the guy calls his band Goth Gay Jew Boy. LAME!

Also, the girl, Mercedes—her parents came over on a boat from Cuba or something. Totally illegal! And they're racists plus they're into voodoo.

These are the kinds of losers I have to put up with in the ELPH audition. MooMoo and VooDoo = f*ing marsupials.

In the comments I see this,

—**B, y r u hanging w/ her?**
Posted by CH3L-C.

—**her 'rents are cousins? Nasty!**
Posted by: ZoEzOe

—**Somebody call immigration on the Cubans.**
Posted by: LadyBug

—**She's inbred. No wonder she never had a frap. I've seen that guy she hangs with staring at Timber, tho.**
Posted by: ZoEzOe

—**Prob has a crush on yer man.**
Posted by: LadyBug

—**Whatev. Who doesn't?**
Posted by: BELLA.

—**but y'd u take her to SB?**
Posted by CH3L-C

—**C, u r missing the point!**
Posted by: BELLA

—**Better watch out or VooDoo'll put a curse on yer A! BTW what's marsupial?**
Posted by: ZoEzOe

—**Marsupial = Wannabe.**
Posted by: BELLA

—**LOL!**
Posted by: ZoEzOe

—**LOL x 2!**
Posted by LadyBug

I'm so mad that my head hurts, my vision is blurry, and I can feel my heartbeat in my temples, my arms, and my chest. My stomach is in knots. My legs are weak. And my skin feels like it's on fire. I don't even know what thing to be the most mad about. That she called Mercedes VooDoo and said that Ari is lame and that my parents are cousins. Or that she didn't mention Ari's band got hit by the U-Tube or that Mercedes takes care of her little sisters. And she even stole my marsupial joke! Who does that? Or maybe I'm most mad because I actually thought she was nice. She's not. She's horrible and my plan totally backfired. Kenji must see me with my head in my hands because I quickly get another IM from him.

> —Those are some seriously mean girls. What'd u do 2 them?
> —Nothing! What am I going to do?
> —Damage control!
> —Huh?
> —Get with your homies!

This I don't understand at all. I need to talk. Out loud! Use real words. I leave my computer and walk up to Kenji's desk. He glances up at me out of the corner of his eye.

"Why should I go home?" I whisper to him.

"What?" he says, taking out only one earphone.

"You said I should get with my homies," I say.

He shakes his head. "That's old school for friends, Zephyr. The people they're talking about."

"Ari and Mercedes!" I gasp. "But how?" I'm panicked. "I don't know where they are." Kenji looks at me like I'm stupid. "What?" I ask.

"Hello!" He points to the computer and pats it. "This is the twenty-first century. IM them."

I jump. "Right!" I say too loudly, causing everyone in the lab to look up at me, but I don't even care. I have to get to my friends. "Thank you, Kenji! Thank you!" I skitter back to my empty computer and quickly shoot Ari a message. That same annoying message "2 Busy 4 U" comes up. I try Mercedes again.

—M, are you there? This is important.

Immediately she writes back.

—u r the biggest bitch i've ever known worse than that puta Bella cuz i was yer friend when nobody else was showed u everything and tried 2 B nice 2 u and u betrayed me and Ari.

I'm so slow at typing that it takes a long time for me to respond. But finally I send this message:

—Please don't be mad at me! She twisted around everything I said and they're saying horrible stuff about me, too!

Mercedes's message comes back almost immediately.

—i don't believe u. u r a liar and a bitch cuz u told her something and that's enuff. and another thing, I'm PUERTO RICAN, not Cuban!

I peck out one last message:

—Please let me explain!

This comes back a few seconds later:

—leave me and ari alone!

Then she signs off. I don't know what to do, so I just stare at the blinking cursor on the screen. This can't really be happening, can it? Just an hour ago I thought I had so many friends and now all of the sudden I have no idea who my friends are. And what happened in between? Nothing except some mean girls typed lies and exaggerations on a computer and sent them out into the world to ruin my life. How can that be? It's worse than any kind of magic that I know. What's worse is that I don't know any spells to combat it.

But then a little box pops up that says I have a new e-mail. I click over to my in-box and see this:

Sender: Mercedes.Sanchez@BAPAHS.edu
To: distributionlist@BAPAHS.edu
Re: URGENT MESSAGE! Please read and forward!

I'm relieved that Mercedes is e-mailing me. Maybe she had a minute to cool off and realizes that this isn't my fault. I open the message.

Hey BAPAHS—want some dirt? Read this and forward 2 everyone U know!

Bella Dartagnan is a bitch and thinks she can ruin other people's lives! Well, here's some news for her! I know a slut who kissed her boyfriend Saturday in the park. Want 2 know who? Zephyr Addler, that's who. Hope you have a great week, beee-yatch!

I don't understand what's going on. Why would Mercedes be sending me this message? And what's a "distribution list"? Suddenly another little box pops up that says I have six new e-mails. I click back to my in-box and see six new messages from people I don't even know. Every message has the same heading: *Forward: Re: URGENT MESSAGE! Please read and forward!* I click through each one but they're all the same thing that Mercedes sent to me. How are all these people getting it? How come they're sending the same message to me if they don't even know me? I'm so confused! Then I start getting instant messages. The first one is from Samurai Son. It says:

—Z,
Ouch!
K

Others are worse. People I don't know are calling me a bitch and a slut and other horrible words. Then some of them are nice. They say, "Way to go!" and "Stick it to her!" and "Bella deserved it!" And a few of them are just scary: "Forget Timber. I'll do you in the park any day!" In a matter of minutes my e-mail is flooded and my instant message board is jammed. I can't take it! I log off as fast as I can and jolt out of my seat. I swear every person in the room looks up. They all stare at me. Some of them elbow each other and point at me. Just as I'm about to the flee the room, Kenji gets my attention and waves me over.

I slump into the empty chair beside him. "What am I going to do?" I whimper.

"Don't worry about it. It'll get shut down in a minute. The webmaster'll see what's going on and put a block on all the forwarding. And your girl, Mercedes, will be in deep doo-doo."

"Why?" I ask, feeling even worse now that Mercedes is going to get in trouble.

"Can't e-mail personal slander. School code of ethics," says Kenji. He shakes his blue bangs out of his eyes. "She'll probably get kicked out of school."

"Oh no!" I gasp.

He shrugs. "Just suspended for a few days. Or maybe her aunt will save her butt."

"This is terrible!" I mumble. "Her parents will kill her."

He smirks. "Why are you worried about her after what she did to you?"

"Because," I stammer. "She's my friend."

He snorts. "Some friend!"

"This is all my fault."

Kenji points to the screen. "Check this out."

"What now!" I groan as I glance up to see the I-Hate-Bella blog on-screen. Of course, I start reading:

Drum roll please! Today's BellaHater Award goes halfsies to Zephyr Addler and Mercedes Sanchez! Zephyr 4 sticking it 2 Bella by tongue

wrestling with TLC. Way 2 Go! And Mercedes 4 outing them. Poor Bella! What's a girl 2 do? Suffer, bitch! You've made everybody else's life hell and what comes around goes around, so read 'em and weep. Yer not the only mean girl in town.

"Who is this BellaHater?" I ask Kenji.

He shrugs. "Nobody knows. I think it's somebody on the inside."

"One of her friends?" I ask, shocked.

"That's a relative term," says Kenji. "Those girls would stab one another in the back for a pair of shoes."

I shake my head. "How awful."

"Who cares," says Kenji. "It's freaking hilarious."

"I can't take another minute of this. I don't care if I never see another computer screen in my life." I drag myself out of the chair.

Kenji laughs. "It's not like you can escape it. Computers are a part of life."

"Not my life," I mutter.

"Anyway," Kenji says as he slips his earphones back on. "It's not the computer's fault people are jerks."

He's right, I guess, but then again, without computers my entire life wouldn't have been flushed down the toilet in five minutes flat.

I do my best to hold it together on my way home because I can't break down on the subway. I'd look like a mental patient if I sobbed on the train and would probably get carted away by the loony police. But, as soon as I hit the park, I start running and I let the tears flow. I'm half out of my mind. Everything has gone wrong today. I hate my school. I hate everyone in it. I hate Brooklyn. All I want to do is go back to Alverland, where I know the rules and the people are really, truly, absolutely nice.

When I get home, I burst through our front door. "Mom!" I yell. "Dad!" I'm crying my eyes out now and want to collapse in someone's arms. I run through the living room and dining room. Both are empty. "Where is everyone?" I yell.

My dad sticks his head out of the kitchen doorway. "Shhhh, honey," he says, and wraps me in his arms. His eyes are red rimmed. I fall into his hug but look over his shoulder into the kitchen. My whole family is gathered around the table. My mom and sisters are crying. Bramble and Persimmon are huddled in Mom's lap. Grove has his hand on Mom's shoulder.

"We've been waiting for you," Dad says.

I think, *Oh no! Someone told them what happened at school. They're so disappointed in me.* I shrink, feeling worse than ever. But then my dad lets go of the hug and looks down into my face.

"It's Grandma Fawna," he says.

"What?" I sputter. "Is she still missing?"

"No, she came back," says Dad.

"Then what?" I ask.

"She's sick," Mom says. It must be serious because elves as powerful as my grandmother don't get sick.

"Is she dying?" I ask.

Mom bites her lip. Bramble covers his ears. Willow lets out a loud wail. Suddenly all of my problems at school float away like dandelion fluff in the smallest breeze.

"We don't know," my dad says quietly.

I can't believe it. I don't believe it! Elves age just like humans for the first sixty or seventy years, but then if our magic is strong, an old elf can linger for hundreds of years. "But Grandma Fawna's magic is so strong," I say.

Dad just shakes his head. "Nobody understands what's going on."

"It's me," I whisper, and start to cry again.

"What?" Dad says, his face screwed up with confusion.

"It's because I've been such a bad elf," I confess. "I've been acting like an erdler. Somehow that got back to her and is taking her magic away!"

"No, it's Dad's fault!" says Willow. "She's dying of a broken heart because he's taken us away from her."

My dad exhales sharply and looks to the ceiling, as if he's trying to control his words. "For the last time, Willow, elves don't get sick because the ones they love go away. It just doesn't work like that." He shakes his head and turns back to me. "Look," he says, and wraps me in his arms again. I press my face against his chest and I sob. "You have nothing to do with this," he assures me, but I'm not convinced. "And neither do I. None of us do. Grandma is just sick," he says emphatically. "Sometimes elves get sick. We need to go back and help her. That's all. We'll figure it out."

I look up. "We're going back?" I ask. "To Alverland?"

"Yes," he says. "Right now. We were waiting for you."

chapter 10

THE FIRST THING we do when we get to Alverland is rush to my grandmother Fawna's house. The path through the woods is familiar and fills me with the reassurance of home, but still, like everyone, I'm worried about my grandma. We reach her porch and quickly but quietly head to the back of the house where she lays on her bed. Her long blondish gray hair spreads across the pillows and spills down over the shoulders of her soft white sleeping tunic. Her eyes flutter open just long enough to see us hovering over her, our hands out, sending her our hearts. Even Persimmon climbs up on the bed and holds her hands over Grandma. I think Fawna tries to smile and I swear I see a glimmer of the usual twinkle in her eyes. I know my mother is relieved to be back here by Grandma's side even though Grandma whispers that we don't need to make such a fuss.

"I'm just a little under the weather," she croaks, sounding like a bull-frog. "But I'm glad you're here."

We take turns kissing her warm soft cheek before Mom shoos us all out.

Even though we're here for a really crappy reason, I have to admit it's nice to be back in Alverland. I'd nearly forgotten how good fresh air, pine trees, and clean water smell. That alone was worth the eighteen-hour car ride. (If only elves had the ability to travel by magic! But no, we're stuck in a smelly van just like everyone else.) I didn't realize how much I'd missed everyone here until we stepped out of Grandma's back door into a circle of hugs and kisses from all our family gathered there. The last person I see is Briar. We cling to each other.

"I missed you so much," we keep repeating between hugs and laughter. When Briar and I finally let go of each other, I see Willow cuddled in Ash's arms, her head on his shoulder, and, at last, a smile on her face.

Everyone huddles around Grandfather Buck beneath the hemlock trees. "Is she going to be okay?" Bramble asks.

Grandpa Buck leans against his gnarled walking stick and sighs. "All we can do is keep her in our hearts," he says.

"Papa!" Aunt Flora smacks her hands against her thighs. "We have to do something else. Especially now that Aurora is here."

Everyone looks to my mom, who leans against the porch rail with her arms crossed. Other than Grandma Fawna, my mom is the best healer in Alverland, but she shakes her head. "I don't know what it is."

"It must have been a mushroom," says Flora.

My mom shakes her head. "She knows which mushrooms are poisonous."

"Yes, but she's been distracted," Flora argues. "Not quite herself since . . . well, you know."

"Since what?" my mother demands in a harsh voice. Everyone is silent for a moment. The little kids all look up from their games and the adults look down to avoid my mother's eyes. Elves hate conflict more than anything.

Dad walks over behind Mom and puts his hands on her shoulders. "Since we left?" he asks gently.

Flora peers up and nods her head.

"Okay," says Dad, simply. "It's good that we know this. Now we can deal with it."

When he says this, my stomach drops. As happy as I am to be back here, I'm afraid this means we'll have to stay in Alverland.

Buck thumps his walking stick on the ground. "The children don't need to be a part of this discussion. You all go on, get out of here, have some fun." He shoos us away. "Not everyone needs to be miserable. That won't help your grandmother." No one moves. Grandpa Buck heaves a sigh and stands up. "Go on," he says, and jabs the walking stick in the ground. We take tentative steps away from our parents. "Don't come back until dinnertime." He strides through the gathering like a goatherd trying to move a stubborn herd.

"You're not going to be a part of this discussion either?" Flora asks our grandfather when he reaches the edge of the forest.

He turns and says, "Words are only words, my dear." He smiles gently toward the house. "And Fawna wants some honeycomb."

My mom reaches out and lays her hands on Flora's shoulder, then looks at us. "Grandpa's right. You kids don't need to be here. Why don't you go gathering? Bring something back for Grandma from the woods. Something she likes."

We all look around cautiously, then slowly, in small groups, the kids drift away into the woods, leaving the adults to talk.

"What should we get for Grandma?" I ask Briar as we hike through the woods to our favorite pond. We've always been super close because we were born a few hours apart on the same day and our moms are sisters.

"She loves marsh mallow," Briar says.

"Is that the pink flower behind the pond?" I ask.

"Have you forgotten already?"

"I never paid that much attention," I admit.

"Yeah, you have to get the roots, then you whip them with eggs and it gets fluffy and gooey," she reminds me.

"Is that the stuff you mix with nuts and honey?" I ask.

"That's it."

"Is it good when you're sick?"

"Beats me!" Briar says, and despite all the unhappiness we both giggle.

"I'm so happy to see you!" I grab her hand. Blotches of sunlight shining through the green, yellow, and orange leaves make pretty patterns on the path at our feet. I notice Jack-in-the-Pulpit plants, their berries turning bright red as fall approaches, and the beautiful deep blue but poisonous lobelia plants scattered around the forest floor. We spent so much of our time when we were little playing games in these woods. One of our favorites was pretending to be erdlers, which mostly meant yelling at each other and acting mad. I never imagined that I'd really know erdlers someday. "When this is all over, I have so much to tell you!" I say.

Briar turns around to face me, walking backward on the path.

"And I want to hear all of it. Every detail. Tell me everything now!" When she says this, the floodgates open and I start talking. By the time we reach the pond, I've filled her in about everything that's happened at BAPAHS and I've got myself into a tizzy, as my mother would say.

"So, you see? I'm absolutely useless!" I yell out over the pond, causing a few wood ducks to swim farther from us. "I should focus on Grandma, but all I can think about is what's going on in Brooklyn. I'm dying to know what Bella and her horrible friends had to say on their stupid blog after Mercedes told everyone that Timber kissed me! And what about Timber? Oh my God, my stomach does flip-flops every time I think of him. Did Bella break up with him? Is he mad at me? Do Ari and Mercedes still hate me? Did Mercedes get kicked out of school? What's going on with Ari's band? Does Timber like me or are we really just friends? Does he miss me? Has anyone sent me an e-mail? Not to mention the audition, which I can't even think about right now." I pick up a handful of little pebbles and throw them, breaking the calm surface of the water. The ducks flap their wings and fly off into the reeds at the opposite edge of the pond. "This is the reason I'm no help. I can't stop thinking about myself long enough to concentrate on poor Grandma! I'm such a bad elf."

Briar's eyes are wide. "Wow," she says. "Wow, wow, wow! You're so much like an erdler now!"

"No!" I gasp. "Don't say that. I don't want to be anymore."

"I do," she says dreamily. "It's so exciting." She picks up a flat stone and skips it across the water. "Better than here. It's so boring with you gone and Grandma sick. Even the Acorn Festival got canceled."

"That's terrible," I say. I try to imagine life in Alverland without the festivals, the singing, the celebration. Those are my favorite things. "What have you been doing?"

"Nothing," says Briar. "I wish I could go to Brooklyn with you."

"There's always something to do there," I admit. "But that won't help Grandma get better." I'm half joking, only Briar doesn't laugh.

"I don't understand how she can be so bad off," I say. Briar shrugs and won't look at me. "Is it me? I mean us? My family. Because we're gone?" She shrugs again and digs her toe into the soft dirt along the shore. "My dad says that's not why elves get sick," I tell her.

Briar looks up at me. It's almost strange to be looking into the face of someone so familiar, who looks so much like me. In Brooklyn I spend most of my day marveling at how different everyone looks from everyone else. "It's good that your mom is back," Briar says.

"You're avoiding my question."

Briar takes in a breath then she says, "Well, I've heard Mom and some others say Grandma is worried about your family and that might have worn her down. Made her kind of weak."

"But we're fine!" I protest.

"Maybe you are, but we don't know that," says Briar as I gaze out over the water, which has become still and mirrorlike again. "You know how it is," Briar says. "Everyone gets so excited about any little thing that happens or changes around here. We talk about you guys all the time. What you're doing. Are you okay. What could go wrong. The little kids even made up a game called Poppy in the City."

I laugh. "What do they do?"

"One kid pretends to be Poppy and all the others hide behind the trees. They're the erdlers. Poppy has to walk through the city and the erdlers try to get her."

"It's not like that at all," I say.

"What is it like?" Briar asks. She lowers herself to a big rock and wraps her arms around her knees. "Tell me more."

By the time I'm done telling her even more about Brooklyn (about the fairy girls, the computer lab, Kenji's blue hair, blogs, BlackBerries, subways, and the strange things erdlers eat like hot dogs from a cart, pizza on a paper plate, and tiny bags of hard salty pretzels) both of our stomachs are growling.

"We didn't get the marsh mallow," I say.

Briar dusts off her butt and points to the far side of the pond. "Over there are a bunch."

We cut through the marshy weeds, pushing low branches out of our way to get to a stand of tall pink and white flowers. Briar plunges her hand down and pulls up the flowers by the dirt-covered roots. After we've gathered two big loads and tied them together with braided maidenhair grass we head back along the path toward the houses. We are quiet but my mind is full of Timber.

What if he came here to find me? What if I was with him out in the woods? I would take him to all my favorite places: the caves where we go camping, Barnaby Bluff where we watch eagles learn to fly, the waterfall where we play on the hottest days, the fields where we gather wildflowers for special celebrations. I'd hold his hand, teach him the names of birds and flowers, and show him all the good things to eat like berries and mushrooms and wild onions. I'd be the smart one, then. The one who laughs at him for all the things he doesn't know because he grew up in a city. Then I'd run through the woods silently like only elves can, hide behind a tree, make him look for me, then jump out and kiss him! I play this last part over and over again in my head until my heart is pumping and my cheeks are flushed. I know that I have to focus on helping my grandmother get better but I also need to find a way to contact Timber or I'll go crazy here.

We find everyone at Flora's. Our cousins have all returned and placed their offerings on the long oak table at the back of Flora's kitchen. We add our bundles of marsh mallow roots to the pile of grapevine wreaths, daisy garlands, bouquets of cattail reeds and switch grass, sparkly purple geodes, a soft pillow filled with lavender, and a beautiful amulet with three hawk feathers.

I pick up the amulet and touch the soft speckled brown feathers. The hawk is Fawna's animal idol. My mother's is a deer. My father's is a cougar. If my magic is ever strong enough, I'll learn my animal idol someday. "Who made this one?" I ask.

"I did," says Willow from Ash's lap.

"Reminds me of that red-tail in Brooklyn," I say.

Willow rolls her eyes and looks away but my mother says, "What red-tail?"

"The hawk I always see in the park or circling our house. I think it has a nest in our tree. It reminded me of Alverland."

My mom knits her eyebrows together and bites the corner of her mouth.

"You okay?" I ask.

She takes the amulet from me. "Was it there that day . . ." She trails off, but I know she means the day she hexed us.

"Yes," I say. "But no one knows about that," I whisper.

Aunt Flora sticks her head out of the kitchen. "Anybody hungry?" she calls. Everyone hurries to grab a plate.

Elves usually eat together since we hunt for meat together, gather wild berries and nuts from the forest together, or work in our grandmother's garden together. Since it's early fall, there is plenty of delicious food. On the table are platters of grilled chanterelle mushrooms and trout, squash and green beans from the garden, fresh-baked brown bread surrounded by jars and jars of jam, and for dessert, my favorite wild blueberry tarts. I grab a plate and dig in.

Everyone's more relaxed now. Even Flora and Mom seem less worried. I haven't seen my own family looking this relaxed for weeks. Mom laughs at a story Uncle Cliff and Aunt Marigold are telling while Dad's full attention is on hearing about all the good hunting he missed. Poppy and Bramble play marbles on the floor with ten of my younger cousins. Persimmon is curled up asleep on Aunt Fern's lap. In the back of the room, Grove strums his guitar while some of my older cousins play fiddle, accordion, banjo, and flute. Across the table from me Willow leans against Ash's shoulder. She looks beautiful and comfortable in a way I haven't seen since we left Alverland and suddenly I'm jealous. I finally understand how she must have felt in Brooklyn, always thinking about what she was missing here, because even though I'm happy to be here, I can't stop thinking about what I'm missing in Brooklyn. Most of all, I'm missing Timber and I wish I knew if he was missing me.

When I wake up the next morning I know what I need to do. First I find my mom whipping up pancake batter in the kitchen. She's singing as she stirs, which is a good sign. "How's Grandma?" I ask and swipe a handful of wild blueberries from the wooden bowl on the counter.

"Better." Mom smiles. "She had some tea this morning. She seems stronger."

"Good," I say. "When can we see her?"

"Probably after lunch," says Mom. She ladles batter into a smoking skillet on the wood-burning stove, then she turns to me. "Tell me more about that hawk."

I pop the last few blueberries in my mouth. "What about it?"

"Did you see it a lot?"

"A few times when we first moved in. Then again the week I started school. And on that day we had the big fight—remember?"

Mom flips the pancakes. "Oh, I remember," she says. "But I didn't see the hawk."

"It landed on the fence and screeched after you hexed us."

Mom pauses with her spatula suspended over the skillet. Her face clouds over.

"It's okay," I assure her. "I didn't tell anybody."

Slowly she puts a stack of pancakes onto a plate. "It's not that," she says, and hands me the plate.

"I'm sure a lot of moms do that," I tell her. "And we deserved it."

Mom snaps out of her dark mood and smiles gently at me. "That was a bad day."

I nod as I smother my pancakes in real maple syrup. "Do you need me after breakfast?"

"No," says Mom. "Just be back for lunch, okay?"

"Thanks." I wolf down the pancakes in five big bites then wash my plate and take off.

I'm halfway down the trail that leads to the road to Ironweed when Briar catches up to me.

"Hey Zeph!" She calls. "Wait up!" She grabs my arm to slow me down.

"Go back," I tell her.

"Why?" she asks. "Where are you going?"

The trees rustle above us, sending a chill across my face. "Ironweed. Now go back."

Briar shrinks back into the shadows. "You can't go there by yourself."

I look at her with the same annoyed look I'm sure Mercedes has given me a thousand times when she thought I was being dumb. "Of course I can," I say. "I live in New York now. I know how to handle erdlers."

"I'm coming with you." Briar steps onto the path beside me.

"Look, I just need to find a computer."

"Are you going to get in touch with Timber?" she asks, her eyes wide.

"Yes," I admit. "I have to. I could barely sleep last night. It's killing me not to know what's happening there."

"Let me come, too. Please?"

"This has nothing to do with you."

"If you don't let me come, I'll tell your mom and dad what you're doing," Briar threatens. "You know they'll come get you."

I sigh. "Fine. You can come."

Ironweed used to seem so big and scary to me. But now, after living in Brooklyn for a while, I laugh when we step onto Main Street.

"What?" Briar whispers in my ear. She tucks her hand in mine and I know she's nervous.

"It's so small and ugly," I say as I look out over one stoplight, four stores, seven houses, one grocery shop, a gas station, and at the far end of town the public library. "Come on." I pull her down the sidewalk.

At first, no one is out, probably because hardly anyone actually lives here, but then an older woman comes out of the grocery store. She looks hard at us, staring, letting us know that she doesn't like us in her town. Usually we drop our eyes, look away, and hurry on, but this time, I stare straight back at her. I have every right to be here if I want. She looks away, muttering, but I don't care. I keep right on walking. Nothing is going to stop me from checking my e-mail.

The inside of the library smells musty. "I used to think this building was so huge," I whisper to Briar, who huddles close by my side. Now I see that it's small and run down. Yellow paint is chipping off the walls, the carpet has stains, and the windows are dirty. The librarian, an old woman with big glasses and a baggy gray sweater, glances up. Her mouth tightens into a frown before she looks down again, ignoring us. I walk right up to her desk and announce, "We'd like to use the computers."

She pushes the sign-up sheet toward me. Which is silly because no one else is here, but I know the rules. I've gotten burned before because I didn't sign in and then an erdler kid came in and wanted to use the computer so I got kicked off. I write my name, then give the dull pencil to Briar to sign up, too. She shakes her head, scared. "I'll show you something you'll like," I tell her, and I put the pencil in her hand.

Briar and I sit next to each other. I open the Web browser on her computer first, then I pull up YouTube. "You can watch videos on here," I tell her. As I scroll down through the featured videos I see Ari's face staring out at me from a little box. My heart sinks. I miss him and still feel awful about what happened, but I can't watch him right now because it'll make me too sad. Instead, I click on a video of two puppies romping around with a tennis ball.

Briar cracks up. "They're so cute!" she says as she watches the clumsy adorable dogs.

"See this box?" I point to the search box with the cursor. "You can type in 'puppies' or whatever you want and watch a bunch of different videos."

"Wow!" she says, her eyes wide, and I know she'll be engrossed in the videos while I check my e-mail.

I log on to the BAPAHS Web site. My stomach immediately tightens when I see the picture of the school with those big green doors. I glance at the clock on the bottom of my computer screen. It's almost ten o'clock on Tuesday so I'd be in algebra right now. I wonder if anyone noticed that I'm gone? Will I be able to make up the work when we go back to Brooklyn? I'll be so far behind! If we hadn't been in such a hurry to leave, I would have brought my books with me. Then I'd have an excuse to come here every day to e-mail my teachers for my assignments and I could also e-mail Timber, or Ari or Mercedes, if they'll ever talk to me again. I glance over at Briar. She's having a great time watching a video of kittens batting around a ball of yarn. I take the plunge and open my e-mail account.

I gasp. I have fifty-six new messages! But when I look carefully, I see that most of them are forwards from the other day. I can't bear to look at that horrible message again so I delete all the forwards and see what's left. Only four. One from the site administrator reprimanding everyone for all the forwarding and another from Ms. Sanchez saying that she's available if I need to talk to her about anything. The third one is a reminder about the ELPH audition next week. My heart sinks again. Even though I wasn't sure I wanted to do it at first, now that the opportunity is slipping away, I realize how much I was looking forward to it. Not just because it was a chance to beat Bella, but because it was my first chance to perform in Brooklyn and figure out if I was good at something other than an elfin festival performance. The last e-mail is from Rienna the fairy girl.

> Even tho i think u suck 4 kissing TLC, thnx for breaking them up. i luv 2 c Bella from Hella cry!

I have to read it a few times to understand what she means but finally it dawns on me that Timber and Bella broke up! I pop out of my seat, then quickly sit back down.

"What's wrong?" Briar leans over and whispers.

"Look at this." I point to Rienna's message.

Briar reads the message then looks at me confused. That must be how I look most of the time in Brooklyn. Now I see why Mercedes and Ari get so annoyed with me. I don't have time to explain everything to Briar.

"I have to find out if they really broke up," I whisper. "But how?" I mutter half to myself and half to Briar. "Who can I e-mail? Could I e-mail Rienna back? She did say that I suck. Maybe she doesn't want to hear from me. Maybe I could e-mail Jilly, the fairy queen. But wouldn't it look weird to ask her if Bella and Timber broke up?"

"I don't really understand this whole e-mail thing," says Briar. "But, if they did break up and he wanted you to know, then he'd e-mail you, right?"

I slump back in my chair. "You're right."

"Why would this Rienna girl be happy that this poor Bella girl is sad?"

"First of all," I tell her, "Rienna has a crush on Timber so she's happy that he's free now. And second of all, there's nothing poor about Bella. She's the meanest one of all. 'Bella from Hella' is right!" Then I sit up straight. "Oh my God. I wonder if Rienna is BellaHater?"

"Huh?" says Briar.

"Never mind," I say. "I just figured out what to do." I'm about to type in the BellaHater blog address when I get a new message in my in-box. It's from Timber! I let out a little shriek.

"Quiet down!" the librarian snaps at me. "Or you'll have to leave."

Briar and I slump down, giggling. "Timber must be online right now," I whisper to her and point to the screen.

"Open it! Open it!" she yell-whispers back to me.

I click on the message.

> Hey Z, I'm in study hall. Wondering y u r not at school 2day.
> Tried 2 IM u last night, but didn't get an answer.

Since I can't IM on this stupid old computer, I start typing furiously, trying to get an e-mail message to him as quickly as possible.

> Sorry I didn't get your IMs! My family had to leave Brooklyn because my grandmother is sick.

I hit send, then wait for a minute until this e-mail comes back:

> Sorry about yer grandma. Is she going 2 b ok?

We continue our slow electronic conversation. I imagine him in the school computer lab, looking really cute slouched behind a screen.

Thanks for asking. We're not sure what's wrong with her so I don't know how long I'll be here.

2 bad. Bklyn isn't the same w/o U.

Briar and I hold hands and grin at each other. "What should I say?" I ask her.

"Ask him if they broke up," she says.

"I can't just ask him that!"

"Why not?"

"Erdlers aren't like that."

"But you're not an erdler," Briar says.

"But he doesn't know that," I tell her. "I have to be more, you know, subtle. Not so honest."

"Why wouldn't you be honest?" she asks.

"I don't have time to explain," I say impatiently as I start typing again. "I have to get this message to him before he logs off."

What's going on in Brooklyn?

I send it and we wait. And wait. And wait for so long that I'm sure I missed him. I'm about to cry when finally another message from him pops up. We both squeal, then cover our mouths so the librarian won't kick us out.

Nothing much happening here.

"What!" I hiss. "What's he mean nothing much is going on?"

"He probably thinks you left before all this stuff started happening," Briar says.

I look at her, amazed. "You think just like an erdler."

"Thanks," she says, smiling.

"But what should I do?"

"You should ask him," she says, poking my arm.

"I can't," I whine.

"Either he likes you or he doesn't, Zephyr. Don't you want to know?" Briar asks.

"No!" My stomach is gurgly and I'm starting to sweat. "It's not that simple. Maybe he's starting to like me, or he thinks he likes me but he's not sure yet. I mean he did just break up with Bella."

"Then we have to help him decide whether to like you or not," she tells me.

"But how?"

"Move over." Briar pushes me out of the way.

"Don't ask him!" I whisper.

"I know what I'm doing!" She pecks at the keyboard while I chew on my fingernails.

> Really? Because right before I left all those crazy e-mails went around.
>
> U saw those, huh?
>
> Yes.
>
> r u upset?
>
> not really. r u?

I'm amazed at my cousin. She's already picking up the abbreviations and she sounds more like an erdler than I do. We wait for his reply.

> hmmm, well, kinda. Bella's pissed as hell and her friends hate me now.

Briar's fingers fly across the keys as she types in "Did u break up?"

"No!" I whisper and grab her arm, but she hits send anyway. I cover my face with my hands. "I can't look. I can't look," I moan quietly.

"There's his reply," she says after a few seconds. I still don't look, until I hear her gasp. Then of course, I peek through my fingers.

yeah, it's over.

Briar and I grab each other's hands and scream.

"That's it!" The librarian marches toward us. "This is a quiet, respectable public library. Not a place for you little derelicts to come and make a ruckus."

I know she's going to kick us out so as quick as I can I type, "Gotta go. Getting kicked out. More later . . ." I hit send right before the librarian pulls the plug.

"You two get out of here," she snarls at us. "And don't come back, you hear? I don't want to see you again!"

Briar and I run down the steps of the library, cracking up. "Did you see her face?" Briar says. "She was so mad. She looked like a snapping turtle!"

I'm laughing so hard I nearly fall over. I have to stop walking and lean against a light pole to catch my breath. "Do you think he got my last message?" I ask her between gasps for air.

"I think it went through. Don't worry. But what are you going to do now?"

"I don't know," I say, and suddenly the whole thing doesn't seem so funny. "Did that librarian say we can't come back?" I ask.

"Yeah," says Briar. "We got banned!" She laughs.

"Oh no!" I moan. "How will I get in touch with him again?"

Briar gasps. "Oh dear. I didn't think of that."

Just then a car drives by. "Go back to the woods!" some jerky guy yells out the window.

"You don't own this street!" I yell back. The car slows down and does a U-turn at the end of the dusty road.

Briar grabs my arm and pulls. "Come on!"

But I'm mad. "I'm not going to let these dumb erdlers tell me what to do anymore," I tell her. "We have every right to be here," I yell over my shoulder as Briar drags me down the sidewalk.

"Stop!" she begs. "You're going to get us in trouble."

The car speeds up and now I am furious at the erdlers telling me I can't be here. Banning me from the only computer in a hundred-mile radius. I'm not just some little meek elf anymore. I spin around and face the oncoming car. Quick as I can I zap them with a little hex to seal their doors for a few minutes so no one can get out of the car and a farting spell just to make them miserable. Then I grab Briar's hand and yank her between two buildings. We run as fast as we can down an alleyway, through someone's backyard, and duck into the woods. We don't stop running until we get back to Alverland.

chapter 11

JUST WHEN I think I can't take it anymore—when I think I'll die if I'm in Alverland another minute beyond the three days we've been here already, I overhear my parents arguing in our kitchen. I pause behind the door and eavesdrop, which I know is wrong, but I can't help it.

"This is important," my dad says.

"More important than your family?" Mom asks.

"Aurora, of course not. But Fawna is getting better every day. She's up walking now. She ate a bit. She's clearly going to recover."

"I'm not ready to go," Mom says and my heart jumps. Does that mean my dad wants to leave?

"I'm not asking you to leave," he says, and I feel my stomach sinking.

"But why do you have to go?" Mom asks. "Why can't we all be together for a little longer?"

"The song is doing well," Dad says. "It's climbing up the chart. I can't lose that momentum. If I'm not out there, touring, gigging, getting some publicity, it could all go backward. You promised me a year to do this. To really pursue it."

"But I didn't know she'd get sick if we left."

My dad sighs. "She didn't get sick because we left."

"That's what you want to believe," Mom answers. "But no amount of success is worth tearing your family apart."

"I'm not tearing our family apart," Dad insists. "I'll be gone one day, then I'll be back."

I have to know what's going on so I step around the door. "Are you leaving?" I ask my dad. They both look at me, surprised, but neither of them answers. "Are you going back to Brooklyn?" He shakes his head no, but my mom nods hers yes. "Which is it?" I ask.

"I've been asked to do a radio show down in Appleton, Wisconsin."

"And then—" Mom says.

Before she can finish, I jump in. "Can I go? Please? Please let me go with you! I never get to go. Grove always gets to go. I know I'm not part of the band, but I'll do anything you want. I'll carry your gear. I'll set up your stuff. I'll sleep in the van. Whatever. Just let me go with you! Please, please, please." I'm practically hanging off my dad's arm, begging him because I know if I can get to Appleton I can find a computer.

Dad laughs. "Since when are you so interested in Wisconsin?"

I glance over at my mom. She's shaking her head back and forth slowly in a way that says she is not happy about any of this. "Your grandmother has been very ill . . ."

"I know!" I whine. "Really I do. And I care about that. More than anything. But she's getting better and it's not like I can help her! All we do is try to stay out of the way."

"Simply having us here, all of us here, helps her," Mom says.

"But I'd just be gone for a day, right Dad?"

"Why do you want to go so badly?" Dad asks me, and I know I'm going to have to give them some sort of reason.

I chew on the inside of my lip. I don't know how much to admit. "I need to check my e-mail. I want to know what's going on in Brooklyn. At school. In my classes. And with my friends. That's all." Obviously I'm leaving out important details, but like Timber said, what they don't know won't hurt them.

"Is that all?" Dad says with a laugh. He reaches in his pocket. "If you want to check your e-mail, you can use my Treo." He pulls out a PDA.

I jump and snatch it from his hand. "How long have you had this!" I yell.

He shrugs as if it's no big deal. "A while. I have to be able to e-mail my manager when I'm on the road."

I'm not even listening because I'm too busy trying to figure the thing out. "Do you get a signal out here?" I ask as I push buttons.

"Only if you climb a tree or go up to the top of Barnaby Bluff," Dad says.

"Can I please have this for a few hours?" I ask.

"Why does she need that thing?" my mom asks Dad.

Dad puts his hand on her arm. "It's okay," he assures her. "You can use it," he says to me, and I'm out of there before they can change their minds.

The sun will go down soon, so I quickly find a tall tree and clamber as high as I can with the Treo in my pocket. I settle myself into the crook of a large branch and wait for the little machine to hook me up to the world. Who knew my dad was so tech savvy? In a few minutes I'm on the Web.

Of course, the first thing I do is check my e-mail. I want to know if Timber got the last message I sent from the library. There's a response to that message in my in-box, but all he says is "ok c'ya l8er" and does not pledge his undying love, which is what I was hoping for. There's also an e-mail with an updated script for the ELPH audition. Part of me wants to open it and practice, but part of me wants to ignore it because what's the use? I probably won't be back in time to audition so why torture myself? I try to tell myself that there will be other auditions, other chances, other scripts, but I'm not so sure and that makes my heart feel like a sapling beaten down by the wind and rain. I leave e-mail and mess around with the keys until I figure out how to get on my dad's instant messenger program. It's Thursday evening, a school night, so the chances of Timber being online are pretty good. I punch in "R U there? It's Z." Almost immediately I get a reply that he's off-line.

I'm so disappointed that I nearly fling the Treo out of the tree! How can he not be online? That's so unfair. Now what am I going to do? Look at stupid puppy videos on YouTube? Of course, I could go to Bella's blog or even to the BellaHater blog to find out what's going on. But first, I decide I should check out something else. I pull up the YouTube Web site and scroll down until I find the GGJB "Not Like You" featured video.

Ari's face fills the tiny window and I feel a strange mix of emotions. I'm happy and sad at the same time. It's the weirdest thing to have both sensations at once. It's like one of those strange erdler contradictions: being nice and mean at the same time; or saying one thing with your words but meaning another with your tone; or acting like someone's friend but really being her enemy. I quickly forget about my emotions though, because I get sucked into the video. I love watching Ari sing his heart out. The melody is catchy and the chorus gets stuck in my head,

You can't make me!
I won't be like you.
You can't make me
into the image of you.

I've got my friends
and I know what to do
to be like me
and not like you.

The video is great. First he's in his house, alone at the piano. Then he's with his band beneath a tree in the park, surrounded by a group of little kids. Next they're standing in the middle of a crowded sidewalk in downtown Brooklyn. Then they're in Chinatown, then Times Square, then Coney Island. Each shot is a different place around New York City and I'm dying of envy! As soon as Fawna's better I've got to get back to Brooklyn.

When the video is over I scroll down and read the comments. Like Mercedes said, most of them are positive but there are a few mean ones, too. That shouldn't surprise me, I guess. By now I know it's impossible for erdlers to always be nice. At the bottom, I see a box that says, "Comment on this Video" and I immediately start typing.

Great! Superb! I loved it! Fantastic! The best video I've ever seen. The music is wonderful and the words are clever, funny, and have heart. Just like you, Ari!

After seeing Ari, I'm curious about what people think of my dad's videos so I type his name into the search box. I can't believe it! Twelve videos pop up, all from live shows. I click on the first one and my dad starts singing. I scroll down and scan the comments. People love him! They think he's amazing. And even weirder, some people say he's sexy. There's also some girl who wants to have my brother's babies. Gross! That's just wrong. I remember Ari saying people talk about my dad and his band on the Web a lot so I put his name in Google then click through some of the links. Mostly it's boring stuff about how good

Dad's songs are or people swapping stories about seeing his band play live in different places around the country. But then I end up in a chat room with some creepy rumors.

—He lives in the woods in the UP of Michigan

—I hear he's a Mennonite.

—Not a Mennonite! Part of a Wicca cult.

—It's a commune. Totally off the grid.

—How can I join?

—Anybody know where? I'm from Michigan. I'd love to look him up.

—Somewhere in the Porcupine Mountains.

—No, near Keweenaw.

—It's called Alderville or something like that.

—You're all wrong. He lives in Brooklyn. He's a fake!

It's strange to see so much speculation about my dad and where we live. I had no idea people were so interested in finding us. Luckily no one's figured it out yet. When I'm bored reading about my dad, which doesn't take too long, I go to Bella's Web site just to torture myself.

I hate seeing her smug face captured in a perfect head shot staring out at me from her homepage. There are links to videos of all the little parts she's had in TV shows, commercials, and even movies. I don't bother to read her public blog entry because I know it will all be lies. Instead, I drag the cursor up to the corner and click on the dog. I type *belladonna* in the password box and the real blog pops up. But there's no entry for today. I skim back through the past week and find the entry from the day after Mercedes sent the mass e-mail about my kiss with Timber.

I took a mental health day today. Needed a pedi. In the religion of Bella, pamper thineself is the 1st commandment. Anyway, I deserve it after all the f*ing b.s. yesterday. What a bunch of freaks forwarding those messages. Whatev. MooMoo can have that jerkface. I was about done with him anyway.

—B, this whole thing sux! i'm here 4 u, girl.
Posted by: ZoEzOe

—looks like MooMoo was 2 scared 2 show her face 2day. Ha-ha!
Posted by: CH3L-C

—did u know her dad is that singer Drake Addler?
Posted by: LadyBug

—never heard of him. must b a LOSER.
Posted by: BELLA

—i keep hearing him on the radio.
Posted by: ZoEzOe

—i kinda like the song.
Posted by: CH3L-C

—f u CH3L, he sux just like his gross daughter.
Posted by: LadyBug.

—wait, the guy's legit? thought they were from some weird cult.
Posted by: BELLA

—maybe but he's got a good song.
Posted by: CH3L-C

My blood boils. It's one thing to call me names or even to talk about my friends, but to say stuff about my dad is just wrong! I really can't stand these girls. I wish I knew who BellaHater is so I could join forces with her and make Bella's life even more miserable than I already have. As I'm sitting here fuming, an IM message box pops up. It's from Timber.

—hey, u still there?

I can't believe it. I'm so excited that I forget Bella and her horrible toadies and start typing away to Timber.

—I'm here!

—they let u in the library again?

—no, a tree.

—huh?

—had to climb a tree to get reception on my dad's Treo

—u r the only person I know who IMs from a tree!

For the first time I get why everyone uses all the short cuts and abbreviations when they write to one another. Punching all these little buttons is annoying. I try to find the quickest way to respond so we can talk more.

—what r u up 2?

—studying

—alone?

—no.

My shoulders tense up and I grip the Treo tighter. "With who?" I type, half afraid of the answer. Is he with Bella? Are they back together? Or worse, someone else? Someone new who got there before me? Is he with Rienna? But this comes back:

—Fred

—who's Fred?

I realize then I don't know much about Timber at all. Who his friends are. Where he lives. What he likes to do.

—my dog :)

—whew! LAL

—LAL? What's that?

Oh no, I think, I got it wrong. I type in, "Laugh Aloud?"

—OMG, u r so hilarious. it's LOL—laugh out loud, but I like
LAL better. more original like u

—is that a good thing?

I wait, wondering if he was being sarcastic.

—of course! who doesn't want 2 B original?

—what if u r 2 original? then yer just different and everybody
thinks yer weird

I type that sentence then reread it on my screen and realize that I'm talking about how I feel when I'm in Brooklyn.

—true, but there's a diff btwn original and weird. Weird is
when u don't have any social skills and u alienate everybody with yer differences. original is when u r yer own
person and everybody wants 2 b like u

Like Bella, I think, but I don't type that in because his message continues.

—u r original, Z. the most original person i've met in a long
time.

I'm blushing. Way up in this tree all by myself, his little words fly invisibly through the air to me and make my heart flutter like a hummingbird. If that's not magic, I don't know what is! I want to tell him how I feel, but I don't want to look like a complete idiot. I'm not sure what to say, so I just type in, "u r different than I thought u'd b."

—what'd u expect?

Now I've really gotten myself into trouble! This is when I need someone here. Mercedes, Ari, even Briar. Anybody who's not as clue-less, nervous, and dorky as I am. Maybe making a boy interested in you is like coaxing a wild animal out of the woods. You're supposed to keep yourself hidden and drop little bits of something yummy to tempt him and keep him on the path toward you without letting him know that you want to grab him.

> —I thought u'd be kinda mean because the way u looked at me the first time I saw you

> —how did I look at u?

> —like a wolf

> —hungry like a wolf? Very Duran Duran, ha-ha.

Now I'm totally lost. Every time I think I'm getting close to finding out how he feels about me, he makes some weird joke or completely changes the subject!

> —what does Duran Duran mean?

> —pure 1980s cheese, baby. my band opened for them once when they were trying to make a comeback.

> —what's that have to do with wolves?

> —nwte

I realized that he's using Bellaspeak and I think I might cry.

> —I'm nwte?

> —no, no. explaining about 80s pop music is nwte. u r twte

> —twte??

> — totally worth the effort

And now I'm smiling again. Before I manage a response, he sends me another message.

> —last time we e-mailed I wanted to tell you that even tho B

& I broke up b/c I kissed u, it's been coming for a long time. i feel bad that it happened that way but not bad that it happened.

My hands shake from excitement as I type.

—me 2

—when r u coming back?

—don't know : (

—2 bad

"Zephyr!" I hear my dad's voice booming through the fading light. "Zephyr! Where are you?"

"I'm up here, Dad," I yell.

"Come on down. It's getting dark," he yells back.

"Just a minute," I call.

"No, now." His voice is getting closer. "You can't be up there all night with that thing. You'll wear out the battery."

"But Dad!" I say, impatient to get back to my conversation.

"Your mother is right," he says from somewhere near my tree. "You do act like an erdler sometimes."

"Seriously, just one minute. That's all," I beg.

"I'm counting to sixty," he says, then actually begins to count out loud. "One, two, three . . . "

I do my best to tune him out while I punch at the keys frantically.

—moose crap! dad wants his treo back. gotta go.

But before I get his reponse, my dad yells, "Sixty! Come down right now or you never get the Treo again!"

"Fine," I mutter as I sign off. "I'm coming." Great, I think to myself as I climb down the tree, the last thing I said to Timber was "moose crap." What kind of weird girl says "moose crap" to the guy she likes?

I'm going to have to find a way to make sure he doesn't think I'm some kind of freakola mountain mama who lives in a shack and uses corncobs to wipe my butt. "Dad," I say when I jump down to the ground. "When can I use this again?"

He puts his hands on his hips and stares at me. It's nearly dark beneath the trees but I can still make out the aggravation on his face. "You were just up there for nearly an hour!"

"But I've been away for almost a week, so an hour is barely any time at all!" I protest.

He holds his hand out for the Treo and reluctantly I give it to him. "You'll not get it at all if you act like that," he says. Then he shakes his head and laughs a little. "Boy oh boy, we've changed, haven't we? A few months ago we never argued like this!"

I look down at the dark forest floor. "I'm sorry," I say. "It's just that . . ."

"Nah," Dad says, and slings his arm around my shoulders. "Don't worry about it." We start walking through the trees. "I know things have been turned upside down and inside out for you lately." He gives me a little hug. "For me, too."

"Are you going to leave?" I ask.

"I'm going down to Appleton overnight but no one is going with me. Not even Grove. I promised your mother. And then . . ." Leaves crunch beneath our boots as we walk.

"What?" I ask.

"Mom started to tell you in the kitchen."

"Tell me what?"

"Our song made the Top Twenty-five. I never thought it would, but it has and my manager might get us a live spot on VH1, a music channel that lots of people watch, so . . ."

"Oh my God, Dad!" I squeeze his hand. Thanks to Mercedes and

186   me, my elf & i

Ari, I finally get what this means. "That's great! It's amazing! You're going to be on TV! Dad, this is huge!"

Dad smiles down at me. "Yes, it is," he says. "It's nice that you understand that. Nobody else here gets it."

"Of course I get it, Dad! Why else did we go there? Auditions! Opportunities! TV, radio! All of those things we can't do here." Then I let go of his hand. "Wait a minute. Are you going to New York, then?"

He stops smiling. "Probably."

"Da-a-a-a-d!" I whine. "Come on. You have to take me." I pull on his arm and beg. "Please, please, please let me come! I have to get back to Brooklyn!"

He shakes his head. "I can't. I promised your mother. And besides, she's right. It's good for Fawna to have you near. All of you. You should really spend some time with her, Zephyr."

"But you're letting Grove go to New York, aren't you?" I say.

"Zeph, come on now. That's different."

"It's not fair!" I shout.

"He's in my band, honey."

"What about school? What about my audition? I need to go back, too!"

"You will."

"When?" I demand.

"I don't know. Eventually."

"But I can't wait. I have to go. Soon! Now!"

"Stop this!" My dad glowers down at me in a way I've rarely seen. I shut up and shrink into myself like a rabbit disappearing into its hole. "Just because you've spent a few weeks among the erdlers is no excuse to become demanding, pushy, and selfish," he lectures me.

I look down at my feet and mumble, "You're the one who took me there in the first place."

"Well then, you can damn well bet I won't be taking you back!" my dad says, and stomps off ahead of me.

I run after him. "No, Dad! Don't say that! It's not fair. You found that school for me. You took me there. I made friends. Started a life. For the first time I was going to audition for something and now you want me to just forget about all of that?"

"Is this about that boy?" he asks. "In the park? The singer?"

I look down at my feet.

He stops short and turns to me. "Maybe your mother is right. Maybe it was all a mistake."

"Why?" I ask. "Because you took me away from Alverland and I was happy?" I've never spoken to my dad like this before. There's never been a reason. But now, I can't sit back and let my mom and dad ruin my life. "I love Alverland. I always will. And I love my family more than anything else in the world, but I want more than this!" I throw my arms out wide to the forest surrounding us. "It's not just about Timber, Dad. I've got something inside me and it's bigger than this place."

"I know," Dad says.

"No you don't! How can you know?" I ask angrily. "You know nothing about my life in Brooklyn!"

He reaches out and puts his hands on my shoulders. I stand up straight and tall and look him in the eyes. "You're right. I don't know enough about your life in Brooklyn but I do know this . . . " He pulls me into a hug. "You're a lot like me, Zephyr. I've always known that."

"Then you should know how important this is to me," I say.

My dad sighs and rests his chin on the top of my head. "You might not believe me, Zeph, but I do understand how you feel. It's just that I also know how important family is and that to truly be happy, you have to find a balance. Which is hard."

I push away from his embrace. "You're not taking me with you, are you?"

He shakes his head. I turn away and head up the path away from him. "But it'll be fine, honey," he calls after me. I don't stop. "Believe me. There will be other opportunities for you. I promise."

His words flit away like bats chasing mosquitoes in the night sky as I walk silently into the cover of the trees. For the first time in my life, I'm so mad at my father that I don't want to be near him.

chapter 12

MY DAD LEFT early this morning for Appleton, alone. "Don't you care that Dad went without you?" I ask Grove while he's shoveling in a huge bowl full of Mom's granola.

"Nah," he says. "Being on the road isn't all that great, Zeph. It's boring. Besides, I like being back in Alverland. It's like a mini-vacation with great food."

I pick through the fruit bowl on the counter. "You mean a mini-vacation with nothing to do."

"Exactly." He drains his cup of tea.

"It's just so boring here," I complain as I rub a green apple against my tunic. "At least in Brooklyn . . ."

"You know, Zephyr, you're always grousing about Alverland," says Grove. "About how no one will try something new. About how it's so limited and you wish you could go with Dad and me so you could perform . . ."

"Duh, I know. That's why I like Brooklyn."

"You're missing the point," he says.

"What point?" I take a big bite.

"Why don't you do something new? Why don't you make a change here instead of expecting everyone to cater to what you want?"

"Why don't you shut up?" I say through a mouthful of tart apple.

"Real nice. You've learned so much in New York."

"You sound like an erdler, Mr. Sarcasm," I say.

"At least I don't act like one. Now, if you'll excuse me . . ." He pushes himself back from the table. "I'm going to go do nothing."

No matter what Grove thinks, for me this whole thing stinks. To make it even worse, Dad wouldn't leave me his Treo. So I'm stuck here disconnected from the world. Since I don't feel like being cheered up by anyone I head for my favorite hideout—a big hollow stump that's shaped like a frog's mouth behind my grandparents' place. I skirt around the edge of their house on a trail half hidden by overgrown ferns and fallen leaves. No one is in the clearing. I slip past the vegetable garden and tiptoe beyond the smokehouse to my frog stump, which is in the center of a half circle of oak and elm trees. I used to come here when I wanted to be alone, but I haven't been here for a few years. When I try to shimmy inside the frog's mouth, I'm too big. I have to settle for sitting on top of the stump to mope.

Not long after I plunk myself down to think endlessly about everything I'm missing—my friends, my classes, the audition, and Timber—who he's talking to right now (hopefully not Bella) and what he's doing right now (again, hopefully not Bella)—I hear someone coming slowly through the clearing. I drop down behind the stump and crouch so whoever's walking this way won't see me. The footsteps stop, though. Great. Like I want to be stuck behind a frog-shaped stump for the next hour. I peek out to see who's ruining my perfectly good alone time. I'm surprised to see Grandma Fawna in a soft white sleeping tunic, leaning heavily on a big walking stick. Her eyes are closed and she lifts her face to the breeze coming down through the colorful fall leaves above her.

I pop out of my hiding place and take her arm. "Should you be out here?"

She opens her eyes and looks at me with a happy smile. "Zephyr, my little chipmunk. What are you doing here?"

"I should ask you the same thing. You should be in bed. Resting." I lead her over to the stump so she can sit.

"Oh now, don't you start. I can get up and take a little walk anytime I feel like it," she says, but she seems relieved to be sitting again.

"You look better," I admit. The color is back in her cheeks and her green eyes sparkle. But still, she looks tired and smaller than I remember.

"I am better," she says simply. She rearranges herself to get comfortable, then pats a place beside her. "Sit down here and talk to me. I haven't had a chance to catch up with you."

I snuggle up next to my grandmother because it's impossible to be near her without curling into her body. Somehow, no matter what's going on in my life, being next to her turns me into a little kid who wants to hold hands and listen to fairy stories.

"Tell me about this place called Brooklyn," she says.

"I like it," I tell her with a sigh.

"That doesn't sound very convincing."

"Oh no!" I say. "I really really like it there. I'm just . . . I don't know how to explain it. It's so strange but since I've been gone, sometimes I feel two things at once. Like right now. I'm happy to be here, but I'm sad not to be there. I miss Brooklyn, but when I'm there, I miss being here."

"Mm-hmm," says Grandma. "A conflicted heart."

I look up into the twisted branches of the oak trees spread above us. "Have you ever felt that way? I thought it was an erdler thing."

"Erdlers might feel it more often than we do. We tend to be a little less complicated about matters of emotion, but still, being conflicted is part of growing up and realizing that there's a wider world than you suspected."

"The funny thing is . . ." I study the overlapping pattern in the leaves and try to figure out how to explain what I'm feeling. "Sometimes I'm not so sure I want to be part of that big world. It can be so mean. But when I think about never going back to my life in Brooklyn, I get really sad because I know I'm missing out."

"That's the dilemma, I'm afraid," says Grandma. The sun winks in and out of the canopy overhead as I listen. "If you want to have big experiences, some of them are bound to be unpleasant. But the good ones can be great if you're willing to take the chance."

"That's exactly it!" I tell her. "Like there's an audition at school that my friends want me to do. At first I was scared and I didn't want to try because I was afraid I'd look like an idiot. But now that I'm probably going to miss it, I wish I were there so I could do it."

"But won't there be other auditions?"

"This one is kind of important to me."

"Because . . . ?"

"It's kind of embarrassing." Grandma looks at me kindly and waits. "The whole thing is not very nice," I admit, but she only blinks. I take a deep breath. "There's a girl named Bella and she always wins every audition. She acts like she's nice, like she's your friend, but really she's very mean. She said some awful things about me and about my friends, who are mad at me now because of what I told her, but it's so unfair because she tricked me and twisted my words. I don't have any way of getting back at her except to beat her at this audition."

"When is the audition?" Grandma asks.

"In a few days, so you know . . ." I trail off.

"You'd like to be there, wouldn't you?" Grandma asks.

I nod and feel tears pressing in the corners of my eyes. A whip-poor-will sings its sad song as if commiserating with how I feel. I quickly dry my eyes. "Sorry," I say. "How silly to cry about an audition."

"Obviously you feel strongly about it."

"I do, because it's not just about beating Bella. I feel like this is my chance, you know? To do the thing I left Alverland to do. To perform. To spread my wings."

"Did you tell your mother all of this?" Grandma asks.

I shake my head no. "She wouldn't understand. Plus she's already got a lot to worry about. And I don't want to tell her everything, anyway."

Grandma nods slowly. She looks out into the woods and is quiet. The whip-poor-will laments and cicadas grind away in the tops of the trees. Finally she turns back to me, "And is there a boy involved?"

I sit up straight. "How did you know that?"

"Usually in a case like this, there's a boy," she says.

"What do you mean, in a case like this? Elves aren't like this."

"Elves and erdlers aren't all that different."

"There's never been an elf like Bella," I tell her.

"Oh, you'd be surprised," she says.

"Name one."

Grandma looks at me. "Those elves don't stay here, my dear." I blink in disbelief. "Where do they go?"

"Away."

"Away where?"

She sighs. "I guess you're getting old enough to ask these questions now, aren't you?"

"Please tell me. I'm tired of not knowing things. I'm not a little kid anymore. I'm fifteen!"

I see a smile crinkle at the edges of Grandma's eyes, but she nods and says, "There are elves who are not nice. I know it's hard to believe, but sometimes, the temptation to use magic for ill will is just too great for some."

"But, if you use your magic for the wrong reasons, you'll get sick and lose it," I say.

"That's right," she says. "But only temporarily. It'll come back. It'll always come back because your magic is a part of you. It comes from your heart. From your intentions. And if your intentions are good, your magic is good, but if your intentions are bad, then your magic will be evil. And if you keep casting spells from those bad intentions for too long, soon your heart will turn dark."

"Dark Elves?" I whisper. She nods. "I always thought the grown-ups made that up to scare us."

She shakes her head. "No, it's real, but rare. There have been occasions when elves have had to leave Alverland and never come back."

"Never come back? That's terrible! I mean, sometimes I don't want to be here, but I always want to come back."

"Oh, it's heartbreaking for everyone. Losing a member of a clan is the saddest thing that ever happens."

"Did you know someone who . . . ?" I start to ask, but Grandma interrupts me.

"So about this boy, Timber," she says.

"Grandma!" I yelp. "I never told you his name. How did you know that? Did Poppy tell you? I'm going to hex her."

"No, no, don't get upset with your sister," Grandma says quickly.

"My mom?" I ask, trying to puzzle through. "But she doesn't know. No one knew except Ari and Mercedes. Until Mercedes e-mailed everyone of course. And then they started talking about it on Bella's blog and the BellaHater blog." I snap my head around to Grandma. "Don't tell me that you read Bella's blog, too!"

"Who's in a bog?" she asks.

"Never mind." I shake my head and laugh at my extreme paranoia. "I'm starting to lose my mind a little bit."

"Well, I'm feeling very tired," Grandma says. "I should really go back and rest now." She tries to push herself onto her feet.

I put my hand on her thigh. "Wait a minute. Stop." We look at each other. "You never answered my question. How do you know about Timber?"

Grandma sighs deeply. "Oh dear," she mutters. "I really must be weak." Then she laughs a little. "I'm getting too old to be sly. I think I've been caught."

"Doing what?"

"I might as well admit it. Get it over with. Stop driving your poor mother and aunts crazy by speculating on what made me sick."

I sit back, holding my breath, waiting as she stares out into the trees again until she's ready to explain.

"I was just so worried about you all. I had to know if you were okay. So I shifted."

"Shape-shifting?" I gasp.

She nods.

"I didn't know anyone could really do it," I say. Then I ask, "Into what?"

She raises her eyebrows and waits. "I think you know."

"How would I know?"

My grandmother twirls the new amulet from Willow around her neck.

I gasp again. I'm starting to sound like a fish flopping around on the shore. "The red-tailed hawk?" She nods. "So that was you! On the branch above Mercedes and Ari when Timber kissed me?"

"And above your house, circling, and on the fence when you threw rocks, and in the park watching. Always watching. I only meant to do it once. But the first time I came, it seemed that things weren't going well. I made it back here, but then I worried and a few days later I had to go back and check on everyone again. I didn't realize how much energy it took to shift and fly all that way, until I got depleted. Then sick."

"Oh Grandma!" I say and throw my arms around her. I hug her tight. "You didn't have to be worried. We were doing okay."

"That's what your mother would tell me," she says with a little shrug. "But you know how it is, a daughter doesn't like her mother to know everything. She wouldn't want me to worry." We both laugh. "So I had to see for myself." We're quiet for a few minutes as I continue to hug my grandma, but then she pats my arm and looks at me seriously. "So what are you going to do about this audition?"

I shrug. "Nothing, I guess. We'll be here and like you said, there'll be other chances."

Grandma gathers herself up. "Zephyr, I'm going to tell you something important. Revenge is never worth it. I want you to remember that. But, if something's important to you for the right reasons, you should always pursue it."

I nod, but I'm not sure what she means. "I don't know what the right reason would be," I admit.

"You have to figure that out for yourself, I'm afraid."

I think hard for a few seconds. "I want to do it for Ari and Mercedes, my friends."

"But do you want to do it for you?"

I think again. "Yes," I say. "I do. Now it's become a challenge. And that's the reason I left Alverland."

"There are no challenges here?" Grandma asks.

I don't want to hurt her feelings but I can't lie. "Learning magic is a challenge, but it's not what I'm most interested in."

"Which is what?"

"Performing," I tell her. "But all the performances we do here are the same every year. I want something new."

Grandma laughs at me. "Well honey, you know that someone had to make up all those songs and plays and dances."

"I know they did, a long time ago, and I like them but they get boring after a while."

"So why don't you make up new ones?" she asks.

I think about this for a moment. "Am I allowed to do that?"

"Who's stopping you?" she asks, but I don't have an answer. After a moment she says, "So what about this boy in Brooklyn?" Grandma has a mischievous twinkle in her eyes.

"Grandma!" I whine but I'm grinning.

"Oh well, young love," she says with a sigh. "And now, deary . . ." She holds her hand out to me. "If you'll help me up, I think I really do need to rest."

I stand and pull her to her feet. I loop my arm through hers and we walk slowly toward the house. "Thanks for talking, Grandma," I say, laying my head against her shoulder. "I've missed you. Sometimes I wish you could come to Brooklyn with us." I look up at her. "I mean you-you, not the hawk-you."

She laughs and pats my arm. "Oh, honey. Thank *you* for talking to *me.*" We've made it back to her house now. "If you'll just help me into this nice rocking chair here on the porch and then do me one more favor."

"Of course, anything," I tell her as I steady her arm while she arranges herself into the chair.

"Run and get your mother. It's time I had a talk with her."

I run, just like Grandma said, but not because I'm in a hurry. I run because I feel like I'm going to explode if I stay still. I know what's going to happen now. It's been coming for so long. Grandma is going to tell Mom about shifting, Mom is going to freak out, and she'll never want to leave Alverland again, which means we'll all be stuck here. Part of me wants to keep running, straight out of the woods, to the highway, on and on until I hit Brooklyn, but my conflicted heart stops me. I know that I have to do the right thing so I go home and tell Mom that Grandma wants to see her. Then I take off for the woods, where I keep to myself for the rest of the day, dreading what I've already imagined.

By the time the sun touches the tops of the trees, I'm too hungry to stay in the woods any longer. I know I might as well get on with my life. There's nothing I can do now except make the best of being stuck here, the way a good elf would. But the thing is, I don't feel so much like a good elf anymore. I'm not effortlessly happy like I used to be. I wonder if this is what happens to the ones who become Dark Elves. Does it start with a tiny slip from perfectly perky to definitely disappointed? The thought scares me. I don't want to leave Alverland forever, but I would like to come and go as I please. I guess it doesn't work that way though.

When I get back to our house, Mom and Dad are on the front porch swing, holding hands. I climb up the creaky steps and sit on the porch rail. "When did you get back?" I ask Dad.

"A little while ago," he says.

"How'd it go?" I pluck mottled green leaves from the ivy vines twisting around the porch columns.

"Fine," he says with a smile.

"Good," I say, because I'm trying here. Trying to be a good elf who doesn't focus on only herself and how sad she is.

"Where were you?" Mom asks.

I shrug. "In the woods."

"I was looking for you."

"Why?"

"I talked to Grandma," she says.

"Did she tell you?" I ask.

Mom nods. "I think I already knew, though. You tipped me off."

"I did?"

"The hawk you kept seeing," she says.

"Oh, right."

"She kept herself hidden from me, though."

"She was afraid you weren't telling her everything," I say as I drop heart-shaped leaves to the ground.

My mom stares at me until I squirm. "I could say the same of you."

I look out at the fading orange day. The porch swing squeaks behind me. I turn to see my dad standing.

"Come on," he says.

"Where?" I ask.

"Grandma wants to talk to us," says Mom.

I bow my head because I don't want my parents to see the disappointment and dread on my face. I'm not sure why they're making Grandma tell me that we're staying here. Maybe they think if it comes from her I'll be less likely to protest. The three of us walk down the path. I'm in between my parents with my dad's arm draped across my shoulders and my mom's arm slung around my waist. Are they trying to comfort me before the bad news, or keep me from running away? I'm too tired and hungry to take off. All I want to do is eat dinner, then go to bed and start again tomorrow.

Thunder, lightning, and hailstones, was I wrong! Turns out shape-shifting isn't the only trick Grandma has up her tunic sleeve. I didn't think anyone could convince my mom to let me go back to Brooklyn for the audition, but Grandma and Dad are on my side.

"For the record," Mom says from a chair in my grandma's living room, "I don't entirely agree with your grandmother and your father. I honestly don't see how this one audition could be more important than—"

"But," interrupts my dad, giving my mom a long, hard look from where he stands in the doorway, "your mother is trying her best to be understanding and supportive of you."

"And . . ." Grandma faces me on the couch. "Sometimes we have to trust our children even if we don't agree with what's important to them."

"You know the others won't be happy," Mom says with a sigh.

"I don't see why it matters to anyone else," I say as I squirm, trying not to jump up and swing on the rafters because I'm so excited.

"You have to understand, Zephyr," my grandmother says. "The only ones who've left before are the ones who didn't come back."

"The Dark Elves?" I ask. Mom and Dad look at each other to avoid looking at me, but my grandma nods.

"Yes, dear, the Dark Elves. So, you see, to the others, the idea of you and your father and Grove leaving is quite frightening."

"But we'll come back," I say. "Won't we?"

"Yes!" says Mom. "Of course you'll come back. We all will. You're just going down with Dad and Grove so they can do the TV show and you can do the audition. Then, when Grandma's better, Willow and I will bring the little ones down and we'll stay in Brooklyn until your winter break, when we'll all come back to Alverland again. You'll have to get used to going back and forth."

"But you see," Grandma explains. "It's not the coming and going that's disconcerting to the others. It's what you might take away or bring back with you."

"What do you mean?" I ask, imagining my pockets full of flowers and berries from Alverland or soda cans and plastic food wrappers from Brooklyn.

Grandma studies me for a moment, then she says, "Change, Zephyr. That's what I'm talking about and that's what scares others the most."

"I'm still me," I insist, but then I stop. "Oh!" I say, blinking as a realization dawns on me. I think back to yelling at the erdlers in Ironweed and hexing them. And how I kissed Timber, then celebrated when I found out Bella broke up with him. "I have changed, haven't I? You know what's weird?" My parents and my grandmother all look at me with their eyebrows up. "I couldn't tell that I'd changed while I was in Brooklyn. I always felt like me, just a lost and slightly dumb version of myself. Until we came back. And now . . ." I think about this for a moment. I remember myself in Alverland before we left for Brooklyn. I think about all the things Briar and I thought would happen. Then I think about all the things that did happen—good and bad. And now, no matter how messed up things are, I still want to go back. "I can't exactly put my finger on how I'm different," I tell them. "But I think I understand myself better now. I mean, who I am and what's important to me. It's like you have to go away from everything you know and then when you come back, you see yourself more clearly."

"You're right," says Dad. "Leaving and coming back is like holding up a mirror. If you never stop to reflect, you don't see how you change."

"But that's exciting," I say. "Not scary."

"Depends on who you ask," Grandma tells me. "For some, there's nothing more frightening than change."

"Like Willow?" I ask.

"Don't be hard on your sister," my mom snaps at me.

"I'm not trying to criticize her," I say.

Mom pushes her hair away from her face and says quietly, "Your sister is a lot like me. Change is hard for us. But you, my dear . . ." —she reaches out and gently lays her hand on my cheek—"are just like your dad. And you know, I love you both dearly."

I lean into my mother's touch. For once, I feel like she totally gets me. "Thank you, Mom," I say.

She kisses the top of my head. "You're welcome."

"Just remember." My grandmother reaches out and lays her soft, wrinkled hand on top of mine. "Everyone here loves you for who you are, so it's okay to be yourself. You don't have to be one person in Brooklyn and another person in Alverland. Just be you."

"You don't know Brooklyn," I say.

"True, but I do know Alverland," she tells me. "And no matter how your choices may fluster some of the others, in their hearts they care about you and will always love you."

"We have only two more days here," says Dad.

"What do you want to do before you leave?" Mom asks.

At first, when she asks me this, I shrug, but then I glance over at Grandma, and an idea hits me like a june bug between the eyes. "I know exactly what I want to do." I jump up and run to the door. "And I have to get started right away."

Briar, Grove, and I stay up most of the night planning. It wasn't hard to convince them to help me. And when we drag ourselves up after a few hours of sleep, we have no trouble getting our brothers and sisters and cousins involved in our plan. We tell the adults that we'll be gone most of the day, but everyone should meet at the clearing behind Grandma and Grandpa's house this evening. Then we lead our troupe up to the bluffs and rehearse all day long.

When we come back down, we find everyone assembled. Grandma Fawna is dressed in a regular tunic but my dad has brought her rocking chair outside and my mom covers her lap with a blanket. Grandpa Buck sits beside her on a stump and grins at us as we take our places in front of our audience of aunts and uncles, moms and dads.

We didn't have time to make up all new songs, so we took the best ones from our favorite festivals and we sing an Elves Greatest Hits medley. The little kids are adorable, belting out the songs and forgetting the steps, but no one cares. We're having too much fun. We also do a few classic skits, "How the Moon Became Round," "How the Spider Learned to Weave," and "Why the Loon Laughs." We've done these many times but it's fun to act out new parts, on a different day, for a good reason. Everything we've chosen for this performance is Grandma Fawna's favorite and this performance is our best gift to her.

For the finale, Grove, Briar, and I play a song I wrote last night. The rest of the kids sit in front of us with drums, shakers, and bells; they join in on the chorus. We stand, Grove with his guitar, Briar with her fiddle, and me with my lute. We fill the woods with our music—a new song for everyone.

Before a bird takes flight
it's safe inside its nest
snuggled with the other birds,
trying to get some rest.

But birds grow fast,
the nest gets small
and pretty soon
it can't contain them all.

Some birds need to soar
Some birds need to fly
Step up to the edge of the nest
And take off for the sky.

If a bird jumps too soon
the world will spin around,
the baby bird will fall fast
and plummet to the ground.

So wait little bird
before you leave the nest,
wait until you're ready
to go upon your quest.

Some birds need to soar
Some birds need to fly
Step up to the edge of the nest
And take off for the sky.

You'll learn to fly soon enough
from the ones who love you best,
they'll let you know the perfect time
to leave your cozy nest.

Your family is your wings
so spread your wings to fly
they'll hold you up, won't let you fall
so you can reach the sky.

And when you finally take that leap
around the nest you'll glide,
just follow the sound of beating wings
your family is your guide.

Fly higher, bird, to reach the sun
but when you're weary rest,

there's always a cozy place for you
back inside your nest.

Some birds need to soar
Some birds need to fly
I'm stepping up to the edge of my nest
And now I'm going to fly.

Everyone erupts into applause when we're done. Our mothers and fathers come to the stage to hug and kiss us.

"What a wonderful job!"

"You kids worked so hard!"

"I haven't had this much fun in weeks," they say. As I look at everyone together, I see the elves I know best—happy, smiling, together. For a minute I feel uncertain about tomorrow. About leaving again and going back to Brooklyn, because no matter how many friends I have or what parts I audition for, there will never be this many people in one place who love me.

Flora finds me in the crowd. She puts her arm around me and hugs me close to her shoulder. "Thank you, Zephyr," she says. "I haven't seen Grandma Fawna that happy in a long time. Or Briar. You're so much like your dad. Your music brings joy to people."

I'm so overwhelmed by her compliment that I stand there stunned and quiet, but very happy. Flora lets go of me and whistles loudly to get everyone's attention. "Hey everybody," she yells. "Let's eat!"

Arm in arm families head up to Grandma's porch, where tables full of food wait. My dad comes to me.

"Great job," he says. "I didn't know you were writing songs."

"I never tried before," I tell him.

"Then you should keep doing it, because you're really good."

"Really?" I ask.

"Yes. But that doesn't surprise me," he says.

I roll my eyes and laugh. "I know, because I'm a lot like you."

"That's right." He turns and points toward the porch. "Now, we better get some of this wonderful elfin food because starting tomorrow we'll be back in the land of prepackaged deli meat and bread from a bag."

I hesitate. Bite my lip and frown. Dad watches me. "You nervous to go back?" he asks. I nod. "You don't have to go."

As I watch my brothers and sisters, aunts and uncles, cousins, and grandparents filling their plates, talking, laughing, there's a part of me that wants to stay. But my heart is conflicted and there's also a part of me that wants to leave this cozy nest. "No," I say to Dad. "I'm ready."

Early the next morning I hug and kiss Willow, Poppy, Bramble, and Persimmon good-bye. Briar has come to see us off, too, but no one else. I imagine our decision to leave isn't popular and I realize for the first time that what I want doesn't affect only me. But like my grandmother said, if my reasons are good, then I'm doing the right thing. I hold on to to Briar for an extra moment.

"I want to come with you," she whispers in my ear.

"I know," I say. "But I'll be back. And you know you can see the erdler world anytime you want." She looks at me, confused. "Don't let that librarian intimidate you. You know how to use a computer now."

She lets go of me. "Right," she says. "I'll do that."

I hug my mother tightly. "I'll be okay," I assure her, but she can only nod. Then Dad and Grove and I hike into the early morning shafts of sun shimmering through the trees, as we leave Alverland for the second time.

chapter 13

"DAD," I ASK when I wake up near Cleveland. We've been gone for only eight hours but ever since I signed off the instant messenger by saying "moose crap" to Timber, I've been trying to figure out a way to let him know I'm coming back. "Can I invite a friend to hang out with me backstage at the TV studio?"

"Sure," Dad says. "How about that nice young man Ari who's so interested in music?"

"You mean in your music?" I ask. Grove and I exchange looks. "I'm pretty sure he's busy with his own band."

"Then your other friend. Mercedes?" Dad asks.

I don't have the heart to tell him that Ari and Mercedes aren't exactly my friends at the moment so I say, "Her parents probably wouldn't let her and anyway, she probably has a lot of homework or has to babysit for her sisters."

"Is there someone else you had in mind?" he asks.

I try to act as casual as possible and to keep all excitement out of my voice. "I don't know. Maybe that guy Timber who sang with us in the park." Dad glances at me over the back of the seat. I quickly look out the window as if the whole conversation is sort of boring. I catch him looking at Grove, who shrugs. "You know he used to have a band with a record deal," I say. "And he really likes your music, too."

"Well then," says my dad. "I don't see why not."

"Great. Thanks, Dad," I say, then I wait for a while. "Oh, by the way, could I use your Treo so I can send him an e-mail to invite him?"

"Ah ha!" yells my dad. "That's what this is all about. You want my Treo!" He laughs triumphantly.

"Whatever," I say. "I'll just go by myself and be really bored. I don't even care."

"Oh now, don't get upset," Dad says. He reaches across Grove and opens the glove compartment. "You can use it." He holds it up, out of my reach. "But only for five minutes."

"Five minutes!"

He looks at me in the rearview mirror. "You want it or not?"

"Yes!" I hold out my hand.

"Five minutes," he says, and hands it to me.

I try to IM Timber, but since it's during the school day, he's not around. I leave him an e-mail, though, asking if he wants to come with us to the taping tonight. At some point, while I'm napping in Ohio, he must e-mail back because after I beg to have the Treo for another five measly minutes, I find his answer.

stone cold, Z! I'm soooo there. Can't w8 2 c u.

Even though I'm not entirely sure what that means, I think it's good, and excitement ripples through my body at the thought of seeing him. There's one other e-mail waiting for me too. It's from Briar@yahoo.com. I open it with a huge grin on my face.

Hi Zeph!
I took your advice and went back to the library. A nice erdler girl named Jenny showed me how to get an e-mail

account. Do you know about MySpace.com? Jenny is going
to help me set up a page so I can make lots of friends.
Miss u already!
xo Briar

I hug the Treo next to my heart. It's nice to have Briar near. Before
I can reply to her Dad puts one hand over the back of the seat and says,
"Hand it over, Zeph."

"Dad!" I whine. "Come on. There's nothing else to do."

"We have an agreement," he insists.

"*You* have an agreement," I say. Grove snickers.

"Shush," I say to Grove. "Before I zap you."

"Ooooh, I'm so scared." Grove laughs.

"Quit stalling," my dad says. "If you want to use it again later, you'll
hand it over now. Your five minutes are up."

I give him the Treo. "Five minutes," I mutter. "That's ridiculous.
Preposterous. You can't do anything online in five minutes."

"That's all I need." He stows the Treo in the glove compartment.
"In fact, that's all I can stand. How can you look at that tiny little
screen for more than five minutes? I swear my eyes will never be the
same. I probably couldn't see a twelve-point buck if it was standing
on my foot."

The remark about the buck sends Dad and Grove into a nine-
million-hour discussion about hunting. Even though I've been track-
ing animals since I was a little kid, I have no interest in reliving every
moment I've had a four-legged creature in my sights. In fact, the only
stalking I want to think about is the kind that involves my finding
Timber. So I tune out Dad and Grove and stare out the window at the
passing trees, hills, occasional farms, and rest stops, until I fall asleep
happily dreaming of returning to NYC.

* * *

We don't have time to go home before we head to the VH1 studio in Manhattan. Which is just dandy. Because after eighteen hours in a stinky van that smells like feet, I certainly want to see the guy who broke up with his gorgeous amazing girlfriend. (Hey, look how good I am at sarcasm now!) I'm sure I look like a troll and smell like a goat. But what can I do? About the only option is to grab a clean tunic out of my knapsack and hope there's a place to change inside.

Backstage, in the green room (which isn't really green but is the place where we wait), everyone rushes around getting Dad and Grove ready. They change their clothes, wash and blow-dry their hair, even put some makeup on them. I've never worn makeup. It's just not something elfin women do, so it cracks me up to see all that gunk on my brother and my dad but it also gives me an idea. Timber isn't showing up for another half an hour, so while the band goes out to do a sound check onstage, I change into my clean tunic then find the makeup person.

She's reading a magazine in front of a big mirror surrounded by lights. "You must be Drake's daughter," she looks up and says when I stand beside her chair. "You look just like him."

"My name is Zephyr."

"Gorgeous name!" she says. "I'm Lucy. What's going on?"

I'm not sure how to ask her for what I want so I poke around her brushes and tubes of color on the counter in front of the chair. "What are all these things?" I ask shyly.

She presses her lips together and squints at me. "Seriously?" she asks. "You don't know?" I shake my head, embarrassed. "Let me guess, you're not allowed to wear makeup?"

"I don't know if I am or not." I pick up some kind of pencil-looking thing. "We just don't have any where we're from."

She holds up a soft wispy brush and cleans it with a tissue. "Do you think your dad would get mad if you had some on?"

I shake my head. "Oh no. I don't think he'd care at all. I mean, come on, what could he say? He's wearing it, too!"

Lucy laughs. She cups my chin in her hand and tilts my face to the left, then to the right. "It's not like you need it."

"Oh but—" I say, then stop.

"I mean you're gorgeous without it. So are your dad and your brother. It's rare to see people with such amazing skin. It almost glows. And this hair." She runs her fingers through my tangled mess.

"It's just that . . ." I glance at the clock. Twenty-five minutes and Timber will be here.

Her eyes follow mine, then she looks at me. "Are you meeting someone?"

A grin spreads across my face and my whole body goes warm as I think about seeing Timber soon. Will he grab me, kiss me, tell me how much he missed me? Will we hold hands all night?

"Ah ha!" Lucy says. "Someone special?"

I nod and smile even bigger. I'm so excited that I might fly up into the Manhattan sky.

"Hop on up here, honey!" Lucy pats the chair and switches on all the lights around the mirror. "And let me work my magic!"

When Lucy's done, I can't stop staring at myself. My hair is silkier and straighter than usual after she washed it and blew it dry. Plus, it smells so much like berries and honey that I want to hold it under my nose and sniff it for an hour. Then she made four thin braids from the front sections that she gathered in the back of my head with a long red ribbon to match the flowers embroidered on my pale yellow tunic. I watched carefully as she brushed color over my cheekbones and eyelids and then took a tiny black wand and filled in my eyelashes so my face is rosy and my eyes look as big and green as lily pads with eyelashes as long as a doe's. The last thing she did was run a tube of something glossy over my mouth to make my lips look moist, as if I'm ready for a kiss, which, let's be honest, I am. I glance at the clock again. Timber should be here any minute.

"So, what do you think?" Lucy asks as we both look at me in the mirror.

I don't know what to say so I turn around and give her a huge hug. "Thank you! Thank you! Thank you!" I gush.

"My pleasure," she says. "And here," she hands me a little bag. "I put together a few things for you to take home. Just some samples to get you started." I hug her again. "Good luck." She winks and points to the mirror, where I see the reflection of Timber coming through the door behind me.

Every bone, muscle, and internal organ inside my body dissolves when I catch sight of him. If it weren't for my tingling skin holding me together, I'd be a big sloppy puddle of elf soup on the floor. I turn in the chair and try to push myself up, but my legs are trembling and I can't quite feel my feet. I'm afraid I'll fall on my butt if I try to take a step. Lucy grabs my arm and hoists me to a stand. I can hear her laughing in my ear, but I don't look at her because I can't stop staring at Timber.

He's even more gorgeous than I remember. I gape at him. I can't blink or talk. Which is mortifying, because for him, all of this seems easy and natural. He smiles that wolf grin as he walks toward me. "Hey, Zephyr."

What should I do with my body? Hold out my arms? Pucker my lips? Tilt my head to the side and close my eyes? I'm freaking out. I can't move. I just stand here, rigid, with my hands frozen by my sides and my eyes open wide.

He gets right up close to me and he stops. "You look different," he says. "Are you wearing makeup?"

That breaks the corpse spell that had me stuck. "Sort of, I guess."

"Looks good," he says with a nod.

"Thanks." I begin to lean in for our glorious reunion smooch, but he presses his hand on the small of my back and gives me a quick little peck on the cheek. Then he pulls back and I blink. What the heck was that? Where were the dancing unicorns and chorus of trumpeter swans to herald our romantic reunion? I press my hand against the burning spot on my cheek where he kissed me. Was that it? What happened to the part where he takes me in his arms and tells me he's so glad that I'm back before we kiss passionately for five minutes?

"So how was your trip?" he asks.

"Boring," I manage to say, covering my disappointment.

"Yeah, being on the road sucks," he says, but then he spies a large flat-screen TV across the room by two blue couches and some chairs. The sound is off but we can see my dad, Grove, and the rest of the band on-stage tuning their instruments and testing the mics.

Timber smiles but shakes his head as he moves toward the screen. "But, man, I miss that. Sound checking, getting ready, being on. It's the biggest rush."

I follow him, still smarting from how casual he's being. "Why don't you start another band then?"

He drops to a couch and shrugs. "Lazy, I guess."

I sit one cushion away because I'm not sure what's going on here. Did I misinterpret everything? Did something happen while I was gone? I try my best to keep the conversation going. "My friend Ari has a band," I say, but then stop when I remember that Ari's not my friend anymore.

"Oh hey, that reminds me. He asked me about you the other day in our improv class."

"Really!" I sit up straight and lean toward Timber. "What did he say?"

"Nothing much. Just asked if I knew where you were, stuff like that."

"Is he all right?" I ask, quietly.

"I guess so. Why wouldn't he be?"

"I don't know." I shrink and slump against a soft white pillow. "I guess, I mean, is he still mad at me?"

Timber stretches his arms over the back of the couch so that his hand is near my shoulder but not touching me. "You did out him, Zeph."

"I what?"

"You outed him."

"What's *outed* mean?"

"You know," Timber says, and raises his eyebrows. "You brought him out of the closet." I look at him blankly because the only closet I've ever seen Ari in is my own when he found my tunics. "You told everyone he's gay."

"I did not!" I protest. "Bella did!"

And there it is. Her name hangs in the air between us like a skunk just sprayed a cloud of stink. Neither of us looks at the other for a moment until Timber says, "You can blame whoever you want, but your girl Mercedes is the one who got busted."

"She got beat up?"

"No, 'busted' means in trouble. She got suspended for sending that e-mail."

"Oh no," I say, holding my head in my hands.

"I think she's coming back to school tomorrow, but she's not allowed to do the ELPH audition."

"That's awful," I mutter.

"Yep, sucks to be her," says Timber, but he doesn't really sound so broken up. I feel terrible, though, about how much trouble poor Mercedes got into because of me. Timber breaks the silence by saying, "Anyway, Ari was sorry to hear that your grandmother's sick."

"He was?" I ask.

"Yeah. Ari's all right. He's a cool guy."

"I thought you didn't like him," I say.

"I never said I didn't like him."

"He said you never talked to him in improv."

"Whatever." Timber pulls his arm away from me. "I didn't know him. I mean, there are like thirty people in that class. What? I'm supposed to be friends with everyone?"

I scoot a little bit farther away from him.

"What's the matter?" he asks.

"You sound like her," I say quietly.

"Like who?"

"Bella," I say. And there it is again! Why do I keep bringing her up? Am I an idiot? Do I want this to go badly?

Timber sets his jaw and looks up at the ceiling. "You know," he says, then stops.

I pull one knee up close to my chest, feeling stupid for ruining the moment.

"The thing about Bella . . ."

My stomach drops because I'm sure he's going to say that they're getting back together. And then what? I'll have to sit here beside him for the rest of the night pretending to be happy for him because we're friends?

"Everyone assumes I must be a jerk if I went out with her," Timber says. "But really . . ." He turns his body toward mine and leans in. "I'm not a bad guy."

I look up at him. He seems so sincere. No wolf grin. Just honest eyes, waiting for me to say something. "I think you're a good guy," I tell him.

"Honestly, I'm kind of a dork, you know?"

"No you're not!" Now I smack his leg. "You're like Mr. Playa," I say, trying to sound like Mercedes.

Timber throws his head back and laughs. "Do you even know what a player is?"

"No," I admit.

"I'm not a player, Zeph. Trust me. I never fit in with Bella and her scene. We looked good together, but we're totally different. She likes to be the center of attention all the time. I'd rather hang back and watch people. She wants to go out and be seen. I like to stick close to home and be with a few good friends. She thinks you have to spend money to have a good time. I'd rather hang in the park. Plus, she likes to party."

"We have a lot of parties in Alverland," I tell him.

"Not this kind," he says.

I shake my head. "No, probably not. We go out in the woods, build a big fire, and stay up until the sun rises, playing music and dancing."

He laughs. "That sounds better than the kind of partying I'm talking about. Bella wanted me to try all this crazy stuff with her, but I wasn't into it, and she'd get all furious with me. Especially when I'd tell her to stop. That's what I like about hanging out with you. I don't have to try to be someone else." He reaches out and squeezes my shoulder. "I can make a dumb joke and you'll think it's funny and not roll your eyes like I'm an idiot. Plus, I like your family and you have cool friends. I hated Bella's friends. Except for Chelsea. She's okay."

"Chelsea!" I nearly yell. "She's the meanest one."

"Not when you get to know her. She's different than they are but she's caught up in trying to be like them. Actually, she and I were always the sober ones, trying to make sure that Bella, Zoe, and the others didn't get themselves into more trouble. She's really okay."

I shake my head. "I refuse to believe that."

Before we can get into a stupid argument about Chelsea, my dad and his band come noisily into the room. Timber and I pop up from the couch.

"There you are!" Dad booms and comes over to shake Timber's hand.

"Thanks for inviting me," Timber says.

"It's nice for Zephyr to have a friend backstage. I know how boring it is waiting. And waiting some more," Dad says with a laugh. "You guys hungry? They've got a spread for us in the other room."

As we're heading for the food tables, another man rushes in. He's younger than my dad and wears a suit jacket over jeans with his brown hair slicked back off his forehead. He's talking loudly and quickly into one of those little cell phones attached to one ear while he's texting on the PDA in his hands. "Drake!" he shouts, then goes back to his boisterous conversation on the earpiece.

Dad shakes his head but grins. "That's Martin," he tells us. "My manager."

"You're not going to believe this." Martin clasps my dad's hand, then pulls him in and bumps him against his chest. "You're all over the Web today." He holds up his PDA. Then he notices Timber and me. "These more of your kids? How many do you have? Like twelve or something. I'm Martin. Nice to meet you."

"I'm Zephyr," I say, shaking his hand. "And this is my friend Timber. Timber Lewis Cahill," I add.

Martin drops my hand and slaps Timber on the shoulder. "Hey my man, I know you. You're that kid. Fronted TLC Boyz. You guys did all right back in the day. Who you with now? What label? Who's your manager?"

Timber shoves his hands down in his pockets and looks uncomfortable. "Well, I'm, you know, kind of between . . ."

"Right, right. Let me give you my card." Martin reaches into his pocket and pulls out a little case. He takes out a card and hands it to Timber. "Keep me in mind." Then he turns back to my dad. "Good stuff going on. They treating you okay? These good people? Got what you need? Wait, I've got a call." He turns away and starts shouting into the earpiece again.

I snicker behind my hand. "He's like a giant squirrel running around looking for nuts."

"Nuts is right," Timber says, and we laugh, but I can tell he's happy that Martin knew who he was and gave him a card, which he tucks carefully inside his wallet.

Martin whips back around toward us. "Yeah so, you're all over the place today." I'm not sure if he's still talking on the phone or talking to my dad. "Did you know that you're in a cult? Maybe even the leader. And you live in the middle of the woods, totally off the grid, by the way. Remind me not to come visit you. I like my electricity and plumbing. And let's see what else?" He glances back down at the PDA. Now I know he's talking about Dad. "Oh right, you're married to your cousin, you have six kids, and you're a Wiccan. Which I don't know, can men be Wiccans? I thought that was only women. I think that would make you a warlock. Maybe I should correct that." He starts pushing buttons on the PDA.

"What's he talking about?" I ask Dad with my heart racing because some of those rumors sound like ones Bella started on her blog.

"Don't know, don't care," Dad says with a shrug.

Martin looks up from the PDA. "It's all good, all good. This kind of crazy speculation only works in your favor. Creates more mystery. More of a persona. People eat that crap up. You'll see. The more people talk, the more that song'll climb. Is there any Pellegrino here? Or Red Bull?" Martin and my dad head off toward the food.

I grab Timber's arm. "What's going on? Why are people saying those things about my dad?"

"It's no big deal," Timber assures me. "You should've heard the stuff people said about me and my band when we were on the charts. I was like twelve years old and there were rumors that I was dating women who were twenty. That I was dying of leukemia. That I was on drugs. That my dad forced me to perform and I hated it. That my mom was having an affair with my manager. None of it was true, of course."

"But didn't it upset you?" I ask.

"At first, then you learn to ignore it, then you learn to use it. Martin's right. This kind of chatter only makes people more interested in the music. Heck, if I had rumors like this about me, I'd love it! I could stage a huge comeback."

I shake my head. The whole thing makes me nervous because some of those rumors are a little too close to the truth. But of course I can't tell Timber that. "I'll be right back," I say to him. I find my dad piling fruit and cheese on a paper plate. "Can I please use your Treo?" I ask him quietly.

He frowns at me. "No, Zeph. Come on. You've got your friend here. Don't start with that again, please."

"But Dad," I insist. "I want to check out those rumors for myself."

He shakes his head. "Don't pay attention, Zephyr. It'll only make you crazy. You have to ignore it. It's nothing new."

"But Dad!" I say.

"Stop," he tells me. "The Treo's down in the van anyway, which is in the parking garage, so I couldn't give it to you if I wanted to. Just drop it."

I walk away, but I'm not ready to give up. I stand off to the side with my arms crossed against my chest.

Timber finds me. "What's the matter, Zeph? You look p.o.'ed."

"I can't get Dad's Treo and I really want to see who's spreading those rumors."

"I don't know what good it'll do, but if you really want to . . ." Timber pulls a sleek white phone out of his back pocket. "I got you covered. Use my iPhone."

We go back to the couches and start Googling my dad. We find all kinds of crazy rumors, most of which are just ridiculous but I want to find out who started the ones about him being in a cult and being married to his cousin. We keep going through chat rooms and blogs until we find a post in a folk music chat room from six days ago—the day after Bella and Timber broke up.

> **—I know Drake Addler's daughter. We go to high school together. She told me that her father is the leader of a cult of pagan atheists who worship trees and marry their cousins. They just moved to Brooklyn so he could brainwash new members through his music. He plans to take his recruits back to the cult in the U.P. of Michigan, to a place called Alverland.**
>
> Posted by: Nightshade

I gasp when I see the name of the poster then I nearly yell, "It's her!"

"Who?" Timber asks.

"Bella."

He rolls his eyes. "You're getting a little paranoid, aren't you?"

"Nightshade," I tell him. "Deadly nightshade. Devil's cherries."

"Now you're starting to sound like the kooks who go to these chat rooms and spread weird rumors about witches and magic and cults."

I shake my head. "No, it's her. The password to her secret blog is *belladonna,* which is another name for the plant deadly nightshade, also called devil's cherries. And this stuff she posted is the same stuff she put on her own blog. Bella is the one who started these rumors."

Timber takes the iPhone from me and puts his hand on my leg.

"Look, even if she did write this one, it's not the only one. People get a little nutty over rock stars, which is what your dad is now. So they post all kinds of weird stuff. Whoever this Nightshade person is, is just fueling the fire and like Martin said, it's not such a bad thing."

"But she knows where we're from," I tell him as my stomach ties itself into knots. "Nobody else does."

Timber blows it off. "So what? People can find that stuff out if they really want to. Plus, most people aren't interested if your dad's in a cult, or where he's from. And anyway, you don't even live there anymore, so what's there to worry about?"

Obviously, I can't answer his question, but I'm still not convinced there's nothing to be concerned about. "Search Alverland," I tell him.

He types it in and we wait. Several links come up for weird things like some Swedish guy's blog and something in what looks to be Arabic, but then at the bottom I see a link to a blog called Drake-o-phile. We click it and find an entry from some nut job who went looking for Alverland so he could join my dad's supposed cult. At the bottom are blurry photos. I jump up from my seat. The first photo is of Main Street in Ironweed. I see the grocery store, the stoplight, the houses, and the library. The second photo is of a path behind a barn outside of Ironweed where we exit and enter the woods. The third photo is grainy and hard to make out, but it looks like whoever took it zoomed in from far away on a group of elf kids in tunics playing hide-and-seek on the rocks of Barnaby Bluff.

"I have to tell my dad right now!" I exclaim.

Timber shakes his head and points to the TV screen. "Can't. They just got called onstage."

I drop back down to the couch. "This is bad, Timber," I say, shaking my head. But he's not paying attention because he's too busy reading whatever that freak Drake-o-phile wrote.

"Hey check it out," he says. "Isn't gothboi your man Ari?"

"How'd you know that?" I ask.

"He IM'ed the other day about a gig he's doing next week. But look at this." He hands me the iPhone and I scan through the comments below Drake-o-phile's photos.

> **—Give the poor man and his family some privacy! They are extremely nice, decent people who don't deserve to be stalked by weirdoes like you. All of these rumors are so stupid and entirely false! Leave them alone and let Drake's music speak for itself.**
> Posted by: gothboi

"Oh my goodness." I feel close to tears. "That's so nice of him."

Timber takes the iPhone back. "You want to IM him and say thanks?" He hands me the phone. I start typing.

> Even tho u r mad at me, I want 2 tell u how much it means 2 me that u defended my dad against those stupid rumors online. I really meant it when I posted on YouTube that u r wonderful and that u have heart. I'm so sorry I ruined r friendship b/c I think the world of u. –Z

"Check it out." Martin turns up the volume on the TV in front of us, then he plunks down on the couch beside me. "They're on. This is going to be hot. Super hot. Your dad is a star, baby, a star! I'm going to take this song all the way to number one!"

Timber elbows me and snickers, but I can't laugh at Martin. I'm so furious that I can barely pay attention to my dad singing or to the fact that Timber is right beside me. Nothing feels more important to me right now than getting back at Bella. No matter what my grandmother Fawna says, sometimes revenge is the only thing you have left.

That night when we get home to Brooklyn, I grab a flashlight and I head straight for my mother's special pantry with all her herbs, tinctures, tonics, and books of remedies. I close the pantry door behind me so my dad and brother won't know what I'm doing. My piddly magic with its silly wart hexes isn't enough for what I want to do to Bella. I know that somewhere in this pantry is a special book. One that is handed down from healer to healer in the family. It was my great-grandfather's. Then it was Fawna's. Now it's my mother's. Some day it will likely go to Bramble, since he seems to be the one with the best magic of all us kids. But for now, I want this book for myself because it holds the secrets of casting powerful spells, both good and bad, and I'm going to need all the help I can get.

As I'm searching, I hear Dad in the kitchen listening to the messages on the answering machine. I try to tune out the noise, but it's hard because the phone is right next to the pantry. Most of the messages are from potential clients for my mom, but then there's one that catches my attention.

"Hello Mr. and Mrs. Addler. My name is Maria Arellano Sanchez. I'm Mercedes Sanchez's mother. I'd like to speak with you about my daughter's actions at school. I'm sure your daughter is very upset, and my husband and I feel that Mercedes must apologize to you and your daughter in person."

I hear my dad muttering, "What? Huh?" Then he calls out, "Zephyr!" I stay quiet. Before he can call my name again, my mom's voice comes through the speaker. "Drake, we have a problem," she says in a quivery voice, and I know something must really be wrong because she'd have to go all the way to Ironweed to use the phone, which no one does unless something awful has happened. I grasp the flashlight tightly, bracing myself to hear that Grandma has taken a turn for the worst, but that's not what it is.

"Today some of the men were hunting and they found a man sneaking around up on the bluffs with a camera," Mom explains. "He'd been taking pictures. He said he wanted to join Drake Addler's cult. The men told him to get out. They said they'd never heard of you, but he obviously knew you were from near here. Everyone is very upset." She pauses. I hear her pull in a shuddering breath, then she continues, even shakier than before. "Everyone says it's the work of the Dark Elves. They're all so angry with us. They don't want the children and me to stay. They've asked us to go before we cause any more harm but Willow is refusing to come. My brother Cedar has offered to drive us down to Calumet so we can get a bus back to New York. I don't know what to do." Then she breaks down and cries.

I've never heard my mother sob. Crying out of sadness is a rare thing for elves. Listening to her weep makes me feel like my chest is being crushed under the weight of a hundred fallen trees, my throat is full of stinging wasps, and my eyes are filled with tiny sharp pebbles. Is this what it feels like to have your heart darken? I don't know and I don't care. All I know is that this is Bella's fault.

I stay paralyzed and sweating, scrunched inside the pantry as I listen to my dad storm through the house, calling for my brother and me. I keep my eyes closed tightly, trying my best to keep my own cries silent until I hear my father stomping up the stairs. Then I open my eyes and wipe away the stream of tears as best as I can while I search for the book that holds the secret to my perfect sweet revenge. My powers might be weakened and my heart may darken, but I will exact vengeance on Bella, no matter what it does to me.

chapter 14

THE NEXT MORNING I dress carefully. I don't choose my best or most beautiful tunic. In fact, I put on the most ordinary one I own. It's rusty brown, the color of fall leaves, and has only simple dark brown stitching around the hems. I pull on leggings, my boots, and my hat. These are work clothes where I come from and today I have work to do.

The last thing I do is put my hunting amulets around my neck. A bear's tooth that my grandfather gave me for protection. A piece of flint Uncle Cedar carved into the shape of a bobcat for stealth. A small bone from the ankle of a deer that Aunt Flora gave me for swiftness. And a polished river rock for clear vision from Grandma Fawna. Plus, I have one other amulet in my pocket. A new one that I stayed up late last night to make.

My dad is gone. He left right after he learned Mom, Persimmon, Poppy, and Bramble were banished from Alverland. He's going to drive along the bus route back toward Michigan until he finds them and can bring them safely back to Brooklyn. Grove is supposed to take care of me, but, of course, he's still asleep and anyway, I can take care of myself.

I shove my books in my knapsack, lock the front door, and head for the subway, prepared for the hunt.

I'm not scared of the big green doors at BAPAHS anymore. I fling them open. Nor am I intimidated by the crowded halls. I weave through the kids, getting occasional stares from people who know more about my business than they have a right to, but I don't care. I'm on a mission to find one person and one person alone. I scan the faces for her face. I listen intently for her voice or for someone else to say her name. I know how to track an animal through the forest—this is no different.

It doesn't take long to find her perched on top of a table in the center of the courtyard, surrounded by Tara, Chelsea, and Zoe. So predictable. She sits cross-legged with a paper coffee cup in her hand, tossing her hair over her shoulder and laughing between sips of her morning brew. Luckily no one else I know is in the courtyard right now so I hide at a corner table obscured by a trash can and bury my face in a book as if I'm studying. I'll bide my time, patiently and calmly waiting for the perfect moment in my pursuit.

The first bell rings and most people gather their belongings. Bella takes her time. Never flustered. Above the rules. This only plays to my advantage. The courtyard empties out. Her gals leave one by one, blowing air kisses to one another as they head off in different directions to their first classes. Bella lingers, finishing her coffee. She's in no hurry and neither am I. I stay put, head down, waiting for my chance. She picks up her books and heads toward the trash can with her empty coffee cup in hand.

As soon as she tosses the cup away, I look up. "Oh, Bella!" I say. "I didn't see you out here. How are you?"

She narrows her eyes at me, cocks her head slightly to the side as if trying to decide how to play this situation. Then she straightens up. "I'm great," she says, and brushes past me.

I join her, step for step. "Hey listen." I put my hand on her arm to slow her down. "I feel really bad about what happened. You know, with Timber."

She pulls her arm away from me as if I'm burning her. "Whatever. I don't care, you know. I broke up with him. And I was going to long before you came along."

"I know," I say. "But still, you've been so nice to me and I just hope that there are no bad feelings between us."

"Okay sure." She slows down and gives me a little smile, but I can see the smirk in the corners of her mouth. "No bad feelings."

Before she can turn away, I reach into my pocket. "So I brought you something. It's an amulet. I remember how much you said you liked mine." I pull out a long green cord of braided silk. On the end I've tied a small linen satchel. "It's got all kinds of things inside for luck." She eyes the necklace curiously. "You know, for the audition today."

She looks up at me. "Are you still doing that?"

"I had to go away for a week because my grandma got sick, so I didn't get to practice." I push the amulet toward her. "I remember the dress you wore to the first meeting. Mr. O'Donnell really loved it and I thought this would look good with it." Bella reaches out and snatches the amulet from me. "I really hope you get the part," I say.

"Oh, I will," she says as she saunters away with the amulet swinging from her fist.

When her back is turned, I close my eyes, press my hands together in front of my heart, and mutter the words from my mother's book of spells,

Beauty fades, quick and cheap.

Hair goes woolly like a sheep.
X marks the skin across the face,
to reveal your heart's disgrace.
Bumps and bruises will appear,
never halting 'til you're sincere.
But you won't see the repulsive maim,
Because your reflection remains the same.

I flick my fingers, zapping her with my truest, dark intentions. I open my eyes just in time to see her trip, look down at the ground for the non-existent rock or stick that caught her toe, then disappear around a corner. I turn and head in the opposite direction, but I stop and nearly trip over myself when I see Timber standing in the courtyard, staring at me.

"What was that all about?" he asks.

"What? That? With her?" I stammer.

"Why were *you* talking to *her*?" He walks toward me, hands shoved in his pockets.

"Oh, Bella?" I say innocently, trying to kill a few seconds so I can think up something to tell him.

"Yes. Bella. I thought you hated her. You said she's ruining your dad's life."

"Well, I decided that maybe you were right." I loop my arm through Timber's and turn him around to walk the other way. We have to get out of here in case Bella comes back. He looks down at me suspiciously. I snuggle closer to his side, like I imagine an erdler girl who can feel one way but talk another might. "Maybe I was being paranoid and like you said, even if she did start some dumb rumor about my dad, it's not the first one. So I thought I should make friends with her." I smile up at him but inside I'm not smiling at all. The lie I told seeps deeply into me, like a poisonous spill soaking into the ground.

He shakes his head and laughs. "You always surprise me," he says. "You're such a nice person. That's refreshing."

I can't meet his eyes after he says that. I drop my arm from his. "Timber," I say and pause.

"Yeah?"

I swallow, forcing myself to stop before I tell him that I'm not as nice as he thinks I am. "You're a nice refreshing person, too," I say, then hurry away so he can't see the darkness in my heart.

He laughs. "You make me sound like a Sprite."

I turn around. "That's not what I meant," I apologize. "Wood sprites can be really unpredictable!"

He looks at me, confused. "The soda?"

"Sorry!" I call to him, not stopping to explain what he'll never understand.

I'm totally distracted in every class for the rest of the morning. All I can think about is whether my spell is working. I keep hoping I'll pass Bella in the hallway so I can get a look at her, but so far, no such luck. That's okay, though, I'm sure I'll see her in the cafeteria, which is where I'm heading, but then Ms. Sanchez stops me.

"Zephyr." She lays her hand on my shoulder. "I'd like to see you in my office."

"But, but, but . . . ," I stutter. My heart races and my palms sweat. Am I busted? How could anyone have figured out that I zapped Bella? There's part of me that doesn't care, though. I'm glad I did it and I hope it makes Bella's life as miserable as mine but still I don't want to get in trouble. "It's my lunch time," I tell Ms. Sanchez.

"It'll only take a few minutes," she says. "Come."

With my head hanging, I follow Ms. Sanchez into her office.

I slip into the same chair I sat in my first day at BAPAHS and once again she rests on the edge of her desk. The daisies in the vase are nearly dead, but I can't save them this time. I may have already cast one too many spells today. I wait for Ms. Sanchez to get on with it.

"So listen," she says. "Usually I don't get involved in conflicts between two students, but this situation isn't exactly normal."

"No, I suppose it's not," I admit, then catch myself. I should be denying everything, but I don't care right now. Girls like Bella will always win no matter what I do.

"But since I'm Mercedes's aunt, I feel like it's warranted that I get involved," Ms. Sanchez says to me.

I look up at her, bewildered. "Mercedes?"

"We know all about the mass e-mail she sent," she says, and relief floods my body, because this isn't about me and Bella. "And by now I'm sure that you know Mercedes was suspended and isn't allowed to audition today." I nod and Ms. Sanchez continues. "That was her school punishment, but her parents feel it's important for her to apologize to you and your family. They've tried calling your parents, but they haven't gotten a response, so I said I would speak to you personally to see if we could arrange something. Perhaps you and your parents could come here to meet with Mercedes and her parents if I mediate."

I squirm in my seat. I can't exactly explain that my mom is on a bus somewhere between Michigan and New York and my dad is trying to find her. "I'll tell my parents," I say. "But it was no big deal. Really I'm the one who owes an apology to Mercedes."

"Let me know if there's anything I can do to make this work," Ms. Sanchez says.

"Is that all?" I ask. She nods and I head for the door, but I pause by her desk. "Are you always so kind to everyone?"

She laughs. "Depends on who you ask, I suppose." Then she comes over and puts her arm around my shoulder. "Developing kindness and compassion is part of becoming mature," she says. "It's something we're all learning and always working on."

"Oh," I say, surprised. "I didn't realize . . ." but I stop because I can't tell her that for me it's backward. Erdlers have to learn kindness, but I've had to learn how to be mean to survive my first few weeks of high school.

When I get to the lunch room I find Timber sitting alone, draining a can of orange soda as most of the other students pack up their stuff. Bella's not around, so I'll have to wait until the end of the day to find out if my spell worked.

His face lights up when he sees me, sending a sparkly chill down my back like an icicle dropped into my tunic. "Hey, I was looking for you," he says. "You ran off so fast this morning."

"Sorry. I had to get to class. And just now Ms. Sanchez needed to see me."

"You in trouble?" He stands and lifts his tray from the table. Before I can answer, he says, "I'm kidding. Do you ever get in trouble?"

"Well . . ."

"Please," says Timber as he crams the remnants of his lunch into the trash. "You're the nicest girl I know."

"I wish you'd stop saying that," I tell him.

"What's wrong with being nice?" he asks.

"I'm not as nice as you think," I say.

Timber puts his hand on my shoulder. His touch is warm and comforting. "Believe me, I know mean girls and you're not one of them," he says.

Now everything is a mess. My family is in trouble. I'm losing what I worked so hard to get in Brooklyn—my friends, the audition today. And, if Timber finds out what I did to Bella, I'll lose him, too.

"What are you doing after school today?" he asks.

"The ELPH audition," I remind him.

"What about later?"

"Why?" I ask, confused.

"I thought maybe we could talk. I could IM you."

"I don't think I can."

"Oh," he says, and shoves his hands deep into his pockets.

"No, I mean, it's just that . . ." I stumble over my words. "I don't have a computer at home so how about if you call me instead?"

"You mean on the phone? A real live conversation with words and sound and everything? Isn't that moving a little too fast? We'd actually have to think of clever things to say with our mouths instead of typing stupid one-liners followed by bouncing smiley faces."

I narrow my eyes at him for a moment. "You're kidding, aren't you?"

"Yes, I am." He slings his arm around my shoulders and pulls me out of the cafeteria with him. "I can definitely call you on the good old-fashioned telephone."

Relieved, I wish I could stay tucked against his side for the rest of the day, where I feel so safe right now. Where no one would dare bother me. Where I wouldn't have to deal with the stupid messes I've gotten myself into with Bella, Ari, and Mercedes. But the coziness of this moment is short-lived because we reach the stairs.

"Where are you going now?" he asks.

"Downstairs," I say. "History."

"I'm going up." He slips his arm off my shoulders. "So, I'll talk to you tonight?"

"Tonight," I confirm as I watch him take the steps two at a time.

"And hey," he calls down to me. I gaze up at him leaning over the railing. "Good luck at the audition!"

"Thanks," I call after him, but the truth is luck's got nothing to do with it at this point.

The audition is held in the auditorium. Mr. O'Donnell, looking much better without the giant sweat rings under his arms, sits at a table on the stage with two women. Next to them is a guy with long dreadlocks adjusting a video camera on a tripod. Across the stage from them is a white screen with a giant cardboard cutout of the ELPH camera. Several girls are already in the seats in front of the stage and others are filing through the doors. I scan the room for Bella, but she's not here yet. I hope I didn't make the spell so strong that she won't even show up. That's not like her, though. Since she can't see what's happening to her, she'll never suspect how horrid she looks. And even if she feels odd, she'll be here because she'd never miss an audition.

I take a seat in the front row so I can turn and watch the door. While I wait, Rienna enters. She's wearing a pale pink tunic, a short suede skirt, and brown leather boots but no fairy wings. She looks really cute and I raise my hand to wave at her, expecting her to ignore me, but she smiles and hurries down to where I'm sitting.

"Oh my God! I didn't know you were back." She plops into the seat next to me and talks a mile a minute. "There were so many rumors about what happened to you when you didn't come to school." I try to look interested in what she says while still keeping an eye on the door. "People said that Bella threatened to kick your butt after you stole Timber and you left Brooklyn because you were scared but I was like, no way, she wouldn't do that. Zephyr doesn't even care what Bella thinks. And anyway, Zephyr could totally kick Bella's butt! And they were like . . ."

I can't quite keep track of what she's talking about, then I tune her out when I see Chelsea come down the aisle toward the stage. I can't believe Timber thinks she's okay. Even the way she walks in her little green minidress is snotty. She looks my way. We lock eyes for a moment.

I expect a sneer or a snide remark from her, but for some weird reason she nods at me quickly then takes a seat on the other side of the room.

"Anyway, now you're back. Which is so awesome," Rienna says. "And hey, I saw your dad on TV. I didn't know that was *your* dad. And your brother! He's totally hot!"

This catches my attention. "My brother?"

"Does he have a girlfriend?" she asks.

I snort. "No."

"I heard he dates models," Rienna says.

I bust out laughing because I can't imagine Grove dating anyone, let alone an erdler model, but then I stop, because I could've never imagined myself kissing the yummiest erdler guy in my school. Good gracious, our lives are so upside down!

Rienna jabs her elbow into my side. "Oh my God!" she whispers loudly. "What the . . ." She points to the back of the room. I turn in my seat to see Bella stomping down the aisle.

She's wearing the same green dress with a brown sash from the first meeting but this time instead of the silver leaf pendant, she's got on the necklace I gave her, which isn't an amulet for luck. I filled it with the worst things I could find in my mother's stash of herbs—bloodroot, hemlock, dropwort, spurge, and yes, even deadly nightshade, a.k.a. belladonna—then I zapped it with hexes of stupidity, lazy tongue, and dizzy spells just for good measure.

As she gets closer I can see that my magic has started to kick in. Bella's normally long silky hair is frazzled and puffy, sticking out in tufts around her head. A red rash has started to take over her bare legs and arms and she scratches vigorously at her stomach and back. Best of all, a faint shadow in the form of an X is beginning to surface from the corners of her forehead, down across her nose to the sides of her chin. Rienna can't stop staring, but I quickly look away, pressing my lips together so that no one can see my huge self-satisfied smile.

When everyone is settled in their seats, Mr. O'Donnell comes to the front of the stage. "Good afternoon, ladies," he says. "Glad you could all make it. I'm joined today by two of my colleagues, Julia Brennan and Grace Lee." Each woman comes forward to join him as he says their names. "Together, the three of us will decide who will be the next ELPH elf." He pauses, as if waiting for us to giggle at his lame joke. A few girls give him a courtesy laugh.

"Usually in a professional audition, each actor performs privately for the casting agents," the woman called Grace says. "But since this is a learning environment, we've decided to let you watch one another."

"When I call your name, please come up to the stage and take a seat on the wooden stool in front of the screen," Mr. O'Donnell says. "Luther, our cameraman who will be taping everything, will give you a cue. State your name clearly, then you have one shot to show us your best work. There's a cue card here under the camera in case you forget your lines, so don't worry."

"You should also know that we're not going to do callbacks since the actual shoot will happen this Saturday," the other woman, Julia, says. "We'll be basing our decision on your performance today and we'll let you know at the end of our session who we're casting. Any questions?" No one raises a hand.

"All right then," Mr. O'Donnell says, clapping. "Let's get started!"

At this point I couldn't care less about the audition. Mercedes is out and Bella will never be chosen in the condition she's in, so I'm a little shocked when Mr. O'Donnell calls me up first.

"Good luck," Rienna whispers to me as I rise unsteadily from my seat.

I've never actually practiced other than that one time with Bella in the studio upstairs. I remember her advice. She said to be a blank slate. Now as I climb the steps to the stage, I realize that she was probably lying and her supposed "help" was probably another ploy to make me look like a fool. I glance out at the girls seated below me. They sit in small groups of three or four, huddled together, whispering. I don't know what they're saying about me, and at this moment, I don't care. I scan their faces until I land on Bella. She squirms uncomfortably in her chair, no doubt trying to scratch the endless itching all over her body. Her hair is even wilder than when she walked in. Some of it sticks straight up from her scalp in knotty puffs and the shadowy X on her face has darkened. Seeing her look like such a freak gives me a boost of energy. This is what I'm here for. This is why I came back. It's my one shot to show everyone what I can do. I remember my grandmother's words. I'm doing this for me and that's all that matters. I turn to face Mr. O'Donnell and the two women.

"Whenever you're ready," he says.

I take my place behind the cardboard camera, which comes up to my waist. I realize then that it's mounted on a small turntable. I look up at the video camera and nod. "Zephyr Addler," I say clearly, then I begin reading the cue card. "To take a great picture with an ELPH camera, all you have to do is point and click." I pretend to push the button on top of the cardboard camera. "Just point and click." I turn the camera to the right and push the button again. "Point and click." This time I turn it to the left. Then I center it again and continue. "When you're done, you'll wonder how it's possible to have so many good shots. But don't worry," I pause and lean on my elbows across the top of the camera, "that's the magic of an ELPH." I give a little wink and smile to finish.

The girls in the audience clap and cheer so loudly that I'm startled. I look out and see that most of them are smiling up at me. Except for Chelsea and Bella, of course, but that's nothing new.

"Thanks!" I laugh because I'm so surprised. I didn't realize that clapping and yelling were part of an audition. It's nice. Almost as if these girls like me.

"All right, all right," Mr. O'Donnell shouts over the noise. "That's enough. Quiet down." The applause dies and I'm left standing there kind of embarrassed but mostly happy.

"So, Zephyr," Julia Brennan says. I turn back toward the casting agents' table. "I see from your résumé that this is your first professional audition, but you've done amateur stuff?"

"Yeah," I say with a shrug because I know I won't get the part. "Sorry, I don't really know how to act, except for acting like myself," I tell her. "But I did my best."

"Obviously they liked you," Mr. O'Donnell says, pointing to the girls in the audience.

"And for never having done this before that was remarkably good," Julia tells me.

"She looks great on camera," Luther tells them.

Grace Lee nods enthusiastically. "I love your energy," she says. "It's right on target. Happy, sweet, but just a little mischievous."

"And this look . . ." Julia motions to my clothes. "Your outfit is perfect!"

"Yes," Mr. O'Donnell agrees. "I see you took my advice and toned it down a little bit from last time. That was a good choice. You did very well. Excellent, in fact. What a great way to start."

"Thank you!" I skip down the steps and back to my seat.

"You rocked!" Rienna whispers to me.

I shrug and shrink down in my seat, relieved that it's over. Each time another girl finishes, I get ready to clap and yell like the girls did for me, but that never happens again and I'm confused. I know I wasn't that good, so why did the girls get so worked up? Do they really like me? I'm skeptical. I don't even know most of these people. I decide it must be something else. Something having to do with my supposed battle with Bella. If only they knew . . .

Rienna is pretty good, but she trips over the last line and gets embarrassed so she leaves the stage with her face bright red. I have to admit that Chelsea is a great actress because she seems sweet, friendly, and engaging when she reads the script—nothing like her true self. Finally after listening to the same six lines over and over again as each girl takes her turn, Mr. O'Donnell calls for my nemesis.

"Bella Dartagnan," he says enthusiastically, then he leans over to Grace and Julia and whispers something to them, probably about how good Bella is. I hold my breath, waiting for her to mount the stage. Only nothing happens. Mr. O'Donnell shades his eyes and peers out at the seats. "Bella?" he says again. "You're here, aren't you?"

Like all the other girls, I wrench around in my seat to get a look at her. She's slumped in her chair, mouth hanging open, a thin line of spit dribbling down her chin. Her hair is a crazy nest poofed out all over her head. Her arms and legs are scratched red and raw and now there is an unmistakable X stamped across her face.

"Bella?" Mr. O'Donnell says one more time.

This snaps Bella out of her haze—courtesy of my stupidity hex. She rises and stumbles toward the stage, seems confused, and starts to walk the other way. Chelsea sticks her hand out and turns Bella toward the stage again, then gives her a little push. Everyone watches as Bella trips up the steps, then bumps the giant camera cutout, which crashes to the floor. Luther rushes over to help set up the prop again. Bella settles herself behind it and when she looks up at the casting agents, they all audibly gasp.

"Bella, are you all right?" Mr. O'Donnell asks.

"Yaaaaw," she slurs. "I'b find. Why bloudn't I blee?"

"What?" he asks.

"I shed bime blind," she insists.

Mr. O'Donnell looks from Julia to Grace, totally confused. "What is that you're wearing?" he asks Bella.

She looks down at herself. "Da blame bling I floor the last slime."

"I think he means your hair and makeup," Julia says. "I'm not sure this is exactly the look we're going for."

Bella stares at Julia for a moment and rolls her eyes. "Butt bever. Can I dust do my laudition?" Then she burps, sending all the girls into a fit of hysterical giggling. I'm laughing so hard that I nearly pee myself. Bella stares at all of us meanly, which only makes everyone laugh harder.

"Quiet down now," Mr. O'Donnell says testily. "You girls settle down." We all shrink in our seats and press our hands over our mouths, trying to stop cracking up. "Let's give Bella a chance." He looks back up at his darling and shudders at the sight of her. "Anytime you're ready."

"To snake a bate snicture with a relph smamera, doll you bave to smoo is doint and smick." Bella tries to push the button on top, but she leans too far forward and knocks the big camera to the floor again. When she bends over to get it, she farts loudly and all of us lose it. That only makes her madder, so she yells her next line. "It's so peasy. Bust foint and jick, woint and wick, gloint and dick." She pounds on the camera top as she says this, then blows a puff of air into the hair hanging in her face. "When you're sun, you'll blunder how's it gossible to bave so fenny rude jots. But don't porry." Then she stops, squints at the cue card, and scratches her belly, then her butt. "Fut's the sline?" she asks, pointing at the card.

"That's the magic of an ELPH," Luther calls out the line to her.

She shakes her head, annoyed. "Vat's gust the, um, uh . . ." Before

looks like he got hit by a truck. His shirt is untucked, his hair's a mess, even one of his shoes is untied. Poor guy. Grace and Julia sit coolly on either side of him, waiting for all of us to settle down.

"This has been a most unusual day," Mr. O'Donnell tells us. "If the shoot weren't already scheduled, I'm not sure what we'd do. Obviously, something was not right with Bella Dartagnan."

I steal a glance at Julia and Grace. They exchange looks and roll their eyes at each other.

"But nevertheless, this is show business, girls," Mr. O'Donnell says. "And no one gets a break. It's cutthroat and, therefore, we had to choose the best of what we saw."

Julia interrupts him. "Which was very good, by the way. Sometimes it's nice to find new talent."

"I agree," Grace says.

"The part of the new ELPH camera elf will be played by . . . ," he pauses for dramatic effect, then he says, "Zephyr Addler."

The other girls erupt into cheers. Rienna throws her arms around my neck and squeals in my ear, but I'm flabbergasted.

"And the understudies," Mr. O'Donnell shouts over the noise. Everyone immediately quiets down. "In case Zephyr can't make the shoot for any reason, are Chelsea Wheeler first and, if she can't make it, Rienna Falzetta."

I'm speechless as everyone rushes over to congratulate me, saying things like, "I'm so glad Bella didn't get it!" and "You kicked her butt!" and "First you took her boyfriend and now her audition, ha-ha-ha!" I look up from the crowd around me to see Chelsea, standing off to the side, arms still crossed, shaking her head. She looks at me and raises her eyebrows as if to say, "Told you so."

"Zephyr, Chelsea, and Rienna," Mr. O'Donnell says. "If you'll come up here, we'll give you all the details of the shoot."

I disentangle myself from the girls. They applaud me one more time as I climb up onstage with Rienna and Chelsea behind me. I turn and look out at the girls. I try to smile, but it's hard because I know these girls aren't really happy for me. They're just happy that for once Bella didn't get the part. This leaves me wondering if I solved anything by sabotaging Bella. Or did I just fuel the flames of some stupid fire?

chapter 15

BY THE TIME I get home, all of the giddiness from the audition has worn off and I'm almost dragging myself up our front walk to the door. Not only am I worried about my family, but my arms and legs feel like they're full of sand, my head is pounding, my throat burns, my stomach churns, and I swear even my hair hurts. All I want to do is lie down and sleep for a hundred years.

I'm expecting the house to be quiet when I open the door, but I'm wrong. The second I step foot in the living room, Poppy, Persimmon, and Bramble come running, screeching like frenzied blue jays, and throw themselves at my legs. Despite my relief that they're home safely, I slump to the floor under the weight of their hugs.

"We rode an erdler bus!" Poppy yells.

"And there's a toilet right there in the bus and I got to pee in it," Bramble tells me.

"But not Willow," Persimmon says.

"She didn't come with us," Poppy tells me gravely.

"She's taking care of Grandma Fawna," Bramble explains.

"See my boo-boo?" Persimmon holds up a finger with a tiny scrape. I kiss her finger then lie back and close my eyes.

"Zephyr, wake up!" Poppy hollers.

"Why are you sleeping?" Bramble pulls on my arms.

"Fephyr, Fephyr, Fephyr!" Persimmon rubs my cheeks with her tiny moist hands.

"I'm so tired," I croak. "I think I'm sick."

"Do you have what Grandma Fawna had?" Poppy asks and my eyes pop open.

Oh no, I think. She's right. I really am sick and it's probably because of the spell I cast on Bella. This realization makes me feel even worse and I moan.

Bramble stands up. "I'll get Mom," he says but I reach out and grab him by the ankle.

"No, don't," I say, and peel myself off the floor. Whatever I do, I *cannot* let my mom know that I'm sick. "I'm okay. Just sleepy. School makes me tired," I tell them. "Help me up." I hold out my arms and they pull me to a stand. "I'm going to take a little nap," I tell them, trying to sound cheery, as if nothing is wrong. "And when I get up, I'll play with you and you can tell me all about riding the bus."

I haul my aching, weary body slowly up the stairs to my room, where I fall asleep before my body hits my bed. I don't even take off my boots or hat or amulets. At some point someone pulls a blanket over me and tiptoes out the door. Once, I wake up sweating, so I kick the covers off. Later I wake up freezing and wrap myself in all the blankets. The room gets dark, gets light, gets dark again. Sometimes I hear the phone ring and my mom saying my name, but I can't answer. I drift in and out of delirious dreams. Timber is a hawk. Mr. O'Donnell is my father's manager. Persimmon auditions for Martin while he talks on his earpiece to Grace Lee, who is my mother. Ms. Sanchez and Mercedes have Xs on their faces and shake their heads at me. Bella stands onstage and tells everyone what I did, then all the girls rush up and knock me down. My mother sits on the edge of my bed. Wait, no. Am I awake?

"Mom?" I whisper, squinting against the sunlight streaming through my window.

She brushes my hair off my face and presses her cool, soft hand against my forehead, then cups my cheek. "You look better," she says. "I think you're past the worst of it. How do you feel?"

I try to sit up but every joint in my body is creaky and achy. "Terrible," I say. Mom hands me a cup of lukewarm tea. I lift it to my lips and take a sip. The liquid soothes my parched mouth and eases the soreness in my throat.

"Do you want to tell me what happened?" she asks quietly.

I slump back against the pillow because I'm not talking. If I tell her, she'll freak out. Plus, no matter what I say, she'll be disappointed in me, which is the worst thing I can think of.

"You know, Zephyr, there's nothing you could do to make your dad or me stop loving you or not want to help you."

"You say that only because you can't imagine how dark my heart could be," I whisper.

Mom actually laughs when I say this. I stare at her, infuriated. "Honey," she says. "You're not the first elf to ever cast a spell and get sick." My mouth drops open, but I close it quickly. I'm not admitting to anything. But still, I'm surprised by how much she knows. "Look at your grandmother, for goodness' sake," she continues. "If anyone should have known better, it would be her. We all do it. I did it when I was young and stupid. Your dad . . ."

"This is different," I tell her. "Grandma was trying to help us and you were in Alverland when you did it."

"Is this about that boy Timber?" she asks, suddenly serious. I close my eyes and shake my head. "Because Dad said he met you at the TV studio and he's been calling here."

"He has?" I open one eye. "What'd you tell him?"

"I told him you were sick."

I close my eye. He called! Like he said. And not just once either.

"Someone else called, too. Another boy."

I open the other eye. "Ari?"

"No." She thinks for a moment. "He had a lovely name. Very percussive. What was it, um, Kenji Nakamura, I think."

Now both of my eyes pop open. "Kenji called me? What did you tell him?"

"That you were sick, of course."

I close both eyes, but this time I'm smiling inside. Timber and Kenji called me? This is bizarre.

"And one other person," Mom says.

I can't help but look at her because I'm dying to know who it could be.

"Mercedes's mother?" She says it like a question and I squeeze both eyes shut. "Is this about your friend Mercedes then?" I shake my head again. Mom sighs. "If I don't know what's going on, I can't help you, Zephyr." I say nothing. "Will you talk to your dad about it?" I don't answer. Mom grumbles. "I don't know what to do here! If you can't talk to me or your father, then who can you talk to, Zephyr?"

My chin starts to quiver and tears squeeze through my eyes, shut tight. "That's just it," I whimper, feeling more alone than I ever have in my life. Mercedes and Ari are no longer my friends. Briar and Willow are far away. And it's not as if I can tell Timber about any of this. "There's nobody." I roll away from her and tuck myself into a little ball, my heart as dark and cold as the far side of the moon.

* * *

I must have slept some more because the next time I open my eyes, it's nighttime again and I hear whispering. I roll over and peer around my room but I can't find what's making the noise. "Who's there?" I ask, my voice stronger now. I see three little heads pop out from inside my closet. "What are you guys doing?"

Poppy, Bramble, and Persimmon creep toward my bed. "Are you going to die?" Poppy asks.

"No," I say, and sit up, definitely feeling stronger. "Of course not."

"Are you going to leave us and become an erdler?" Bramble asks.

"Why would I do that?" I reach over and turn on my lamp.

Persimmon climbs on the bed with me. "Do you have a boo-boo?"

I pull her onto my lap. It feels good to hug someone. "Inside," I tell her and she frowns at me. "I was naughty," I explain. She opens her eyes wide.

Poppy scoots onto the edge of my bed and leans close, eager to hear about my catastrophe. "What did you do?" she whispers.

"You know how sometimes we get mad and hex each other, then we get the sniffles?" Poppy and Bramble nod. I take a deep breath. "Well, I did that, but I did it to an erdler." It feels good to admit it. Like I've opened a window into my heart and let a little light back in.

"Did you get in trouble?" Poppy asks.

"I don't think anybody knows," I say, then I get wise. "And you can't tell anybody. It's a secret."

"I won't tell," Poppy says, but I already know that I've made a huge mistake.

"Poppy, I'm serious. You've never kept a secret in your life. But this time you have to."

"I know a secret," Persimmon says with a mischievous grin as she wiggles off my lap.

"Persimmon!" I sit up. "Don't tell secrets. That's naughty." She's already out the door.

"I know a secret! I know a secret!" she sings as she heads for the stairs.

I try to scramble free from my covers, but they're twisted around my legs, plus I'm weak from not eating in two days. "Poppy, Bramble," I command. "Go get Persimmon. Bring her back in here."

They aren't listening to me. They've joined hands and are skipping around in a circle, shouting an old elf nursery rhyme, "Shame, shame, you were bad. Mommy cries, go tell your dad. Weepy, weepy whip-poor-will, you were naughty, fall down ill!" And they collapse to the floor, giggling. They do it over and over again, louder and louder.

I finally get loose from the covers and fall out of bed. Persimmon has started down the steps, one at a time, holding on to the rail, singing at the top of her voice. "I know a secret, secret, secret. I know a secret, ha-ha-ha-ha-ha!"

"Persimmon," I insist. "Stop. You come back here. I'll give you some candy."

This stops her. She turns around and starts to take a step toward me, but not before my mom comes out of the kitchen. "What's your secret, Persimmon?" Mom asks, and I know that this time, I'm truly busted.

The next day is Friday, but I'm still too weak to go to school. Timber called again yesterday, but I was asleep and he didn't leave his number so I can't call him back. Plus, I probably shouldn't be gabbing on the phone anyway. Persimmon told Mom and Dad my secret. And although my parents are truly furious with me for casting a spell on Bella, bigger problems have come up.

One of my uncles was in Ironweed the other day to pick up supplies when he overheard that more people have come snooping around, asking about Drake Addler's cult in the woods. My dad is upset but Martin says any press is good press. On top of that, Aunt Flora has called a few times because Briar has been giving her a lot of trouble. She's been disappearing and refuses to say where she goes. I know she's with her new friend Jenny on a computer at the library in Ironweed because we've been e-mailing back and forth whenever I've been able to get Dad's Treo. I tell Mom that, hoping it will ease everyone's worries about Briar, but it only seems to make it worse. Briar says that everyone in Alverland is angry with my family, saying that we've brought all this attention and darkness to our clans by entering the erdler world.

Just to complicate matters, Mercedes's parents keep calling our house, asking to come over for Mercedes to apologize. My mom has assured them this isn't necessary, but they won't let it go. My parents finally gave in and invited them over this afternoon. So, lucky for me, the fact that I hexed Bella is low on the list of horrible things to deal with at the moment.

"Do erdlers eat dried apples?" Mom asks as she moves the armchairs for the fiftieth time.

"I hate to tell you this," I say. "But no matter how you rearrange the furniture or what snacks you serve, we're not going to seem normal."

"But why?" she asks, dragging a ficus tree from one corner of the living room to the other.

"Because," I tell her, sinking down onto the sofa so she can't move that. "We're not like them."

The doorbell rings. We both freeze and stare at each other. "Oh stars!" she says, pressing her hand against her forehead. "Why did we ever agree to this?"

"Go get Dad," I tell her. "I'll answer the door." I take a deep breath.

Mercedes stands between her parents on our front step. I smile despite myself because I'm happy to see her. I wish I could throw my arms around her shoulders and hug her, but I know I can't. Instead, I open the door wide and invite them in.

Mercedes is like a little clone of her mother, who bustles into our house and fills it with incredible energy. Her father is more upright, severe, and quiet. When my parents come into the living room, he holds out his hand and says, "I am Victor Sanchez. Thank you for having us over."

My mom forgets herself and steps forward as if to hug him. I shoot her a sharp look. She stops, blushes deeply, and says, "Welcome," with outstretched arms. "To our home."

"Please sit down," Dad booms, motioning to where the chairs used to be, as if he's inviting them to sit on a lamp and a table.

Yeah, I think to myself. Real normal.

"What a beautiful place you have!" Mercedes's mom, Maria, exclaims. "All these plants remind me of my grandmother's house in San Juan."

"Oh!" my mom says, clearly pleased. "That's so kind of you." I can tell that she's fighting the urge to hug Maria.

As soon as we all settle ourselves Mr. Sanchez clears his throat and places his hand on Mercedes's knee. "I think you have something you'd like to say."

"Yes, *Papi*," Mercedes says in a small, meek voice that I've never heard before. I blink, wondering where the feisty, eye-rolling, joke-cracking girl I know has gone. She takes a deep breath and rubs her hands against her thighs. "I would like to apologize to Zephyr for spreading a rumor about her through e-mail."

"And . . . ," her father says.

"And sorry to Mr. and Mrs. Addler for causing your family any, you know, distress."

"Because . . . ," her father says, staring hard at her.

"Because it's wrong to gossip about people." She glances at her father, who stares harder. "Because it's hurtful," she says. He still stares. "And, and, and . . ." He looks harder at her. *"Papi!"* she pleads. "What? I'm sorry. I was wrong. I know it. I apologized. Jeez. I already got suspended from school and missed the audition and you took my computer privileges away for a whole month. Come on!"

I burst out laughing. Mercedes glances at me and grins, but her father isn't pleased. That's when I know that we'll be okay. I pop up from my chair. "I'm the one who should apologize, Mr. Sanchez," I say quickly before he can make Mercedes say anything else. "You were right, Mercedes," I tell her. "I should've never trusted Bella. I didn't know how mean she was. I told her so much about you because I was excited to be your friend. I told her all the things I like so much about you and about Ari. The things I think are great. And she twisted it all around. Made it sound awful, like I was gossiping, but that's not what I meant to do."

In an instant, I go from laughing and talking to crying and talking. "And what's so horrible is, you and Ari were my friends. My first real friends here and because of her, I lost your friendship and that's worse than anything." I bury my face in my hands. "I miss you guys!"

"Aw, Boo!" Mercedes says. She comes over and reaches up to put her hands on my shoulders. "It's okay. I'm not mad anymore. I miss you, too."

I turn to her and wipe my eyes. "Really?" I ask.

"Really," she says. "And my *papi* didn't even make me say that part," she adds with an eye roll. I throw my arms around her and hug her tight. She hugs me back. I can see Mrs. Sanchez beaming from the couch, nodding to my mother, who looks relieved.

"Would you like some tea? And some snacks?" my mother asks.

"That's not—" Mr. Sanchez starts to say, but Mrs. Sanchez interrupts him.

"Yes!" she says. "I'll help you." She leaps up from the couch and follows my mom to the kitchen.

The Sanchezes end up staying for dinner. My mom and Maria talk nonstop about family. And it turns out that Victor spent a lot of time hunting when he was a kid, so he, Dad, and Grove trade stories for an hour straight. At some point, Mercedes and I manage to sneak up to my bedroom with a plate of peanut butter cookies and milk (cow's milk, that is). We lay on the floor and fill each other in on our last few weeks. She tells me all about how she had to clean the house every day and go to church and the botanica with her *abuela* plus babysit for her sisters. I tell her about the ELPH audition, skipping the part about hexing Bella, and fill her in about Timber.

"Do you think he actually likes me?" I ask her.

"Duh," she says. "He talks to Ari about you all the time in improv."

I break a cookie in half, scattering crumbs on the plate. "Really?"

"Yeah. And he's been calling you. So I'd say that he's into you." Mercedes dunks her cookie into her milk.

"How do I find out for sure, though?"

"Ask him out," she says with her mouth full.

"You mean on a date?"

"Sure. Why not?"

"What if he says no?"

She reaches for another cookie. "Then you know for sure."

"You sound like my cousin Briar."

"She must be brilliant," Mercedes says, then she adds, "If you go out with Timber that'll stick it to Bella more than anything."

"Well," I say, ducking my head. "That's not why I'd ask him out."

"You really like him, don't you?" she asks.

I nod.

"Then you should definitely call him." Mercedes dunks a second cookie, then pops it in her mouth. "Ask Ari. He'll tell you."

I toss my cookie to the plate because I'm not hungry anymore. "Ari won't even talk to me."

"Mercedes, Zephyr!" my mom calls up the stairs. "The Sanchezes have to go home."

We pick up the plate and glasses and head downstairs.

"Don't worry about Ari," Mercedes tells me. "He never stays mad that long. By Monday everything will be fine."

"I hope so," I say. "I miss him."

Mercedes and I hug by the front door. "Good luck tomorrow with the ELPH shoot," she tells me as she goes out with her parents.

"You won't be doing that," my mother says.

"Why not?" I ask. "I'm not sick anymore. I can do it."

"Not a chance," says Mom. "I discussed it with Maria. You're not going anywhere tomorrow. You're grounded."

"What!" I yell. "For how long?" I can't believe she's doing this to me.

"A week," she says.

Maria turns around and winks at my mom. "You go, girl," she tells her.

"I'll give you a call once I mix that arthritis remedy for your mother," Mom says to Maria and waves good-bye. Then she pulls me inside and shuts the door.

"You didn't discuss anything with Maria," I say to my mother. She raises her eyebrows at me. "You wouldn't because that would mean telling her about *us*. That we're not, you know, *normal*."

"I'm not quite that stupid, Zephyr," Mom says. I'm speechless.

"What did you tell her?" Dad asks, as surprised as I am.

"I told her that Zephyr disobeyed me about the audition but then she got the part so I didn't know what to do. And Maria said it was simple. If you disobeyed me, then you should not do the shoot and you should be grounded."

"But Mom!" I protest. "You don't understand. Bella pushed me too far. I cast that spell on her because it was the only way to stop her from spreading more rumors about Dad and hurting our family."

"Did you ever think about asking her to stop?" Dad says.

I can't even help it, I *have* to roll my eyes at that one. "You don't ask a girl like Bella to stop being mean. That's who she is."

"Because she feels threatened," Dad says.

I shake my head. They are so clueless! "No, you don't get it. She has all the power. Everyone is afraid of her."

"Exactly," says Dad. "She's afraid of losing that power. And you threatened her."

"I did not!" I yell. "I never threatened her. I was so nice to her until . . ."

"No, no," says Mom. "She felt threatened by who you are, not by what you did."

"Huh?" I ask, not sure who's more in the dark here, me or my parents.

"Look at it from her perspective," Mom says. "A new girl comes to school. She's beautiful, interesting, kind. People like her immediately."

"I hate to burst your bubble about me, but that's not how it happened. I was the biggest dork in the world when I first came to school."

"You may have felt that way," Dad says. "But that's obviously not how other people saw you."

"Otherwise," Mom adds. "Why would you have friends like Ari and Mercedes? And why would Timber take an interest in you? And why would Bella think you could be competition for the audition?"

"But what am I supposed to do about that? I can't help what people think of me and if they feel threatened by who I am."

"That's right," says Mom. "You can't control what people think about you or how they treat you. You can only control how you treat others and how you react to the way they treat you."

I slump against the wall and cross my arms. "So you want me to change? That's not fair!"

"Not at all," Dad says. "That's the point."

"You guys are making *no* sense," I tell my parents.

"If you had stayed true to yourself in this situation, Zephyr, you would have never cast an evil spell," my mother says. "You would have been kind and compassionate. You would've come to us for help when the problem got out of hand. But instead, you acted like an erdler. And therefore, we're treating you like one. That's why you're grounded."

I hang my head because I know in a way they're right. "But," I say, "what you're asking me to do is really hard."

"Yes," says my mom. "It is. But we expect more from you than just merely being normal."

"You have to be true to yourself," my dad adds. "True to who you are on the inside." He taps his breastbone as he says this and I think about the shadow in my heart. "And who you are, Zephyr, is an elf. Be proud of that. Be fierce about it and protect that part of yourself because in the end, that's all we've got."

chapter 16

HERE'S ONE THING I know for sure about being a teen-ager in the erdler world: being grounded sucks! My parents called Mr. O'Donnell and told him that I wasn't allowed to do the ELPH shoot. They also made it abundantly clear: no phone, no Treo, and no friends visiting. The only thing I'm allowed to do is go to school but at least that's gotta be interesting.

I get to BAPAHS early on Monday morning. There are only a few people in the hallways but most of them glance at me and say, "Hey" or "What up?" At first I look over my shoulder, trying to figure out who's behind me that everyone's saying hello to. Then I realize that it's me they're talking to, so I chirp, "Hi" and "Hello" back because when I say, "What up?" it just sounds silly. I find Ari and Mercedes at their usual table in the courtyard, huddled over Ari's BlackBerry.

"Zephyr!" Mercedes says when she sees me. She opens her arms and I lean down for a quick hug.

Then I look at Ari. "Hi," I offer, timidly.

"Hey, Zeph, what's new?" he says.

"Well, er, um, lots of stuff, I guess," I stammer.

He cracks up. "She's so easy to fluster," he says to Mercedes. Then he turns to me. "Obviously like a million things have happened to you in the last couple of weeks. How's your grandma?"

"She's better. Thank you for asking," I say, then I blurt out, "Does this mean you're not mad at me anymore?"

"For what?" he asks.

"You know," I whisper.

"For telling everyone I'm gay?" he nearly shouts as he looks all around dramatically. "Yeah, about that . . ."

I drop down into the seat next to him. "Ari." I place both of my hands on his forearm. "I am really, really sorry," I plead and I wish I could tell him that I get it. That I have a secret, too, and if everyone found out, my whole life would change. But, of course, I can't say that, so I just say, "Please believe me, I didn't mean to ruin your life. If I had known how sensitive an issue it is, I would have never, ever told Bella. Like I told you, where I come from it's just not a big deal who you love and I thought since you named your band GGJB that it was something you were okay with other people knowing. Now I can't even believe that I was so stupid—"

Ari interrupts me. "The thing is, Zephyr, I'm not sure what I am. What I told you was that I think I *might* be gay. And I never told anybody but you and Mercedes what GGJB stands for. So what really bites is that now I've been labeled. I'm officially the gay guy."

"Everyone thought you were gay anyway," Mercedes says.

"Yeah, but the problem is, I didn't get to decide when or if to confirm that or deny what other people thought. It should've been my choice, my decision."

"If there was some way I could take it back," I tell Ari. "Or maybe I can tell everyone that you don't know what you are."

"You can't, Zephyr. We both know that. It's out there."

I bury my face in my hands. "I'm just so sorry!"

"Actually, I'm dealing with it okay," Ari says. "I mean, I already had a therapist before this happened, so you know, it's just more fodder. And according to Dr. Melfi . . ." Mercedes giggles, but I'm not sure what the joke is. "I mean Dr. Farmingham," Ari says. "I can either choose to break ties with you for outing me because I no longer have a 'safe relationship' with you . . . ," he says using finger quotes.

"Oh Ari!" I say, my heart breaking at the thought of truly losing his friendship forever.

"Or," he continues, "I can forgive you and we can work to 'rebuild our trust.'" More finger quotes.

"Maybe you should do a ropes course together in the woods," Mercedes says with a snort.

"Yeah, and we'll do a trust fall at the end," Ari adds.

"Only make Zephyr be the one who falls off the log," Mercedes says, giggling.

"Right," says Ari laughing, too. "And I'll drop her on her butt."

"Wait, you guys are being sarcastic now, right?" I ask.

"Our little Zephyr," says Ari. "She's growing up so fast!" He reaches over and tousles my hair. "I guess I can't stay mad at you forever. It wasn't entirely your fault. And the fact that you've apologized like ninety-eight times does make a difference."

"Yeah, yeah, we're all friends again," says Mercedes as she scrolls through Web pages on Ari's BlackBerry. "Moving on. Zeph, did you see the post of Bella's ELPH audition on YouTube?"

"Are you kidding? I'm totally grounded. Not only did my parents take away the ELPH shoot, I'm not allowed near anything that looks like a computer. I'm surprised they let me use the microwave."

"You've got to see this," Ari says. Mercedes hands me the BlackBerry, which is set to a BellaHater entry from the weekend.

Well, Dorothy, dreams really do come true. Check out this link on YouTube and you'll laugh your butt off!

I click on the link. Up comes the video of Bella's flubbed audition. Mercedes and Ari are laughing so hard I'm afraid they'll fall out of their chairs. But I don't think it's funny. "That's so cruel to post it on YouTube," I say, still feeling guilty for zapping Bella.

"How can you say that?" Mercedes nearly shouts at me.

"She's been so mean to us," says Ari.

"Yeah, but we can't control how people treat us," I tell them. "We can only control how we treat other people."

"She's so Dalai Lama about everything," Ari says.

"Seriously, girl, did you o.d. on Paxil this morning?" Mercedes asks me.

"But something was wrong with her," I say.

"Yeah," says Mercedes. "She was high."

"Drugs?" I ask. Only I know it couldn't have been drugs. It was me who made her act like that.

"Oh please, that girl has been using since eighth grade," Ari says. "Her parents sent her to rehab."

I gasp. "No!" My stomach clenches.

"It's been coming for a long time. She drinks like a fish and has been caught with cocaine twice," Mercedes says.

"And I know for a fact she buys pot because my cousin's a total stoner who sold her some weed last year," says Ari.

"Are you sure?" I ask.

"Ask Timber," says Mercedes. "He'll tell you. Her daddy is some big-time lawyer so he always gets her off when she gets busted, but this audition thing apparently sent her parents over the edge. It's all so very Lindsay Lohan."

"Timber told me that this is probably the best thing that ever happened to her because the drinking and drugs were getting really out of hand." Ari takes the BlackBerry from me. "Let's see what else BellaHater has to say." He goes back to the blog and I read over his shoulder:

> **So this week's BellaHater award goes to Bella herself, because nobody could have made a bigger ass out of her than she did. Way to go! Of course, she didn't get cast as the ELPH elf. That went to none other than Zephyr Addler who told me she didn't care who got the part as long as it wasn't Bella.**

"That's weird," I say. "The only person I told I didn't care about the part was Chelsea."

Ari and Mercedes look at each other, then at me. "Are you serious?" Ari asks. Before I can explain, he says, "That dawg!"

"Two-timing, back-stabbing skank!" Mercedes says, but she smiles, too.

"I think I love her!" says Ari.

"What are you guys talking about?" I ask.

"Duh, Zeph." Ari leans in close. "Now we know who BellaHater is."

"Who?" I'm completely lost as usual.

"It makes perfect sense," says Mercedes. "Who else could it be?"

"This is brilliant." Ari stands up. "We mustn't waste this opportunity, girls! Come on."

Mercedes follows Ari across the courtyard. I pick up my bag and tag along behind them, calling out, "Where are we going?" Ari walks smack dab into the center of the courtyard and plops himself down at Bella's empty table.

"Awesome," says Mercedes, slipping into a seat beside him.

"What are you doing?" I ask.

"Hey Zeph, did I tell you that my band has a gig on Saturday?" Ari asks me as casually as can be.

I drop into the seat across from him. "Are we really going to sit here?"

"The show's at South Paw on Fifth Avenue. All ages night. Think you can come?" he says.

I'm flummoxed and don't answer. Then I feel a tap on my back. I look over my shoulder, afraid of who it might be, but standing behind me is Kenji. "Hey Zephyr," he says. I turn all the way around in my seat. "I heard you were sick so I drew this manga for you." He pulls a notebook out of a graffitied messenger bag strapped across his chest. The cover of the notebook has an amazing drawing of a tall girl in the middle of a forest. She has long blond hair and giant eyes and she wears a long green tunic with a quiver of arrows on her back.

"Check it out!" Mercedes says. "That's totally you!"

"No way," I say, but now that she says it, I think she's right. "Is it really supposed to be me?" I ask Kenji.

He shrugs. "Sort of. I guess I based it on you. And well, you said you'd never seen manga before so I thought maybe you might like it." He hands the notebook to me.

"Wow!" I say, flipping through the pages. The cartoon me has all sorts of adventures being chased through the forest by vampire girls. "This is the coolest thing anyone has ever given me." I look up when I say this and see Timber standing on the other side of the table, staring at me, but he's not smiling. My heart revs and a surge of excitement then panic goes through my body.

"What's that?" he asks, squinting at the notebook in my hand.

Ari and Mercedes look at each other, trying not to lose it.

"Kenji made it," I say, but I'm flustered. "Do you know each other?"

"What's up, man?" Kenji nods to Timber.

"Hey," Timber says back, but not in a friendly way.

At that moment, the fairy queen, Jilly, who seems to have lost her wings, stops by our table. "Hey Zephyr," she says. "Why didn't you do that ELPH shoot?"

"Um . . . ," I say, looking from Timber to Kenji, then Ari to Mercedes.

"She was sick," Ari answers for me.

"Where are Rienna and Darby?" Mercedes asks her.

"Don't talk to me about those skanks," Jilly says. "We're totally not friends anymore."

I try to catch Timber's eye to make sure he's not mad at me, but then Kenji says, "Speak of the devil." He points to the side of the courtyard and everyone turns to see Chelsea, Rienna, and Darby walk through the door.

"Are they hanging out?" Mercedes asks.

"Who cares?" says Jilly. "They deserve one another."

"Is it just my imagination," Ari asks, "or are they dressed alike?"

When he says this, I notice that all three of them are wearing tight tunic tops, short skirts, and knee-high boots.

"Guess somebody took her role as the ELPH a little bit too seriously," jokes Kenji, and everyone but Timber and I laugh.

"Oh, oh, oh!" Mercedes smacks our arms. "This is going to get good. Check it out." She points in the opposite direction and we all turn to see Tara and Zoe coming through the other set of doors. Jilly, Darby, and Kenji take a step away from the table, but Timber stays his ground.

"Let the games begin," says Ari, rubbing his hands together.

Mercedes stands up and moves back. "Does this thing have video on it?" she asks, fiddling with Ari's BlackBerry.

"I got you covered." Kenji pulls out his phone and aims it toward Ari.

Tara and Zoe scurry toward the table with angry looks on their faces. From the other direction, Chelsea, Rienna, and Darby march through the middle of the courtyard, which has become a lot more crowded since we first got here. I have the urge to sink down and hide under the table, but everything happens so fast. Ari climbs up on his chair, then steps onto the top of the table. "Hear ye! Hear ye, BAPAHS! I have an announcement to make," he shouts.

All faces turn toward Ari. He waits another second, until Tara and Zoe are on one side of the table and Chelsea, Rienna, and Darby flank the other side. Timber is in the middle, looking as confused as everyone. The courtyard is nearly quiet, but Ari cups his hands over his mouth and shouts, "Chelsea Wheeler is the BellaHater! I repeat, Chelsea Wheeler is the BellaHater!" A small buzz ripples through the crowd, then it turns to laughter, shouts, and jeers as Ari climbs down and moves back.

"Is that true?" Timber asks Chelsea. "Are you the BellaHater blogger?"

Chelsea's face goes from shock to anger to firm denial but she doesn't say anything.

"What are they talking about?" Tara asks Zoe.

Mercedes hands Zoe Ari's BlackBerry with the BellaHater homepage displayed. "See for yourself," she says. The crowd begins to press forward.

"This is awesome." Kenji keeps his phone trained on the action. But I think it's terrible and I wish I knew how to stop it.

"Did you really do this?" Zoe asks Chelsea.

"I don't know what you mean," Chelsea snaps.

Zoe waves the BlackBerry close to Chelsea. "This! Did you do this?"

Chelsea pushes Zoe's arm away and snarls, "Get out of my face!"

Timber shakes his head in disbelief. "It was you, wasn't it?" he asks. "Who else could've gotten the pictures and would've known so much?"

The crowd of kids moves in closer to the knot around the center table.

"If this is true, Bella's going to kick your ass," Tara tells Chelsea.

"Bella isn't here," Chelsea says. Then she tosses her books onto the table in front of me. I scoot back quickly and hop out of the chair.

Tara catches Chelsea on the shoulder with the flat of her hand. "You can't have this table," she says.

Chelsea steps onto the chair Ari used, then she turns and sits on top of the table, facing Zoe and Tara. "Oh yeah?" she says. "Who's going to stop me?" Rienna and Darby grab the other two chairs before Zoe and Tara can get them. They plant themselves at Chelsea's feet.

Zoe gets right up in Chelsea's face and waves the BlackBerry again. "Bella's coming back this weekend, and if this is true, then all hell is going to break loose!"

Some kids in the back chant, "Cat fight! Cat fight!" but before anything else can happen, the crowd parts because the pixie is pushing her way through. "Break it up! Break it up!" she yells. She grabs Zoe by the arm and yanks her away from Chelsea, sending Ari's BlackBerry skidding across the ground.

"Crap!" Ari yells as he scurries after his darling machine.

Ms. Sanchez emerges from the crowd behind the pixie. "Let go of her! That's not the way we handle students," Ms. Sanchez yells at the pixie, who has Zoe's arm in a death grip.

"There better not be a bruise on me," Zoe shouts, rubbing her upper arm, "or my parents will sue you!"

"Oh really?" the pixie says, standing up to her full height, which isn't all that tall.

"Yeah, you better apologize to me," says Zoe.

"Now wait a minute, everyone just calm down," Ms. Sanchez pleads.

"Well then, Zoe," the pixie says. "I'm so very sorry . . . that you're such an IDIOT!" Then she turns on her heel and pushes back through the crowd, which has erupted into cheers.

"We'll discuss this in a staff meeting, Prunella!" Ms. Sanchez shouts after the pixie.

"*Prunella?*" I whisper to Mercedes. We duck our heads to hide our laughter.

The first bell rings (and I jump, of course). "Everyone get to class," Ms. Sanchez yells over the noise. "Go on. No late passes. Get out of here." Groups of kids peel away and filter through the doors, talking excitedly about what just happened. Ms. Sanchez turns to our group in the center of the courtyard. She shakes her head. "I don't know what's going on but it better stop right here and right now. Do you all under-stand me?"

"Yes, Ms. Sanchez," we say.

She points to Kenji. "You. Erase everything." He sighs and pushes buttons on his phone. We all hear it beep. Then she turns to Zoe. "You. Come with me. The rest of you get to class."

In the chaos of the courtyard, I lost track of Timber so as I walk to my ensemble, I'm nervous. I realize now how quickly erdlers turn on one another. One minute people are best friends, the next they're mad at each other, the next they're making up or breaking up and becoming friends with someone else. I hope that never happens to Ari, Mercedes, and me again, but with Timber, I'm not sure what we were to begin with so I have no idea what we'll be now that my friends outed Chelsea as the BellaHater.

When I get to class, I see Timber in the front row. There are two open seats beside him. He's got his head down on the desk, probably trying to block out the noise of everyone discussing what just happened outside. I stop in front of him and tap his shoulder. "Mind if I sit beside you?" I ask, pointing to the chair on his left.

He looks up, sending a warm tingly ripple across my skin. "Sure," he says.

As I sit down, Chelsea walks into the room. She pauses in the doorway and scans the seats. Everyone gets quiet. The only open place is right beside me. I glance at Timber, but he's looking away. I wonder if he still thinks Chelsea is the best of Bella's friends or that I'm the nicest girl he's ever met. Then I remember what my mom and dad told me when they grounded me. I look up at Chelsea and despite my urge to scowl at her, I try to think what a good elf would do. A good elf would not perpetuate all the meanness of this morning, so instead of being nasty, I look at Chelsea and I say, "How was the ELPH shoot?" She blinks at me a few times, probably trying to figure out if I'm being sarcastic, so I add, "Did it go okay?"

She walks to the seat beside me and says, "It was great!" Then she mutters, "Sorry you were sick."

"That's okay," I say. "There'll be other auditions." And that's all the niceness I can muster for Chelsea today. I turn my attention to Timber. "You okay?" I ask.

He sits up. "Sure," he says. "Why wouldn't I be?"

I shrug, deciding to let this morning in the courtyard fade away. "I'm so glad to be back at school," I tell him. "I was losing my mind at home. Especially since I couldn't talk to you."

"You must've been really sick," he says.

"Yes, but then I was grounded."

"You?" he asks. "I can't imagine you ever do anything wrong."

"Um, well," I laugh nervously. "I'd explain, but N.W.T.E." Timber snickers when I use the abbreviation and I'm beginning to think we'll be okay.

"How long are you grounded?" he asks.

"Until Friday," I say. "No phone, no computer, no nothing."

"Can you go to Ari's gig on Saturday night?" he asks.

"Are you going?" I say. He nods. "Then hopefully I can, too."

"Cool. You want to go together?" he asks. "Unless you're going with that other guy, what's his name? The manga dude?"

"Kenji?" I ask as I lean across my desk and stare straight into Timber's blue eyes. "No, Timber," I say. "I'd really like to go with you."

chapter 17

IT'S SATURDAY AND Mom and I are in the kitchen, making snacks. Timber, Mercedes, and Ari are all coming over so we can watch an interview my dad did for a show called *Inside Lives* on MTV to dispel rumors that he's in a cult. This is big stuff, because it's the first time we get to watch the television my dad finally convinced my mom we should buy so we can seem more normal.

"Dad called," Mom tells me as she chops up fresh veggies. "He says he's bringing back a surprise."

He's on the way back from Michigan, where he took the MTV camera crew. "I bet he killed a deer and tied it to the top of the van," I say as I arrange homemade crackers around a mound of goat cheese.

"I could go for some good venison sausage this winter," she says.

"Mmmmm," Bramble pipes up from under the kitchen table, where he's feeding an abandoned baby chipmunk with an eyedropper. "I love sausage. And candy."

"Candy!" yells Persimmon, who is busy removing every pot and pan she can reach from the cupboards.

"What time are your friends coming?" Mom asks.

"Around six thirty. The interview isn't on until seven and Ari's gig doesn't start until nine." I glance at the clock. "Wow, it's already six. I should go get ready."

"I can finish up in here," Mom says.

I stick the cheese and crackers in the fridge, then head upstairs to change into a clean tunic and try out the makeup that Lucy from the VH1 studio gave me, just in case it turns out that I'm on a date with Timber. Mercedes has promised to take me shopping for new clothes next weekend. It's not that I don't like my tunics anymore. In fact, I love them. But since Chelsea, Rienna, and Darby are now walking around looking like some weird urban version of an elf, sometimes I want another choice. One nice thing about the erdler world is that you can change. One day you might be a fairy and the next day you might be an elf. But I think the trick to changing your look is always knowing who you are on the inside, and that's not so easy.

As I'm getting dressed, I hear the front door open. "Anybody home?" my dad yells. "I have a surprise!"

I slip on a couple of amulets and run down the stairs to find out what it is, but when I get halfway down, I stop. Standing in the doorway behind my dad is Grandma Fawna.

Mom comes through the dining room, wiping her hands on a kitchen towel. When she sees Grandma, she bursts into tears. "Oh, Drake!" she says as she runs to Fawna and wraps her arms around her. Poppy, Bramble, and Persimmon run into the room. They see Grandma and jump up and down, yelling and laughing and hanging on her legs.

"Is it really you?" my mom asks while she hugs Grandma. "I can't believe you're here."

"I tried to talk her out of it," says Dad.

"I had to see this place for myself," Grandma says. "And not just from a bird's-eye view." She winks at me.

"But the others?" I ask. "Are they mad?"

Grandma shrugs. "I'm here because I want to be. The others will have to accept that for now."

Dad looks at me. "There's someone here for you, too." I assume he means Timber, Mercedes, and Ari, but then Briar comes in.

"Oh my God!" I scream, just like an erdler. I run and grab her. We cling to each other, hopping up and down, screaming with excitement. "I can't believe they let you come! Is your mom freaking out? How long can you stay?" I ask her. She looks at my dad.

"We're going to see how this works for a while," he says.

"I had to beg," Briar says. "But it was totally worth it!"

My mom looks around and asks, "Where's Willow?"

Dad puts his hand on her shoulder as he shakes his head. "She didn't come, but I do have some good news."

"She stayed behind?" Mom dabs her eyes with the kitchen towel.

"Do you want to tell her, Fawna?" Dad says.

"Ash asked Willow to marry him," Grandma tells us.

Mom clutches her hands against her chest. "Oh my baby!" she moans, but she's smiling.

Briar squeezes my hand. "He made a picnic and took her up to Barnaby Bluff. He had all these flowers for her and a garland of late roses for her hair. He sang her a song that he wrote about her. Then he proposed."

"How sweet!" Mom says. "Sounds like someone I know." She leans against my dad and he kisses her on the forehead.

"I can't believe my sister is getting married," I say.

"Do we get to go to the wedding?" Poppy asks.

"Of course!" Mom and Dad say together.

"They're planning it for the spring," Grandma tells us. "She's staying with Flora until then."

"It's like we swapped," Briar says with a laugh.

Just then, Timber, Mercedes, and Ari come walking up to our front door, which stands wide open. As usual, my heart races when I see Timber grinning at me. I introduce Briar and Grandma to my friends. Of course, being elves, they immediately hug everyone and wink at me when they get to Timber, which makes my cheeks go red.

At seven o'clock we gather around the new TV in the living room. Mercedes and Briar have hit it off, not that that should surprise me. They're both so funny and full of energy. I'm going to have a hard time keeping up with them! From my place on the floor, I lean back and look up at Timber, who sits behind me on the couch. As usual, every time I see him, my stomach gets all fluttery. He's deep in conversation with Grove about the best road food and whether someone named McDonald has better hamburgers than a girl called Wendy. Ari is asking my dad's advice on what to play if he gets an encore tonight. I look over my other shoulder at Grandma Fawna. She sits quietly and happily, taking it all in.

I reach up and put my hand on her leg. "I'm so happy you're here," I say.

She grins. "Me, too. But I have to say I prefer flying here to riding in a van." We both crack up.

"What?" Mom asks.

"Oh, nothing," Grandma tells her and squeezes my hand.

"Hey look," Dad tells us, pointing to the TV. "Here it comes!"

We all quiet down as he turns up the volume.

"Drake Addler has been mesmerizing fans with his unique blend of rock and roll and traditional folk music for several years now," a woman's voice proclaims over footage of Dad and Grove and the rest of the band playing at some outdoor festival.

"Daddy!" Persimmon yells and runs to point at the screen.

"Get out of the way," we all yell at her, laughing.

"But is there something behind the star's power over his fans?" We all oooh and aaah, then giggle as the camera closes in on a photo of my dad looking slightly demonic.

"Drake grew up in the upper peninsula of Michigan, outside this little town," the woman informs us and we see Dad walking down Main Street in Ironweed.

"God," Mercedes says. "I knew you were from the middle of nowhere, but that place is so small it doesn't even qualify as nowhere."

"I think it looks cool," Ari says. Briar, Grove, and I groan.

"I spent a lot of time hunting and fishing in the woods around here," Dad says on-screen. "And when I wasn't doing that, I was playing my guitar and writing songs, of course."

"All that time to play paid off with his new hit song, 'Aurora Dawn.'" A close-up of my dad singing the song fills the screen.

"It's about your mom, isn't it?" Mercedes leans over and whispers to me. I nod and smile. "That's so ridiculously sweet," she says.

"I know it almost makes you want to barf, doesn't it?" Briar asks. Mercedes pretends to gag and they both laugh.

In the next shot, my dad sits in a television studio across from a pretty woman with long legs. "There are rumors that you're in a cult," she says.

"The leader, in fact," my dad says sarcastically.

"Are you denying it?" she asks.

"I'm just an ordinary guy," Dad says. "Like most fathers, I can't even get my kids to do what I say, let alone an entire cult."

The camera cuts to a shot of us sitting around the table. We're all dressed in jeans and T-shirts and pretending to like roasted chicken. Everyone starts yelling and laughing so hard we can't hear the dialogue.

Poppy, Bramble, and Persimmon crowd the screen pointing to themselves.

Mercedes smacks my leg and howls, "What are you wearing?"

"Where are your tunics?" Briar shouts in my ear on the other side.

"What are you eating?" Fawna asks my mother.

There are also shots of the park, the Brooklyn Bridge, Dad reading with Poppy, Bramble, and Persimmon on his lap, then a totally embarrassing one of me studying at the kitchen table.

Timber leans over and says into my ear, "You look good on-screen." I turn and smirk at him. "Really. You would have made the best ELPH elf."

"Thanks," I mumble, embarrassed, but happy.

"Check it out! Check it out!" Grove shouts over all of us. We turn back to the screen.

The long-legged woman, now in hiking gear, stands on top of Barnaby Bluff. My heart gives a little skip as I think of Ash proposing to Willow up there. "We've combed these woods," she says, motioning to the forest below her. "Asked people who claim to be experts on Drake and who've been searching for his cult for weeks and this is what we've found."

The last shot is of my dad sitting on the frog's mouth stump behind Grandma Fawna's house. Only there's no house there. No garden. No smokehouse. No other houses off in the distance. Nor any of my uncles and aunts and cousins moving silently and happily through the woods. I squeeze Grandma Fawna's hand. Her power is back and stronger than ever. The invisibility spell she cast over Alverland lasted long enough to convince the erdlers that our homeland is nothing more than a myth. My dad looks at the camera and shrugs. "Like I said, I'm just an ordinary guy." And then it's over.

"I always knew it," Ari says with a nod.

Everyone laughs and talks about the show for several minutes while my mom and I bring out the snacks we made. Then I stand back and look around the living room. For the first time in Brooklyn, I feel at home. I'm surrounded by people who like me and love me and accept me for who I am (even if not everyone knows the entire truth). I realize then that I'm happy. Truly happy.

While we all fill our plates with food, I notice that Timber has pulled his iPhone out of his pocket. He frowns at it as he touches the screen, then he seems to be reading something that makes him unhappy. I stand next to him. "What?" I ask.

He looks at me. "Oh nothing," he says, trying to shove the iPhone back in his pocket.

"Something upset you," I say.

"It's nothing. Really. Nothing important."

I stare at him until he sighs and says, "Bella is back from rehab."

"And she e-mailed you?" I ask.

"Sort of," he says. "She e-mailed a lot of people."

By this time Mercedes and Briar have figured out that something is up. They join us.

"What's going on?" Mercedes asks.

"Bella's back," I say. "And she sent out an e-mail."

"This I've got to see!" Mercedes holds out her hand for Timber's iPhone but he won't give it up.

Ari walks over. "You better do what she says," he tells Timber.

"All right, I surrender." Timber laughs as he relinquishes the iPhone. "I know when I'm outnumbered."

Mercedes, Ari, Briar, and I crowd around the small screen to read the message:

I'm back from the spa and better than ever. Don't think it's that ez to get rid of Bella. #1 on my yatch

list is Chelsea Wheeler, you back-stabbing, two-faced slut from hell. Your blog might be gone, but I have not forgotten.

"Chelsea took BellaHater down?" I ask.

"She didn't cop to it, but the whole site vanished," says Ari. "Not a trace left."

"You still think it was her?" I ask.

"It was," Timber tells us. "She told me the truth, but I don't think she feels bad about it."

"Look," says Mercedes, pointing to the iPhone. "There's more from Bella."

We all read:

And the next yatch on my list is Zephyr Addler. So watch yer backs girlies, bc when you least expect it, I'll be there.

"Is she threatening you?" Briar asks, her eyes wide.

"I'll whoop her butt into next Tuesday if she even comes close to you," Mercedes says.

Timber shakes his head and plucks the iPhone from my hand. "You don't have to worry. She's all talk."

"Besides . . . ," says Ari as he slings his arms around Mercedes's and Briar's shoulders. "We've got your back."

"Thanks, guys," I say, wrapping my arms around the three of them. Ari, Mercedes, and Briar let go of me, then wander back over to the food, but Timber hangs back.

"You okay?" he asks.

I look up at him. "I guess so."

"You really don't have to worry about her," he says seriously.

"That's not what I'm worried about. In fact, I'm not actually worried about anything. I'm more confused about something," I admit.

"What is it?" he asks.

I glance over my shoulder at my Grandma Fawna. She sits in a rocking chair in the corner of the room, happily watching everyone. I think back to my conversation with her in the woods when she told me that I have to do things for the right reasons and the only person who can know those reasons is myself. Then I look over at my parents. I think about their words, encouraging me to be myself. I take Timber's arm and lead him around the corner, into the front hall.

"When I first got here, I spent all my time trying to figure out how to be like everybody else so that I'd fit in," I tell him. "But now after everything that's happened, I realize that I don't want to be like other people and I don't have to change a lot about myself to find good friends."

"Yeah," says Timber. "I think you're right."

"But the thing is, I don't know what I'm supposed to do with you."

He shifts uncomfortably.

"So I'm just going to be me."

"Okay," he says.

"Here goes." I reach out and take his hand in mine. "You make me laugh and you're interesting and I enjoy talking to you and I get excited when I see you and I think that you're a good, decent, kind person. So maybe it's dumb, dorky, and socially awkward of me to say this and maybe I'll sound like a third grader instead of a normal, average girl but I want you to know that I like you."

At first, Timber tosses his head back and laughs. "You crack me up!" he says, but he quickly tugs on my hand and pulls me close to him. "And you're far from normal or average." Then he looks down into my face. "And for that reason, I like you, too," he tells me. When he tilts his head to the right this time I'm ready. I tilt my head the other way, close my eyes, and we finally, truly, fully kiss.

Twenty minutes later, we're ready to leave for Ari's gig. Ari has invited Grove to go with us and, of course, we all want Briar to come, too. As we're heading for the door, my mom pulls me aside. Oh no, I think, she saw Timber kiss me and she's going to freak out. But instead, she adjusts my amulets and says, "Be careful, okay?"

"Mom," I moan. "We're not going very far and I'm going to be with Mercedes and Timber and Grove. What could happen?"

"Well, you have to watch out for Briar," she says. "This is all new for her."

"I know," I tell her, trying not to roll my eyes.

She sighs and puts her hands on my shoulders. "I'm proud of you, Zephyr," she says.

"For what?" I ask, totally confused now.

"For coming here, to Brooklyn, and trying new things and making friends and showing me that we can have a life outside of Alverland."

"Wow, Mom," I say. "Thanks. That was actually really cool of you to say."

She pulls me into a hug. "You have nice friends, Zephyr," she tells me and I smile up at her. She lets go. "So have fun."

I wave and turn to join my friends out on our walk. "I will!"

"And remember." Then she grabs my arm and pulls me back to her quickly. "No matter what else happens . . . no magic in Brooklyn!"